W9-CJM-203

the charmer

A HOT ROMANTIC COMEDY

A HOT ROMANTIC COMEDY

AVERY FLYNN

This book is a work of fiction. Names, characters, places, and incidents are the product of the author's imagination or are used fictitiously. Any resemblance to actual events, locales, or persons, living or dead, is coincidental.

Copyright © 2017 by Avery Flynn. All rights reserved, including the right to reproduce, distribute, or transmit in any form or by any means. For information regarding subsidiary rights, please contact the Publisher.

Entangled Publishing, LLC
2614 South Timberline Road
Suite 109
Fort Collins, CO 80525
Visit our website at www.entangledpublishing.com.

Amara is an imprint of Entangled Publishing, LLC.

Edited by Liz Pelletier
Cover design by Liz Pelletier
Photography from Wander Aguiar

Manufactured in the United States of America

First Edition September 2017

For my in-laws (who have no idea that I write romance books) for raising one helluva son. Thank you. xoxo

Chapter One

Surrounded by Harbor City's elite decked out in Armani and Michael Kors, Hudson Carlyle couldn't take his eyes off of *her.*

Even in little kitten heels, she barely stood above people's shoulders. Her long dark hair was pulled back into a ponytail, but a few strands of hair had escaped from the hot-pink elastic band and hung like limp string down her back. Then there was the dress. Boxy and black, it stopped mid calf and left *everything* to the imagination. She could have been smuggling one of the ant colonies they were supporting with this fundraising cocktail party at the Harbor City Museum of Natural History under the damn thing. There was absolutely nothing about her to make a guy like him pause for a first look, let alone come back for a second and a third—except that's exactly what he was doing. Why? Fuck if he knew. All he could think was that underneath her oversized black glasses were two startlingly blue eyes and a pair of cheekbones that had him itching for a paintbrush and a blank canvas.

A soft cough pulled his attention away from the mystery

woman and over to his mother, who'd clearly caught him ogling. *Shit.* Hudson Carlyle's mother was a barracuda in a bun, and there was no missing the danger signals in her steely gray eyes. He'd seen them before, when she'd set her matchmaking sights on his older brother, Sawyer. And now she was looking at him, her youngest son, with that I-just-found-the-perfect-sacrificial-lamb gleam in her eyes.

Rubbing the back of his neck, he tried to ignore the prickly sensation crawling along his skin and focus on the party before him.

At least the throngs of wealthy guests would help distract Helene Carlyle from whatever mission she was about to undertake. Well, that and the fact that the fundraiser they were attending was in the middle of the Harbor City Museum of Natural History's Ant Lab—which was exactly what it sounded like. *Shudder.*

Each wall of the lab was made up of two sheets of glass with ant colonies sandwiched between them. If it wasn't for the fact that he loved his family, there was no way in hell he'd ever be caught dead here. He'd much rather be hunkered down in his cabin, finishing up the paintings he'd sold. Or rather, that "Hughston," one of Harbor City's most sought after—and mysterious—artists had sold.

His chest tightened at the thought of all the little white lies he'd been telling his family for years to keep his double life a secret. They thought he was nothing more than a rich playboy, only interested in the next cover model he could get naked, and that was just how things needed to remain.

Still, when his family needed him, he came—even when it was to a place where the walls were literally crawling with bugs. *Double shudder.*

"Let's mingle," his mother announced in that well-bred tone that brooked no argument, then she hooked her arm through his and started walking.

He shook his head. *And I guess we're "mingling" now.* Because of his height, he could look over the crowd and see the throngs of charity guests parting as though he was walking Queen Elizabeth across the red carpet, a person nodding at them here, another trying to gain their attention there. His mother acknowledged them with a gracious nod but didn't stop. She was guiding them toward Hudson's older brother Sawyer, who was standing next to, but not actually *talking to*, his former best friend Tyler Jacobson.

His mother continued as they went, "While I appreciate you being my escort for this fundraiser, I really wish you had someone of your own to bring."

Hudson let a lazy half smile curl his lips and raised one eyebrow teasingly—a move that usually annoyed his mom as much as it made the city's sexiest socialites sigh and lose their better judgment. "Be careful about saying 'escort' too loudly," he warned. "We wouldn't want to give people the wrong idea about what it is I do with all of my free time."

She raised a matching eyebrow. "Considering I know almost every person here, and they all most definitely know who *I* am, we can safely assume that no one is going to mistake my son for an escort."

"A guy can dream." He shrugged with a laugh, his gaze again settling on his brother and Tyler. The animosity between the two men had lessened over the past few months, but they were nowhere near the friends they'd been for decades.

"A mother has dreams, too," Helene said with a pitiful sigh that she must have practiced for hours. She dropped her gaze before looking back up at him with all the innocence of a honey badger.

"Give it up," he said, his steps stalling out as he caught that familiar gleam in her eyes. She pretended her attention was riveted by the soon-to-be-divorced Masons arriving together, but he wasn't fooled. "Don't you dare look at me like that.

I *know* that look. It's the same one you started shooting at Sawyer before you began Operation: Matchmaking Mama. I'm immune."

"I'm sure I don't know what you're talking about." She squeezed his arm, a devious smile tugging at the corners of her mouth—a mouth almost exactly like the one that greeted him from the mirror every morning, except right now, hers looked more like a shark baring its teeth. "But you do look very handsome saying it."

"Mother, you should leave the charm to me. It's scary looking on you."

She patted his cheek, a little harder than she needed to, and then shook her head. "All that charm won't always get you what you want. Not in the long run."

"Don't worry. It does everything I need in the short term." He winked at her then resumed walking, this time guiding *her* to Sawyer's side. He needed to hand Helene off before she sank her claws in any farther, and his brother owed him. "And the long run? My massive bank account will take care of that."

If Helene Carlyle were the kind of woman to snort, that's how he would describe the sound leaving her throat unexpectedly. As it was, he had to imagine she'd delicately sneezed.

"That attitude might fool most people, Hudson Bartholomew Carlyle, but it doesn't fly with me," she said, her attention zeroed in on his brother and former friend who were pointedly ignoring each other while Sawyer's wife, Clover, talked animatedly with Tyler.

Out of the corner of his eye, he noticed the young woman in the boxy dress weaving through the crowd, heading straight for the same target as he was. She almost looked elegant for a moment, but as she neared Sawyer and Tyler, she tripped over her own feet.

His muscles tensed, wishing he was close enough to catch her, but Tyler and Sawyer quickly reached out to stop her fall. She said something to Tyler as she pushed her black glasses up from where they'd slipped down almost to the end of her button nose. Despite her being only a few feet away, her voice was so soft that Hudson couldn't hear what she said, but it was followed by a gruff "no problem" and a nonchalant "no worries" from the men. The interaction seemed to jolt Sawyer and Tyler out of their silent standoff, though, and for half a second, it looked like they'd actually talk. But instead, both nodded good-bye to the woman and headed in opposite directions, Sawyer tugging his wife Clover along with him.

Douchebags. It couldn't be more obvious that the two wanted to be friends again, but neither of them would do a damn thing about it. Although he had to admit, bro-code and all, he blamed Tyler for the rift. It wasn't like Sawyer encouraged Tyler's fiancée to end up naked in Sawyer's bed. Sawyer had sent her on her way, but Tyler insisted everything was his brother's fault. Ridiculous pride.

Hudson's ire started to rise further as he studied his mystery woman, who was still watching Tyler's retreating form. Sadness darkened her eyes, giving the tip of her nose the slightest red tint. As an artist, Hudson had spent his life studying people and learning their secrets so he could better paint them, and one thing was certain about this woman— she was unquestionably in love with Tyler. Poor thing. She was definitely not his type. Tyler liked 'em tall, blonde, busty, and bitchy.

"You need to fix that, Hudson," his mother said, pulling his attention away from the woman—again.

"Me?" he asked, following her gaze toward Sawyer. "Why is this my problem?"

"How I manage not to flick your ears on a regular basis, I have no idea." The words were stern, but she couldn't hide the love in her tone. "He's your brother, and he needs your help—I need your help."

He grinned down at her. "Fixing a broken bromance isn't exactly my thing."

"Fixing things has *always* been your thing. Sawyer and Tyler have regained some of their footing as friends, but they haven't been able to make total amends. I need you to facilitate that process—without either of them knowing, of course."

Now that would be an accomplishment.

"Why, Mother," he said, shaking his head as if she weren't the original fixer in the Carlyle family, "that sounds downright devious. Who would have ever thought it of you?"

This time Helene definitely snorted. "We all know you're not above a little tinkering to maneuver people to where they need to be. Just look at how you helped Sawyer and Clover get together." Her gaze stopping on someone just over his shoulder. "You know people. You understand what makes them tick—you always have. Take that woman, for instance. What can you tell me about her?"

Hudson pivoted and spotted the woman his mom had caught him checking out earlier, the same one who was still mooning over Tyler, staring at the clueless idiot—now talking to a tall blonde—like he'd just run over her cat. What could he tell his mom about the mystery woman? A lot. What could he say to his cunning mother without giving away his immediate fascination with the mystery woman? Not much.

The petite brunette had an air about her that sucked him right in and made him want to get her on canvas now, but for the life of him, he couldn't figure out why, and he definitely wasn't going to share that tidbit with his matchmaking mama.

"I can't tell you anything important about her, Mom," he said, forcing himself to look at anyone but the woman. "She probably works here. Well, and she obviously has a thing for

Tyler."

"I noticed that, too. She keeps circling around to talk to him and never quite gets up the courage, even when she almost fell right into him."

His fingertips itched just like they always did before something in the world shifted. "And why are you so interested?"

"There's just something about her, isn't there? I can't place my finger on it, but it might just be what Tyler needs. You could help her. No one has quite your way of charming people into doing what you want. If you could help her win over Tyler, then I do believe Tyler and Sawyer would be able to fix their friendship themselves. He just needs help getting over that dreadful ex before he can forgive and forget."

"What are you saying?" he asked. The image of his mystery woman with Tyler left a sour taste in his mouth, like he'd just licked chalk.

"I'm saying that love conquers all." She got that misty look in her eyes, and the lines around her mouth softened just like they always did when she thought about his dad, who'd died a few years ago. "Now, go do that fixing thing that you secretly do so well and help your brother get back his best friend, and then *maybe* we can get you to use that talent for the benefit of Carlyle Enterprises. There's more to the family business than just sneaking cookies from Mrs. Esposito in the company cafeteria. You do know you have a corner office collecting dust, don't you?"

"I have an office?" He winked at her and then shifted his gaze back to Tyler Jacobson.

Hudson cocked his head and grinned as his favorite kind of plan started to form in his head—one that helped the people he cared about and allowed him to get what he really wanted, all while keeping his secret life...well, secret. Oh yeah, this was going to work like a charm.

• • •

Felicia Hartigan's life would be so much better if she could just get back to her honeypot ants. Of course, as her boss had pointed out rather specifically to her earlier today, that wasn't going to happen if Harbor City's rich and bored didn't donate money to the natural history museum's ant lab. So here she was. Lucky her.

"It could be worse," said fellow researcher Stan Gabrys. Tall and thin, with red hair that had started to go wispy, he was currently trying to pull off a Van Dyke beard that always made her think "magician" when she saw him. "One year, we had to put on a show-and-tell demonstration."

"I love talking about my ants." Sure, she was a researcher, but as an academic, she couldn't overlook an opportunity to educate.

Stan grimaced as a rosy flush creeped up from the silver hook of his clip-on tie. "We had to dress up like the ants we researched."

Felicia imagined herself dressed in a giant bubble to represent how the honeypot ant gorged itself on food until it looked like Violet from *Charlie and the Chocolate Factory* so it could feed the other ants in the colony when there wasn't enough food to be found. The picture was even worse than having to go out like she was now, in her cute new classic little black dress rather than her regular T-shirt and jeans (with the cuffs tucked into her socks if she was out in the field). *Why am I still single?* She mentally shook her head.

"So, who's the guy over there talking to your rich friend?" Stan asked.

An excited buzz started in her stomach. "Tyler Jacobson?"

She only had one rich friend, and *he* was the reason she was here, despite her boss's insistence notwithstanding. Everyone else here was either Harbor City elite—and therefore out of her social strata—or someone she worked with, making them a big, giant no-no. She didn't mix her ant species, and she didn't mix her work and personal lives. Felicia believed in boundaries, the importance of evidence-based science, and that success came with never deviating from the plan. In this case, that meant not giving up on getting Tyler Jacobson to really see her. And if he was looking at her, then spending the birthday check her mom had sent her early—*"Thirty days before thirty! Go have some fun," she'd written*—on this flattering black dress had totally been the right move.

Stan shook his head. "No, I've met him before. You introduced him at another one of these things. It's the guy he's talking with, who keeps staring."

Felicia glanced in the direction Stan motioned with his head. Since animal classification was kind of her thing, she assessed and categorized the man talking with Tyler in an instant. He was tall, with longish light brown hair, and lean muscles that he used to his advantage as he exuded the easy confidence of the obnoxiously rich. His lazy smile proved just how often he got his way. Just as she was thinking it, he turned and zeroed in on her and that smile of his went from nice enough to dangerous, as if he not only knew what kind of panties she was wearing, but how to get her out of them, too. He was too tall, too handsome, and too full of himself. To put it bluntly, she would classify him scientifically as Family: Man, Genus: Not for Her.

Now, Tyler Jacobson? He was all dark hair, blue eyes, and brains. Smart wasn't the new sexy. It was the *only* sexy as far as Felicia was concerned. Super-stud over there with his I-have-sex-for-breakfast-every-day grin didn't stand a chance in her world.

She turned around and shrugged. "No clue."

"Well, he's coming this way with that Travis dude," Stan said.

"Tyler," she corrected as heat pricked her cheeks. Out of habit, she smoothed her hair back and straightened her spine to add as much as she could to her five-foot-nothing height.

This was it. *This* was why she allowed herself to be pushed into doing exactly the opposite of her usual Thursday night plan of a hot bath, a single glass of red wine, and the latest issue of the *Journal of Myrmecology*. With her birthday only a month away, she still had time to check off *Make Tyler Fall for Me* on the list of career and personal goals to hit before thirty that she'd made when she was fifteen. There were already black check marks by every other item on the list (graduate first in her class, land a premium research position, move across the harbor from Waterbury to the big city), and she wasn't a woman to leave things undone.

. . .

Hudson had never been more thoroughly ignored by a woman in his entire life. Women loved him. He was funny, charming, and knew exactly what to do to with his tongue to make a woman's toes curl and her eyes roll back in her head as she screamed her thanks to God, the fates, and anyone in between that he'd been born with a mouth like that. Plus, he had more money than some island nations. That in itself usually got him a slow, appreciative look.

However, Felicia—she of the black burlap-sack of a dress, messy hair, perfect bone structure, and mysterious something in her eyes that only a paintbrush could figure out, had attention for Tyler alone. For his part, Captain Clueless was too busy scoping out everyone else at the fundraiser to notice. It chapped Hudson's ass and made him even more curious— and if that wasn't karma telling him to go fuck himself, then he didn't know what was.

Really, he should excuse himself, make a quick stop at

the bar, and then find one of the many society darlings to run off with and work out the crazy taking up space in his head. Instead, he couldn't move.

The way the light bounced off her features. The way she hid behind those big glasses. The certain something that could only be discovered by getting her on canvas. They all made the center of his palms itch. He had to paint her. It wasn't a choice. It was a necessity. Good thing for him, she had an obvious, if totally baffling, thing for Tyler, and the man had no fucking clue. That meant his plan to kill two birds with one ant researcher was going to work out just fine.

As she continued to rattle on about honeypot ants— seriously who knew scientists could have such dirty minds? What other excuse could there be for that name—she flashed a wasted smile at Tyler, one that emphasized the fullness of her bottom lip. Hudson would have to mix just the right acrylics to get the shade right, but it could be done. It *would* be done. When the other guy in their little foursome *(Steve? Stan?)* walked a few feet away with Tyler, and they started talking about the disaster that was the latest Harbor City Warriors game, Hudson leaned down—way down—to whisper in Felicia's ear.

"You want Tyler." He hadn't meant to blurt it out or make her uncomfortable, but he sensed this woman wouldn't tolerate beating around the bush. It was refreshing, honestly, to be able to say exactly what he was thinking with a woman. Of course, she'd probably fight admitting it to a stranger. He needed to tread carefully if he wanted to get her to agree to help him. Or let him help her, more precisely.

A pink blush stained her cheeks as her hands fluttered around in front of her like she was about to go all Jackson Pollock on him. "I don't know what you're talking about," she finally said, her soft voice hard to hear with the crowd around them.

"It's okay, sweetheart. We're in the tree of trust." He gave her the smile that always got him extra cookies from Mrs. Esposito. "You like him, but he hasn't noticed."

"Of course I like him," she huffed. "We've been friends almost our entire lives. Well, he's been friends with my older brother Frankie for that long."

Sounded to him like the buttoned-up ant researcher was protesting too much. "And at any point during the very long and supposedly storied history of your friendship, has he kissed you?" There went that blush of hers again. He tried to clear the teasing, subtle, spicy amber scent of her out of his head before it took his thoughts in a different direction "Pressed up against you?" She tugged the juicy flesh of her lip with her teeth. "Slid his fingers—"

"That's enough," she said, her voice a quiet squeak. "What are you, the Non-Relationship Police?"

He waited a beat, just long enough to watch her skin return to its pale, creamy color. Then, unable to stop himself, he teased. "I'm your fairy godmother wrapped in this extremely awesome, sexy package. It's okay to swoon a little. I won't judge."

Her jaw muscles worked overtime fighting a smile before she said in a low tone, "Let me guess, your massive ego turns into a magic wand?"

"That's not what most women call it—well, except the 'massive' part." He winked and almost laughed out loud when her eyes widened.

One of her dainty hands snagged a glass of champagne from a passing waiter, and she tossed the whole thing back like a trooper. When she set the empty glass back on the bar, her shoulders shook with silent laughter. "I can't believe you started this conversation about one man and expertly turned it into a dissertation about your own junk."

"I wouldn't call this a 'dissertation.' More like a thesis

statement at this point, wouldn't you agree?" He spied a waiter at the end of the bar refilling his tray with bubbly, and Hudson subtlety nodded for service. While this conversation was turning to one of his favorite topics—himself—he needed to steer things back to Tyler.

"But I think I can help you snag Tyler without the aid of my 'magic wand.'" He squashed the immediate revolt in his pants and grabbed two flutes of champagne from the offered tray. He handed one to Felicia, curious if she'd pound this one back, too.

"You think so, do you?" she asked, all eyes for Tyler while she sipped at the bubbly liquid. Pity.

"Thinking doesn't factor into it. I'm just that good," he said, watching her work out the possibilities with that super fast mind of hers before she tossed the rest of the champagne back like they were in a frat house. He smiled. *That's my girl.* "This is all about the heart. You want Tyler to see you as a woman—his kind of woman—and I can help you do just that."

When it came to what made women irresistible, he knew it all—one of the many benefits of being a lifelong connoisseur.

Felicia's face lit up with wry amusement, and she managed to get her soft voice above a murmur. "Are you offering to make me over into what the patriarchy has decided is attractive?"

"No," he said, slipping off the superficial charm like a snake shedding its skin. "I'm offering to help you get what you've wanted, probably since perfect Tyler first became friends with your older brother Freddie."

"Frankie," she said reflexively.

"Whatever." He shrugged, knowing the key to getting her to agree was in appealing to her scientific mind. Earlier, he'd gotten a glimpse into the way she thought while she'd excitedly explained to him and Tyler about her ant research. She was methodical. And driven. "You don't strike me as a woman who gives up on what she wants without at least an experiment."

For a second, he had her. He would have sworn it in a court of law.

Then, that perfect bottom lip of hers straightened out and flattened. "I don't, but I'm also not the type to trick a man into believing he's getting a different sort of woman. Thank you for the offer, but I think I've got things under control."

With a little tilt to her stubborn chin and a shake of her head, she turned to leave, but he shot out his hand to stop her. It started as a tingle the second his fingers curled around her forearm and built to a vibration that shot straight to his dick the longer he held her. He should let go. He didn't. He stepped closer, eliminating the distance between them. He was supposed to be persuading her, not picturing all the things he'd like to do to her and wondering what sounds she'd make when he did them.

"Look, Matches, there's no doubt about it, my ego is huge, but my reputation is well earned." He studied her gaze carefully. "No one else out there can help you get Tyler as well as I can. You've been trying for years, haven't you?" He watched, fascinated, as her skin turned rosy. "Yeah, that pretty pink blush tells me everything I need to know. You want him, and I can make sure you get him."

Of course, he had zero plans for her to actually end up with Tyler. His instincts said this woman was *more*. Definitely more than Tyler deserved. Sure, he'd agreed to help mend fences between Tyler and Hudson, but he could do that without Felicia ending up with Captain Clueless. Tyler had been Sawyer's best friend, not his, and he owed no loyalty to the guy who'd made his brother's life miserable for the last umpteen years. No, he had a much better way to mend their friendship, while at the same time showing Felicia she deserved more than her stupid childhood crush. He was going to save her from herself. Then, of course, she'd owe him and let him work her out on canvas.

"And what do you want in return?" she asked, her voice breathier than it had been before.

"To paint you." Her eyebrows reached her hairline in a split second, and he rushed to assure her. "No one would ever know." No one *could* know, or he'd risk exposing his secret life.

"Is that the new 'let me show you my etchings'?" she asked, looking down at where his fingers pressed into her flesh, though she didn't try to free herself.

"Tick tock, Matches." Adrenaline surged through him, shrinking his world until she was the only thing in it. "What's it going to be?"

She flicked her gaze up at him, her blue eyes scrutinizing him behind her thick glasses. "Why are you calling me Matches?"

The truth came out before he could think of a charming lie. "Because they're small, but when you stroke them just right, they can burn the whole place down."

Her jaw flexed, and she started to say something before shaking her head. "I'm sorry, but I'm going to have to pass on your generous offer," she said, her voice quiet but firm. "If you have any ant lab business or donations to discuss, which I very much doubt you do, you can find me at the lab during regular business hours."

Then she turned and walked across the ant lab, disappearing behind a door marked STAFF ONLY.

Hudson was still trying to understand what had just happened when Tyler—apparently back from talking sports— elbowed him in the ribs, a shit-eating grin on his face.

"I've known Felicia my whole life," Tyler said, goodwill toward her but nothing more incendiary in his tone. "She's the youngest of seven and the total runt of the litter—not that it's ever mattered. You might not think it because she's got that whole quiet nerdy girl thing going on, but you don't want to go up against her. She'll knock you on your ass, Pretty Boy."

Yeah, she'd just delivered a metaphorical swift kick to the nuts. But Hudson would get back up. He always did—it was part of his charm.

Chapter Two

Back in jeans at the ant lab the next afternoon, surrounded by her favorite creatures, Felicia felt her shoulders inch down from where they'd lodged up by her ears since her run-in with the too-charming-for-anyone's-good Hudson Carlyle. The man and his so-called offer to help her win over Tyler had burrowed under her skin and burned like a fire ant's bite the whole night.

Being back in the cubicle farm, not so unlike an ant colony, she settled into her chair and waited for her computer to boot up. Just as she took a sip of Earl Grey from her YOU HAD ME AT ANTS travel mug, her boss Eddie Sledge stopped next to her cubicle, a sheen of sweat making the top of his bald head shiny. Her muscles tensed. A glistening dome always meant trouble—usually from the higher ups.

"There you are, Felicia," Eddie said, his voice unnaturally loud and his eye doing that weird twitch thing that happened whenever he was nervous.

"What's up?" Whatever it was, it better not concern her because she had work to do. Not that she'd ever *say* that out loud. But she'd *think* it at shouting volume.

Eddie's left eye twitched. "We have a special guest with us this morning who wants to get a tour of the ant lab in general and of your honeypot ant research colonies specifically."

The pop of excitement at the idea of someone else who loved honeypots was tempered by the reality of her workload. It wasn't all fieldwork and data collection. She had to get published—the true currency of power in any scientific field. She may be down to one item on her do-it-by-thirty list, but she was already tackling the items on her to-do-by-thirty-five list, and those included becoming a peer reviewer for the *Journal of Myrmecology*. To do that she had to get published—and often—so the editors would think of her when they refreshed the review board as they always did in three-year cycles. After that, she'd be one step closer to joining the journal's scientific advisory board, which was key to moving from researcher at the ant lab to department head someday.

"I'm behind already on the article I'm putting together to submit to the *Journal of Myrmecology* because of the fundraiser last night."

"I understand." Eddie's head bopped up and down in a staccato beat. "But this guest...well, he could really help out the lab."

That answer meant only one thing. "He has deep pockets, huh?"

"And you know funding isn't what it used to be."

No, it sure wasn't. As grants became tougher to get, and other funding sources dried up, getting the money to run a stellar program like the Harbor City Natural History Museum's Ant Lab had become a full-time job for Eddie, which explained the rapid hair loss. And God knew she needed the practice keeping her blue-collar opinions to herself when she was around the well-heeled elite if she ever wanted to run the department.

Of course, that wasn't normally a problem. Last night's slip had been because of the champagne she'd shotgunned, obviously. Taking a deep breath, she made up her mind not to mess up this opportunity.

"Okay," she said, setting down her travel mug next to her messenger bag stuffed with notes. "Who's the sucker?"

"Me," a deep voice said, filtering from just outside of Felicia's cubicle.

She froze. *That* voice. It was one she'd heard all night telling her that he could help her get the man she'd always wanted. Hudson Carlyle. The butterflies in her stomach split up into Team Annoyance and Team Anticipation as she turned and saw him watching her from over the top of her cubicle—the one she couldn't see over even when she stood on her tiptoes.

"Mr. Carlyle," Eddie squeaked. "I didn't realize you were so close."

"I studied with an elite group of ninjas for years," Hudson said with a straight face, coming around to stand next to Eddie in the doorway. "Old habits die hard."

In jeans that probably cost more than her monthly grocery bill, a dark green cashmere sweater that would cover her electric bill—but perfectly set off the flecks of green in his brown eyes—and with his light brown hair artfully messed up, he looked delicious. If Felicia went for that hot rich guy with too much charm, which she most definitely did not. Forget broad shoulders, hard abs—she could tell even if they were covered—and an ass that was made for a beefcake calendar, she cared about what was inside a person, not the sexy facade.

So, you're admitting he's sexy, Hartigan?

She wasn't dead, just smarter than the average socialite he probably banged and forgot about, and therefore she was able to see through his lame attempt to torment her some more.

"*You're* the one who wants to learn more about the honeypot ant?" she asked, tight and quiet and trying her hardest to keep her disbelief to herself. And obviously failing, from the way Eddie's eyes went wide and the shine on his head actually got brighter.

The sexy grin on Hudson's face transformed into more of a smolder as he gave her a slow up and down that sent Team Anticipation into kamikaze spins.

"Honeypots," he said, pausing for effect after the word. "have *always* fascinated me."

Internally, she rolled her eyes and fought to keep her words steady and firm. "I'm sure there are plenty of places where you can study up."

"But none quite as good as the natural history museum," Eddie said in a rush, narrowing his eyes at her. "Our facility is head and thoraxes above other research facilities. Aren't we, Dr. Hartigan?"

Eating her groan at his horrible ant pun, she nodded in agreement. "Without a doubt."

"Then I can't wait to discover all of your secrets." Hudson held out his hand toward Eddie, who shook it. "Thanks for helping to set this up, man. I really appreciate it. I'll be sure to put in a good word for the lab at the next Carlyle Foundation meeting."

Eddie swallowed the promise hook, line, and sinker, the poor optimist. Unless her IQ and powers of observation, which had been honed out in the deserts of Arizona while watching honeypot ants for days on end, had failed her, Hudson had probably never been to one of his family's foundation meetings in his life. The air of the lazy and bored rich clung too heavily to his designer clothes for that. Too bad there wasn't any avoiding this uncomfortable tour.

"Well then," she said, pasting on her snooty scientist

smile. that probably made her look a bit deranged, but it was her go-to defense mechanism when she was nervous. "Let's not delay in enlightening you further."

"Looking forward to it," he said, stepping to the side and allowing enough room for her to pass him, but not so much that she missed inhaling the woodsy musk of his cologne.

Team Anticipation flat passed out in her belly, and she tripped over her feet. Hudson's arm shot out, and he caught her, his fingers curling around her elbow. A tingling awareness zipped through her before settling with a quiet buzz between her legs.

"Careful there," he said, his voice grittier than the playful tone he'd had just a moment ago.

Oh no. This isn't allowed. Deviating from the plan only meant disaster, and the plan began and ended with Tyler Jacobson.

"Thank you." She slid her arm free. "Let's get on with it."

"You're the boss," Hudson replied, the teasing timbre back. "Show me the way."

Ignoring the wink he gave her, and the prick of disappointment that came out of nowhere, Felicia strode toward the glass-encased honeypot ant colony that formed the heart of her life's research.

• • •

Turns out, the honeypot ant was disgusting.

Hudson took a step back from the eight-by-ten glossy close-up photo of an ant with its middle so engorged it looked like someone had glued an ant head and legs onto a yellow marble. If he never saw *that* in real life, he'd die a happy man.

"So," he said, turning back to Felicia, who wore a twisted sort of glee on her face, obviously enjoying playing up this part about her ants as they toured the public portion of the ant lab. "It drains itself whenever someone else in the colony is hungry, and then that ant eats it?"

"When necessary, yes."

And she looked like a regular human being. Sure, her jeans were rolled up at least three times at the ankles and her T-shirt was so loose he—again—had almost no clue what was underneath, but there was no hint that underneath her french braid lay the brain of a gross-out queen. What else were people missing when they saw her? There had to be more. No one knew the art of the con quite like him. She was good, but not good enough to fool him. Matches was hiding something, and he needed to know what.

"And you study these things voluntarily?" he asked, moving on to look at the glassed-in colony, thankfully with no engorged ants visible to the naked eye.

"I've even gone out to Arizona and done field research, counting the colony's foragers, nest maintenance, and protector ants before excavating the nest and taking the ants back to a research facility."

He took a long look at the colony; it took up a good chunk of the wall. "How do you excavate an entire colony?"

Her blue eyes gleamed. "With a backhoe."

Turning back to her, he tried to imagine her in the hot desert sun, sweaty in an almost see-through tank top and short shorts (what could he say, he was a dude) digging up an entire colony of unsuspecting ants. Part of him zoomed in on the picture of her in those shorts, but the rest of him couldn't help but picture the unmitigated joy of being in her element that would show on her face. It would be hell to get it just right on a canvas, but if he could, it would stop a gallery walker in their tracks—a real only-a-Hughston-painting moment.

"So, you're like an alien who lands on a foreign planet, studies the creatures, and then destroys their home before taking them back onto your spaceship for further study?"

Her narrow shoulders tensed, and the pointed chin of her heart-shaped face went up a notch. "That's one way to look at it."

"How do you look at it?" he asked, loving how easy it was—despite her quiet voice and deep blushes—to get her all sparked up for a fight.

"As though I am obtaining evidence about ant colonies so we can better understand them and their place in the world. So perhaps one day we don't take them for granted and lose another species important to our planet's ecosystem."

Okay, it made sense even to him. "We're all in it together."

"Yeah, we are." She gave him a considering look, her eyes narrowing behind her glasses. "I didn't expect that coming from someone like you."

The words were no more out of her mouth when she shoved up her glasses with a shaky finger, and a mottled red creeped up from the crew neck of her T-shirt. Obviously, she hadn't meant for those words to exit out her sweet mouth. He wanted to give himself a little pat on the back for guessing correctly that she was a tell-it-like-it-is kind of woman, but her words stung a little.

How many times had he heard it before? It had to be at least a billion. *"Like me?"* It wasn't that he didn't encourage everyone to think there was nothing going on behind his pretty mug, but coming from her, it settled uncomfortably across his shoulders. "Oh, I see," he said, closing the distance between them in two long strides. "Is it the deep pockets or the hot bod that throws you off?"

The red went all the way up to her chin with one giant splotch on each cheek. "I...I..."

"Let me let you in on a secret," he said, stopping just out of arm's reach because all he wanted to do was touch her. "I never had a choice about the money or the looks. I've had them both since I was born. You know what I also have? A fully functioning brain." Fuck it. Another step, and he was close enough to brush the silk of an escaped strand of hair behind her ear. "I would have thought that someone who believes in evidence-based science would have waited to make some more observations before developing a hypothesis, but what do I know?" He pulled back from the edge before he cupped the back of her head, threaded his fingers through her braid, and held her where he wanted her. "I'm just the handsome, rich dilettante."

Where in the hell had that come from? He was usually cooler than that—especially when he was the one who wanted people to think there wasn't anything more to him than a cocky grin and a well-earned reputation for debauchery. He didn't know what it was about the diminutive ant researcher, but she got him right in the soft underbelly that he hadn't even realized was unguarded. He didn't like it. Fuck that. He *hated* it, but he couldn't ignore it any more than he could pretend not to see there was more to Felicia Hartigan than she let the world see, too.

His words hung between them as the ants went about their business not giving a shit about how the museum air suddenly smelled like it did before a summer storm—electric and full of possibilities. Inches of open space, that was all that stood between his mouth and hers. Her lips parted, and the tip of her pink tongue wet the bottom one. The pulse point at the base of her neck thrummed, drawing his gaze to the long, creamy column.

"All right, children, stay together," a chipper female voice called out. "Don't get separated from your buddy."

Hudson and Felicia both turned as if in a trance. A group of about twenty kindergartners in blue blazers and plaid skirts, walking two by two, wandered into the ant lab, heading straight toward the manmade ant mound big enough to crawl through. They didn't even look at Hudson and Felicia, but it didn't matter. By the time he'd turned to look at her again, her eyes had cleared, her pulse had slowed, and the moment was gone. He shifted his stance to accommodate for the fact that his pants were tighter than they'd been when he'd left his apartment this morning.

"You're right," Felicia said, straightening her glasses with hands that no longer trembled, her low voice steady. "I made up my mind about you before we'd even spoken." She exhaled a deep breath and met his gaze head on, her cheeks still pink. "It was wrong. I'm sorry."

For once, he didn't have a quip or a sly remark. In the world he'd grown up in, direct confrontation was frowned upon. And admitting you were wrong? Practically unheard of. He didn't know how to process it, so he fell back on what he knew best.

"Are you saying that just because I could fund your entire lab?" He kept his tone light and teasing but couldn't miss the way Felicia's intent, observant expression didn't falter.

"No. When I'm wrong, I admit it, and I was wrong." She held out her hand with its clear, close-clipped nails and delicate, tiny tattoo of a honeypot—not the ant, an actual yellow pot that said honey—inside her wrist. "Will you accept my apology?"

He took her smaller hand in his. Her handshake was firm and professional, but that didn't stop a sizzle of awareness from making him wonder once again what she was hiding under all of those baggy clothes. Yellow underwear to match her tattoo? Soft rose that matched how he imagined her nipples? His cock thickened against his thigh. Shit. He *needed* to stop thinking like this in a crowded lab with a bevy of kindergartners nearby.

"Apology accepted," he said.

She smiled up at him, and his dick did more than twitch in his pants. *Fuuuck.*

Abruptly, he released her hand, stretched out his fingers to get rid of the tingling sensation in them, and mentally marched on with the real reason he was here and not the *whatever* that was snapping between them. "So, show me something less disgusting, and then let's talk about how I'm going to get you what we both want."

She cocked her head to the side. "What's that?"

"Tyler Jacobson, of course."

Her eyebrows went up high enough to be seen over the top of her glasses, and she honest-to-God laughed at him. "No offense, but while I'm sure there are a lot of people who think you're devastatingly attractive, I doubt Tyler is one of them."

"You think I'm hot, huh?" he asked, latching on to the one part of her declaration that made his pulse quicken.

He counted. One. Two. Three. And there it was. The color in her cheeks that suddenly appeared made him think of pink lemonade and cotton candy. Judging by the way her jaw tightened, she wasn't as much of a fan of her body's reaction.

"And that brings our tour to an end." She started walking back toward the door marked STAFF ONLY.

"While you've been studying ants and observing their behavior, I've been doing the same with people," he called out, his voice easily carrying over the chatter of the school kids' giggles. "I can help you."

Her step faltered, then slowed. *That's it. Turn it over in that big brain of yours.* Finally, she stopped and pivoted to face him.

"How?" she asked.

"We'd start with the hair." It was a silky dark brown, almost black color that naturally caught the light. "You should wear it loose more."

"A makeover?" she scoffed. "What is this, some dumb movie where the girl takes off her glasses and then everyone falls at her feet?"

He took another look at the worn sneakers, baggy jeans, and loose-fitting T-shirt. "No, we have more work than that ahead of us. This is more of a *My Fair Lady* project."

"You've seen that movie?"

"It's my mom's favorite, and I've been forced to sit through it a time or two hundred." And he'd sat through it every time she wanted to watch it after his dad died unexpectedly. It had been a rough three years of mourning for his mom, and he had done anything he could think of to make Helene smile— or at least not look quite so lost.

"Does that make you the professor?" Felicia asked.

"Exactly."

"No way." She shook her head. "I don't believe in changing myself for a man. I'm a scientist. A girl from across the harbor in Waterbury. I don't do false lashes, fake boobs, or a knock-off personality."

"Good." The mental image of her like that put a foul taste in his mouth. "You wouldn't be nearly as interesting if you did. What I'm talking about is"—he searched for the right word to pull her in—"an experiment. You don't like my hypothesis that with a little visual tweaking you could catch Tyler's attention so that the real you could reel him in for good? Fine. But you see it all the time in the animal kingdom. I bet even your ants do things a certain way to attract a mate. It doesn't make them bad or shallow or any less genuine. But if you want to make Tyler really wonder what he's been missing all these years, you need to shake things up a bit—not change, but tweak. So, what do you say?"

She crossed her arms and pursed her mouth, the move making her nose scrunch up, and he held his breath. He'd made his case. All she had to do was say yes, and everyone would win. Felicia would land Tyler, he had no doubt about it, and she'd be happy. Or, even better, she'd realize when she actually had a choice of Tyler or no-Tyler, she was definitely better off no-Tyler—the guy was way too much of an idiot for someone like Felicia, who, let's face it, probably only wanted Tyler because she couldn't have him. So he'd help get her the thing she wanted most, and he'd hope like hell that at the end, she'd want someone else—him, at least for the moment. He wanted her on his canvas and in his bed until he figured out what it was about her that was so damn captivating. He wouldn't deny it. Not to himself anyway.

Felicia would be happy he set her free of her childhood crush to find a man who was better than either himself or Tyler to share her life with. Then, Captain Clueless could find himself a woman. Any woman but Felicia.

He couldn't stop the grin overtaking his features. Sometimes, he was just too fucking brilliant.

"Nice try." She lifted one shoulder in a half shrug. "But not in this lifetime, which means this is the end of your tour."

Hudson's grin melted into a frown as he watched her walk away, not exactly sure what had happened to him, the supposed legendary charming Carlyle. Being turned down for the second time within twenty-four hours by the same woman was a new experience for him. He couldn't remember the last time he was turned down even once. Felicia was anything but usual, though. Fascinating? Stubborn? In desperate need of his help? Yes, to all of the above. Turning the problem over in his head, he lingered in the ant lab trying to understand how such small creatures—or people for that matter—could pack such a big punch.

Chapter Three

The days were still sunny with blue skies, but an early October chill had already rolled up Sixteenth Street along with a biting breeze that sliced through Felicia's light jacket as soon as she walked out the museum's side door a few minutes after she'd told Hudson good-bye. Using her taxi app had been a good call and—bonus!—it was already waiting for her. Hustling across the sidewalk before the light changed and the massive stream of people hurrying home from work grew even thicker, she straightened her spine and popped out her elbows a little and tried to make herself seem as big as possible. She felt a little ridiculous, but when you were five feet and one-half inch on a *tall* day, you had to do what you could to avoid being trampled in the Harbor City crush.

She fought her way through the dense crowd across the wide sidewalk and reached for the door handle of her ride. Before she could wrap her fingers around it, though, a large hand with a few specks of blue paint on it beat her to it. Her jaw tightened. Oh no. No one was snagging her ride home. Ready for battle, she turned and looked up...right into the face of Hudson Carlyle.

He shot her a cocky grin. "What a coincidence."

That's what the kids were calling it these days, huh? "Stalk much?"

"Not at all. I was chatting with your boss Eddie and happened to spot the same cab as you. No reason we can't share, is there?" He opened the door.

"It's unlikely we're going the same way." It was expensive to live *anywhere* in Harbor City, but the people in his tax bracket lived uptown, not on the East side where her one bedroom apartment was.

"There you go assuming again before your facts are in," he said.

Ugh. She closed her eyes and counted to ten. She *hated* when he was right—and he was. She was doing it. *Again.*

"Come on." She slipped into the cab, her heart beating a little faster than normal—because of annoyance, obviously—and slid across the seat until her hip was against the opposite door.

Hudson got in behind her, his broad shoulders taking up entirely too much space, and closed the door.

"Where to?" the driver asked as he pulled into traffic.

Hudson looked up from the mile of space between them, a grin playing on his lips, and stared at her expectantly. The challenge did *not* go unnoticed. He wasn't going to say anything, the manipulative pain in her ass. First, he sabotaged her morning with that so-called tour. Then, she couldn't stop wondering about the kiss that had almost happened between them—she *swore* he was going to seal the deal before the real tour group walked in, and she was *not* excited at that possibility. She. Was. Not. And now, he'd elbowed his way into her ride home.

"I promise I just want to share a cab," he said. "Ladies first."

She didn't believe it, but he didn't give off a stalker vibe, even though she'd accused him. Oh, Hudson was determined, all right, but her danger alarms stayed quiet, and her gut didn't rumble. Sometimes a cab ride really was just a cab ride.

The cabbie cleared his throat.

Felicia huffed out a sigh. "Forty-fifth and Havston."

"You got it." The driver nodded and cut off two cars in his effort to hurry up and get in the left-hand lane before the traffic congestion bottled them in.

Cars blurring past them, she swiveled in her seat and gave Hudson her best glare—the one that made her six-foot-six redwood tree of a brother, Frankie, shiver in his steel-toed workbooks. It had exactly zero effect on Hudson. Wait. It *did* have an effect—the glutton for punishment relaxed against the seat, somehow managing to all but eliminate the space between them, and winked at her.

That actually worked on women? What a frightening thought.

Thinking tall thoughts, she straightened her spine and pressed back her shoulders. "Is this where you try to go all Henry Higgins again?"

"Nope." There went that lazy curl of his lips. "I changed my mind."

Well, that answer sucked all the wind out of her sails. She slouched back against the seat. "Good."

It was exactly the answer she wanted. If it wasn't for the fact that he gave in *waaaay* too easily. But for someone who'd shown up at the ant lab with some bullshit story about wanting a tour, to a guy who just *happened* to go for the same cab as her, his giving in didn't fit. Sitting there, surrounded only by the sound coming from the in-taxi TV as the traffic went from a flowing stream to a plugged-up sink, she turned it around in her mind but couldn't come up with an explanation. He was up to something, but she couldn't unwind his logic, and it made the tips of her ears itch.

She couldn't take not knowing.

"Decided I wasn't a good makeover candidate, huh?" she asked, breaking first.

"No." He shook his head and went back to watching the news updates on the tiny screen attached to the back of the front passenger seat.

That's it? No way. He hadn't stopped running his mouth since they'd met. Now they were stuck in a cab in the middle of a traffic jam, and he decided to turn into Silent Bob? Nope. That wasn't happening. There was no way he could outlast her in this game. Satisfied she'd be proven right, she focused all her attention on the TV screen and not the almost hypnotizing way the muscles on his forearms moved, or the mysterious flecks of paint on the back of his hand. All she had to do was wait.

One.

Two.

Three.

Nothing. Not even a twitch. He'd gone as still as the cars around them.

The question burst out before she even realized the words had formed. "Are you going to tell me?"

He slowly turned his gaze to hers. "Do you really want me to?"

"That's why I asked." She could take it. Small but mighty and all that.

Hudson gave her an appraising look, cool and clinical. It didn't give even a hint the man she thought she had categorized down to genus and family the other day. "You don't want it enough."

She flinched. "What?"

"You're a smart woman, determined, and you've definitely got spark," he said as he reached out and tucked a stray hair behind her ear. "But I don't think you really want to snag Tyler's attention."

What? "But…" Words failed her. She had nothing because that made about as much sense as nest maintenance ants all of a sudden becoming queens.

Hudson took his wallet out of his back pocket and grabbed a wad of cash. "Come on, let's do this over food. I'm starving."

She looked around. "But we're stuck in traffic."

"Exactly," he said, handing a few bills to the cab driver. "So, we might as well get out."

"B-B-But," she stammered, a little queasy at the idea of changing plans once she'd mentally committed—even if was just dinner plans. "I have leftovers in the fridge."

"Come on, Matches, my treat." He got out, holding the door open for her. "I know of a great place right around the corner."

This wasn't like her. She didn't abandon cabs in the middle of rush hour, or go to dinner with men who knew exactly how sexy they were.

"Best shakes you've ever had in your life," Hudson said. "Come on. Live a little."

Her stomach picked that moment to let loose with a loud growl. Hudson cocked an eyebrow. Done in by the dare-you expression on his face and her own hunger pangs, Felicia scooted across the backseat of the cab and got out on to Hamish. They walked a couple of blocks before coming to stop in front of Vito's Diner on the corner of Fifth. Out of the corner of her eye, she took in Hudson's designer clothes and two-hundred-dollar haircut before directing her attention back to the diner with its winking neon sign.

"This isn't what I was expecting," she said.

Hudson didn't say anything; he just gave her a knowing grin and opened the door. It smelled like cheeseburgers and homemade fries—in other words, heaven. They took two seats at the counter, bracketed on either side by the pie display sitting on the counter and the cash register on the other.

He slid the laminated menu over to her. "You have to get a shake or you'll regret it for the rest of your life."

She had a minute to glance at the huge list of offerings— everything from all-day breakfast to colossal sandwiches and chicken-fried steak—before the waitress stopped by, pad at the ready.

"How's your brother and his sweetheart of a wife?" Donna, according to her name tag, asked Hudson.

"They're good. How's Vito?"

"Growly as usual and refusing to do his business in the yard in this weather. What can you do? An old dog is gonna do what an old dog's gonna do—or not doo-doo." She shrugged. "What'll it be?"

"I'll have the patty melt, an order of fries, and a strawberry shake," Hudson said, not even glancing down at the menu in front of him.

"Gotcha." Donna scribbled a note on her pad and turned to Felicia. "How 'bout you, hon?"

Everything looked amazing. She debated ordering what most of Hudson's dates probably ordered—a glass of water and a wedge of lemon—but to prove to herself that he had no more effect on her than one of her brothers, and that this was most definitely *not* a date, she ordered what she really wanted. "Double bacon cheeseburger, large fry, side salad, blue cheese on the side, cup of fresh fruit, and a large vanilla shake."

"Gotcha," the waitress nodded, sending her french fry earrings bobbing.

After Donna took their menus and left, Felicia looked up to see Hudson staring at her with what looked like awe.

"Are you taking some home to a starving, house-bound

neighbor?" he asked.

"Very funny." She rolled her eyes. "I had to skip lunch because of an unscheduled tour for some big muckety-muck."

He *tsked*, but there wasn't a flicker of regret on his face. "I hate it when that happens."

A giggle just bubbled out. It wasn't a sound she normally made, but it wasn't like she spent a lot of time around someone as teasingly incorrigible as Hudson Carlyle. She was used to people like her family. Loud, straight to the point, and without the ability to let go of a bone once they got hold of it. There were red Irish, black Irish, and then so-bull-headed-their-ancestors-got-kicked-off-the-island-for-rebel-activities Irish. The Hartigans fell into all three categories. And just like the rest of them, she couldn't let anything go.

"Now," she said, "tell me the real reason why you think I don't *really* want Tyler."

"Because if you did…" His gaze dropped to her mouth and lingered just long enough to take weight. "If you *really* wanted him, you'd have him by now."

Heat rushed to her cheeks, and not for the first, millionth, or last time in her life she cursed her pale-but-at-least-not-freckled skin. "Flattery? That's your new angle?"

He shrugged. "It's the truth."

She didn't know what to do with that, so she did what she always did when confronted with things she'd analyze to death later—she ignored it and barreled ahead. "You're wrong, but let's put that to the side for a minute. Why do you want to help me? You don't even know me."

"Would you believe I'm a sucker for a pretty girl who blushes?"

Of course, Donna picked that moment to drop off their shakes. She looked from Hudson to Felicia, an indulgent smile on her face. "You're a sucker for every kind of girl, Hudson Carlyle—and this one, as pretty as she is, has enough lights on upstairs to know it."

Mentally high-fiving her fellow woman, Felicia held up her shake in salute. By the time she turned back to Hudson, he was already in shake nirvana, seemingly oblivious to the burn the waitress had delivered. Since joining him seemed like the best choice, she took a sip of her shake. The creamy ice cream hit first, followed by a wallop of vanilla bean that gave a whole new meaning to the flavor vanilla. Intent on her shake, she didn't even realize Hudson had stopped until he spoke.

"I need your help," he said, stirring his shake with his straw. "Tyler and my brother used to be tight, then Tyler's fiancée tried to bang Sawyer the night before she and Tyler were supposed to get hitched."

"Oh my God!" That filled in a big blank spot. "I knew *something* had happened, but I had no idea what. He wouldn't tell anyone."

"Would you in that situation?"

"After my best friend slept with my fiancée? Probably not."

Hudson scowled. "Sawyer didn't sleep or anything else with her. He kicked her out."

Ouch. "So why the big bust-up between them?"

"No clue, but it's gone on long enough." Determination added some gravel to his tone.

"And you want to get them back together?" she asked, still trying to understand why his brother's friendships were so important to him. "What are you, a matchmaker or Henry Higgins?"

"Both." He looked away but not before she saw something flash in his eyes that was more raw and real than anything else she'd seen from him.

Whatever he was hiding, he wasn't about to fess up over shakes and diner food. Not yet, anyway. But that part of her that loved to work out puzzles and observe until she'd figured out exactly why someone or something behaved in a certain way was already taking notes. Hudson might act like just another rich playboy, but there was more to him than that. She couldn't believe she hadn't noticed it until now.

Before she could dig in, though, Donna delivered their food, and the next twenty minutes were filled with devouring their meal and questions from Hudson about the secret life of ants. By the time Donna collected their empty plates, he'd eaten half of Felicia's fries in addition to his own and managed to get her to spill all the salacious secrets of the honeypot ant and their neighbors in the Arizona desert, the harvester ants.

"So, it's an orgy?" he asked, his light brown eyes huge. "An actual ant orgy?"

"Pretty much," she said, licking stray ketchup from her finger. "The future harvester ant queen flies out to a spot where all the other future queens and fertile males are. Everyone has sex—a lot of sex—and then the females go and start a new colony with the unborn progeny from the orgy."

"And what happens to the male ants? Do they go to the new colonies, too?"

"They all die." She added just enough cartoon-villain glee to her voice to make him laugh—a real laugh. One that made it sound like he pretended to laugh a lot but never really meant it—but this time he did. "Life's hard if you're not the queen. Really, it's hard if you *are* the queen. All you do is pop out babies fourteen to fifteen years, you never leave the colony, and when you die, so does everyone in the colony."

"So, what I've learned tonight is that you're just a simple girl with a nice job studying vicious insects who gorge themselves to marble proportions and die after sex."

Her first instinct was to argue, but…he wasn't exactly wrong. And dammit, he was gifting her with what was probably his patented I'm-too-charming-for-words smile. She shrugged. "Pretty much."

"Tell me why this big crush on Tyler."

Okay, that was a sharp left turn.

She could lie, make up a version of the truth that didn't hit her so close to her vulnerable center, but he'd finally been honest with her. It would be pretty shitty not to do the same. After taking one last sip of vanilla shake for courage, she started to explain.

"I grew up the youngest of seven. I'm also the smallest, by almost a foot. The family joke is that when I was born pocket-sized—and I hate that term—my parents knew it was time to stop." She sighed, hating that joke a little more every time she heard it. "Add to that the fact that they are all your typical Waterbury Irish—loud, fun, and destined to be cops or firefighters or nurses or teachers—and I'm a nerdy girl who studies ants for a living and, well, you get the picture." She sucked down more vanilla shake for strength. "Don't get me wrong, my family is great, and I'd cut anyone who ever said a bad thing about them, but it wasn't always easy growing up where it was so obvious that I didn't fit in. When Tyler's family moved into the neighborhood, I was in sixth grade, and it was like a rock god was living next door. He was scary smart— so much so that he got a scholarship to a fancy Harbor City private school—hot, and he always seemed at home no matter who he was with—and he's still that person today."

"And you want him, but have never made a move?" he asked, getting right to the sharp, jagged point of the problem.

What could she say? Nothing. She let a sharp shake of her head speak for her.

He swiped her shake, plopped his straw down in it, and took a hit of the good stuff before continuing the interrogation. "Why not?"

Now, wasn't that the billion-dollar question? After turning the problem over in her mind for what felt like forever, she'd finally zeroed in on an answer when her mom had sent her the thirty-days-until-thirty present. "I've been scared to go after what I really wanted, I guess."

"So why change that now?"

"My thirtieth birthday is in less than a month." And getting Tyler was the only thing left on her do-by-thirty list. "Plus, there's the cat thing."

He raised one eyebrow, silently asking her to explain that statement.

"It was just a silly comment that my brother Finian, Frankie's twin, made when I'd gotten a cat last year. He'd said it was the first of many, and everyone in the family had laughed." She idly traced the alphabet on the table. "He didn't mean anything by it; he'd just been busting my chops. However, I haven't been able to get the mental picture out of my head. Tyler will have a wife and a family someday, and I'll have thirty-two cats." She sighed. It wasn't that she needed a man to be happy or successful, but she wanted a family, a spouse, a life away from her beloved ants, which never even noticed if she was around or not. She needed someone, for once, to notice *her*.

"Nothing like a milestone to bring things into focus," Hudson said quietly.

"Exactly." She snagged back her shake before he could finish it off.

"So, let's do this," he said, turning on his stool so that their knees touched, sending a spark of almost tangible and definitely thrilling *yes* straight through her. "I'll help you get Tyler in bed and out of it, if that's what you decide you really want."

Of course, that's what he thought her thing with Tyler was, an itch to be scratched rather than a love story she'd been writing in her head since middle school. "You just had to add that last bit, didn't you?"

"Yep." He winked and took back his straw and put it in the measly bit of strawberry shake he had left. "And of course, you agree to let me paint you as payment."

Maybe it was the sugar rush from the shake, but partnering up suddenly seemed like a good idea. Hudson wasn't anyone's idea of Henry Higgins, but she had a feeling she just might be Eliza Doolittle—or at least someone who didn't want to end up alone with thirty-two cats.

"I'm probably going to regret this, but fine. Let's do this." She picked up her glass and clinked it against Hudson's. "Not sure why you want to paint *me*, but just to be clear, absolutely positively no way am I posing nude. Fair warning."

An absolutely, positively wicked gleam sparkled in his eyes. "Whatever you say, Matches."

Chapter Four

After paying the bill, despite Felicia's attempt to get him to halve it, Hudson held open the door for her, and they stepped outside into the cool fall night. The streetlights had blinked on while they'd eaten, and the streets had cleared—well, as much as they ever did in Harbor City—but there wasn't a cab in sight. A crisp breeze brushed past them, and she shivered and huddled deeper into her thin coat.

"How far up are you?" he asked after he scanned the area for a cab and came up with nothing.

"About fifteen blocks." She jerked her chin eastward.

Okay, that was doable. Harbor City was a pedestrian city; everyone hoofed it—even the mayor. "Let's walk."

She crossed her arms and rubbed her palms up and down her arms. "It's kinda cold."

"It's in the high fifties. Come on." He shrugged out of his thicker coat and draped it over her shoulders. "Try something new."

She narrowed her eyes in a glare, the rush of color in her cheeks a telltale sign that she was gearing up to give him a what for. "I've walked home before."

"Yeah, but never with me, Matches."

Not giving her time to formulate any objections, he started off in the direction she'd pointed. He made it three steps before she caught up. For once in his life, he kept his mouth shut about winning that little argument and just enjoyed one of life's small victories.

The walk back to Felicia's house took less time than Hudson had expected for fifteen long city blocks. Maybe it was because when Felicia wasn't telling him—verbally or with a look—to go fuck straight off, she was actually kind of fun, pointing out her neighborhood's little oddities. Maybe it was because he couldn't stop noticing the way the streetlights brought out the dark auburn highlights in her hair, or the way she couldn't seem to talk without using her hands. Maybe it was because even though she was a solid foot shorter than him, she actually walked faster than he did—definitely a woman on a mission.

"What's the rush?" he asked ten blocks in.

"My cat is going to be nuts by the time I get home." Her pace increased as they hustled across the street to beat the light. "Honeypot is kind of an asshole."

"First, aren't *all* cats assholes? And second, you named your cat Honeypot? Obsess much?"

Her chin went up, and she hooked a right on Elmhurst. "Cats are regal creatures. Well, most of them are."

"Not Honeypot?"

"No." Caught by the no-crossing light at the corner, she nudged him with her elbow then pointed at the building they were next to. A plaque set in the concrete declared that David Carlyle had laid the cornerstone in 1970. "One of yours?"

His gut tightened as he stared at the reminder of his family legacy. "My grandfather."

The light changed, and they strode across the street.

"What's that like, knowing your family built Harbor City?"

Part of him wished it was an exaggeration, but it wasn't. Carlyle buildings dotted the skyline of this city and dozens of others across the globe. Hotels, office buildings, skyscrapers, and more all bearing the Carlyle name. Carlyle Enterprises had been one of the most prominent international building companies for decades, and he had an office in the company's Harbor City headquarters that he visited once a quarter whether he wanted to or not.

Hudson reached for the breezy charm he usually employed as cover, but couldn't do it. Something about the honest and curious look Felicia had on her face made it impossible. "It's amazing and awful all at the same time."

"How so?" she asked.

"There are unending bottles of champagne, pretty girls everywhere I turn, more money than I could spend in five lifetimes, and certain...expectations." Yeah, that was one way to put being assigned a job as suit-wearing, spreadsheet-loving businessman from birth when all he'd ever wanted to do was paint—not that what he wanted actually mattered.

"Like what?" She stopped in front of the black iron railing for a short flight of stairs that led down to a basement apartment, her piercing gaze trained on him like she was determined to classify and catalog him.

"Oh no, don't look at me like that. I'm not one of your ants to study."

She opened her mouth—no doubt to argue—but a horrible, blaring yowl burst from the window of the basement apartment at the bottom of the steps. It was the kind of ear-splitting screech that bored straight into a person's eardrum before stopping as suddenly as it started.

Felicia sighed. "And this is me."

He took in the eight steps leading down, past the window

with decorative bars over it, to a red door, but movement in the window dragged his attention back. Sitting on the other side of the glass was a one-eyed orange tabby cat with a good chunk missing from one ear. It looked like one of the animals they showed in the animal rescue commercials to get people to donate—but more feral.

"*That's* Honeypot?"

"Yeah, and he's an escape artist, so I'd better say good-bye now." She took off his coat and held it out to him. "Thanks for the burger and shake."

Ignoring the coat, he pulled his phone from his front pocket. "Let me have your phone real quick."

"Why?" She eyeballed him suspiciously.

"So I can call myself from it, and then we'll have each other's numbers."

As Honeypot wailed in the background, Felicia handed him his coat and her phone. One quick text later, and her digits showed up on his screen.

"All set for tomorrow." He handed her back her phone.

"What's tomorrow?"

"We begin Operation: *My Fair Lady.*" With any luck, Tyler would be on the ropes within a few weeks. He ignored the sinking feeling in the pit of his stomach that his plan could backfire because she was actually in love with Tyler, not just holding onto a childhood infatuation.

Shaking her head as if she still wasn't sure this was a good idea, Felicia headed down her stairs and unlocked the two deadbolts on her front door while he watched from the top of the stairwell, still holding his coat. Her neighborhood wasn't a bad one, but the fact that she didn't have a doorman as an extra layer of security had him glaring at the other people walking by, even if they didn't give her apartment a second glance.

"Oh shit! Honeypot!"

Hudson spun around in time to see a flash of orange heading straight up the steps toward him. Acting on instinct, he reached out and grabbed the fur ball as Felicia rushed up the steps, arms stretched out for the mangy cat. Just as he brought the cat up to his chest, Felicia's footing slipped, and she tumbled forward. Shifting the cat into one arm, he grabbed Felicia with the other so she fell into him instead of onto the unforgiving cement steps. She landed against him with a *whomp* that had both of them grasping for their balance. By the time he'd regained his footing, she was pressed up against him like a starving man against a bakery window, and he *finally* got an inkling of what she was hiding under all those ill-fitting clothes. Small, perky tits. Narrow waist. High, round ass. As if that wasn't bad enough for his sanity, he made the mistake of looking down at her. Her lips parted as her breath came out in a soft little sigh, and she had a hazy, slightly unfocused look in her eyes that had him wondering if that's what she looked like when she slid her body down onto a hard cock. It had to be. If it wasn't, then she'd shortchanged her lovers, because he wasn't sure if he just wanted to stare, kiss, or paint her more at that moment.

"Hudson," she said, her voice husky. "You saved my cat."

The mostly evil animal picked that moment to show its gratitude by digging its claws into his arm and letting out a hiss that would have sent the nastiest guard dog scrambling for cover.

Felicia blinked and stepped back, her face still soft but now with a wary tightness around what had been her pliant mouth. "We better get her inside before she shreds you."

She grabbed his coat and headed down the stairs. Keeping ahold of the squirming cat, he followed her inside and shut the door behind himself before releasing Satan's best friend. The cat took off before its paws even hit the cream carpet, tearing through the tiny, dimly lit living room and through one of the two doors on the other side of the room. Felicia hustled after the cat, shutting it in what must be her bedroom.

"Sorry about that," she said, crossing over to him. "She's a little skittish—oh my God, she got you."

He glanced down at the skinny streaks of red on his forearm, below where he'd pushed up the sleeves of his sweater. "It's just a couple of scratches."

"Still, you don't want to ruin that sweater." She laid his coat across the back of her couch and hustled into the galley kitchen off the living room and tore off a paper towel. "Here let me."

She brushed aside his outstretched hand and pressed the towel to his arm. The move brought her in close, making it impossible to miss the flowery scent of her shampoo or the way the dim light from the single lamp in the living room highlighted her cheekbones and the fullness of her bottom lip. His arm wasn't bleeding anymore, but she kept patting it, her fingers glancing over his skin—not teasing but making him all too aware of her softness in contrast to his hardness. His heart rate ticked up, and the rest of the world started to dim. *God, if she looked up, he'd—*

She looked up. The pink tip of her tongue wet that bottom lip he wanted to suck into his mouth. Even with her glasses on, there was no missing how her pupils had dilated, highlighting the flecks of gray in her blue eyes. The air grew thick around them. Blood rushed south, making his jeans tight and his thoughts dirty.

She must have sensed it, too, because she shivered against him. "All better?" she asked in a whisper.

"Not yet," he managed to get out before crashing his mouth down onto hers.

Her lips, so soft, parted as she moaned—a sound that went straight to his cock. Never a man to leave a woman wanting, he slid his tongue inside. God, she was responsive to every thrust, every parry, meeting him halfway and putting her own twist on the kiss. Matches. Never had a nickname been so well-picked because he was a twelve-alarm fire now. Too bad the only thing that was going to put it out was his own hand. Hating it, but making himself do it anyway, he broke the kiss and stepped back from her.

It took a few seconds, but he could tell the exact moment when reality knocked lust down for the count in that quick mind of hers. The blush was back. This time it skipped the varying stages of pinks and went straight to scarlet.

"What was that?" she asked in a hushed tone.

Her breath was coming in fast, lifting her chest and making him all too aware of the delicious curves he now knew without a doubt she was hiding. He needed go slow or he'd spook her. But at least one suspicion had been confirmed: she wanted him as much as he wanted her. If only that brain of hers could let go of the ridiculous notion she was meant for her childhood crush. He'd have to tear that idea down one brick at a time, for both their sakes.

"That," he said, picking up his coat, "was lesson number one in seduction. Believe me, there will be more."

She straightened her cockeyed glasses and strode to her door, her head high even as she fanned her cheeks with the air of a woman who made the movement so often she didn't even realize she was doing it. "I know how to kiss already, thank you very much."

He wasn't going to argue that, but he wasn't going to fuck up his opportunity for another kiss—and more—either.

"Don't hate, Matches." Walking toward her, he slid his arms into his coat—not that he needed anything to keep him warm because that kiss had taken care of that. "Everyone has room for improvement, even little secret spitfires like you who moan so pretty when someone else's tongue is in their mouth."

She gasped and yanked open the door. "Good-bye, Hudson."

"Did you already forget what I said before?" He paused just inside the opening, so close to her that all he had to do to touch her again was move the slightest bit to the right. There was no missing the electricity zinging between them, or the way her breath caught. A slight shift, a small pivot, and he'd have her up against the door, her legs wrapped around his hips as he rocked his iron-hard cock against her sweetest spot. The temptation almost won out, but he managed to resist. "When it comes to us, it's always until next time."

Walking out that door was almost as hard as he was, but he did it anyway. Felicia thought she was in love with Tyler, he reminded himself as he walked down the block to hail a cab. He refused to acknowledge the twisting of his stomach at the thought of Tyler kissing her the way he just had. Not that he was in love—*Good God no not even close*—he was just feeling oddly...territorial when it came to Matches. Ideas were already forming just what "lessons" tomorrow had in store.

Chapter Five

Hudson hated mornings. Oh sure, there were people who weren't morning people. But he was barely a noon person. The fact that he'd stayed up until almost four sketching ideas when he really wanted to be at the cabin painting hadn't done a damn thing to improve his mood. So why was he ass to elbows on the subway with tourists on their way to see the sights before the weather turned frosty? Because of the woman who had stared back at him from ten new sketches when he'd finally strode out of his penthouse at the ass-crack of nine in the morning.

After getting off the subway, he made a quick dip into the coffee shop with a grand-opening sign hanging in the window a block from Felicia's apartment and then walked the rest of the way to her place, balancing a tray of drinks and a box of pastries. His foot was barely on the top step before Honeypot's yowling began. It went in his ear and straight to the middle of his brain like an extra-long ice pick. And he'd been worried about someone breaking into her apartment. That beast was better than any alarm. Luckily, since both of his hands were full, Felicia had opened the door, stepped out, and closed it behind her by the time he'd hit the last step.

Her hair was pulled back into a long ponytail, damp tendrils clinging to her neck, and her glasses were on, but the rest was a whole new vision. Sweat gleamed on her skin above the scoop neck of the blue sports bra covering her perfect just-a-handful-sized tits and below the band that wrapped tight around her rib cage. A pair of black and blue running pants clung to her shapely legs and stretched over her heart-shaped ass that had him considering all the possibilities. Sure, she thought she was hooked on someone else, but Hudson wasn't dead, a monk, or legally insane.

"What are you doing here?" she asked, swiping a small hand towel across her forehead as her gaze landed everywhere but on him.

He forced his attention back up to her face, which didn't make his blood rush straight to his cock any slower. "Bringing you breakfast."

"Is that from Grounded Coffee? They just opened up a new location down the block." She clutched the small towel to her chest and leaned forward and sniffed the box, a look of total bliss on her face, and tugged her plump bottom lip between her teeth. Obviously, the temptation of sugar beat out Felicia's shyness. "I've been dying to get some. I can't wait to get that in my mouth."

He wouldn't pop a boner at the dirty image that appeared in his head at her statement. He wouldn't get a hard-on. He would just get a halfsie. That was totally acceptable. *Yeah, if you're fourteen, asshole. Get it together.*

"Is this your way of making up for last night?" she asked, taking a peek from the box to his face.

Too much of his attention was taken up by the way a bead of sweat was doing a slow slide down her collarbone before disappearing beneath her sports bra for him to make any sort of mental connections. "Last night?"

"Don't pretend." She slapped the towel over her shoulder and planted her hands on her hips to give him the stare down—or stare up since he had a foot on her. It would have been more effective if her cheeks weren't bright red already. "You know exactly what I'm talking about. That can't happen again." The words came out in a rush as if she had to get them out quickly or risk losing her courage. "If we're gonna do this, it has to be like prison visiting hours. No touching."

"You've visited someone in prison?" He had a hard time picturing doe-eyed Felicia Hartigan and her ant obsession anywhere near hardened, convicted felons.

A nervous giggle escaped. "I binged *Arrested Development*."

Okay, that made more sense. "So, you also know there's always money in the banana stand."

Her mouth twitched, but she stomped out the smile before it could fully form, and stubborn Felicia rose to the surface. "Last night needs to be a one-time thing."

"You didn't like the kiss?" The one that had gotten him hard and made her soft and pliant against him. Oh, that was definitely happening again. He'd tried to convince himself otherwise all the way home last night, but by four a.m. in the middle of the worst insomnia ever, he'd rationalized it was for everyone's benefit if he and Felicia explored this attraction. Made perfect sense. "It *felt* like you liked it. It *sounded* like you liked it." That little moan had found its way into his very naked dreams last night.

"Liking it doesn't matter." Light pink splotches dotted her cheeks. "It can't happen again. Deal?"

Since agreeing to things he had no intention of doing had pretty much been his M.O. since birth, and definitely since he'd become vice president of client relations (or as he liked to think of it: Flirt in Chief), putting a charming little white lie out there didn't even make him twitch. "Deal."

"Good." Her smile took up the entire bottom half of her face and only looked fake because he was a man who knew all the tricks. "Come on inside. You can bond with Honeypot while I take a quick rinse off."

He shifted his stance, his zipper taking the brunt of the movie playing in his head at the idea. "Sounds like a plan."

And it would give him the opportunity to remember the entire point of this little excursion. This was Operation: Hey Tyler, You Dumbass, She's Hot. Any action between him and Felicia, and there would be some, would be of the educational variety—not the fuck-I-forgot-my-brains-at-home variety. Keep it surface. Keep it fun. Keep it focused on making all the people happy so he could go secretly paint in his cabin in peace. Basically, it was his life as he'd been living it for as long as he could remember. And if his dick took notice of Felicia's pert ass as he followed her inside her apartment? What could he say, he was an artist—he had an eye for beautiful details.

. . .

The cold water from the shower couldn't hit Felicia's face and pour over her sweaty body fast enough. That kiss had been the bane of her existence last night, and now Hudson was here in another pair of ass-hugging jeans and carrying pastry. That should be illegal. It sure as hell wasn't fair.

The kiss was an anomaly, a statistically insignificant event. It didn't change anything. The goal was Tyler. It had always been Tyler. And less than thirty days from now, she will have achieved that goal. Deviation led to chaos, and she wasn't into chaos. She'd had more than enough of that growing up to last a lifetime. The Hartigan household had been loving, but a totally, gleefully, no-holds-barred free-for-all. And for a quiet girl who liked books and bugs—not necessarily in that order, it had been more than a little overwhelming at times.

It wasn't until Tyler's family moved into the neighborhood that she finally stopped feeling like quite so much of a freak in her own skin. He was her ideal man. They were perfect for each other. Now all she had to do to successfully complete this experiment was factor in the new variable—better known as Hudson Carlyle—to get Tyler to finally notice her as more than just Frankie Hartigan's little sister and the adorkable girl next door.

Refocused, she scrubbed the five-mile run off her skin, rinsed the shampoo-conditioner all-in-one out of her hair, and got out of the shower. A fast buff-dry and comb-through later, she grabbed an ancient Ant Life T-shirt and yoga pants, grateful that for her, bras were almost always optional. Dressed, damp hair hanging down her back, she hurried out into the living room before Honeypot got a chance to snag all of the pastries or take another swipe at Hudson—both were totally possible.

Of course, none of the above turned out to be the answer. Hudson lounged—his shoes abandoned on the floor—on her powder-blue tufted chaise beneath a print of her favorite Hughston painting. Honeypot lay curled up on his stomach, purring loud enough to make the walls vibrate. Shocked didn't begin to cover it. That cat barely tolerated her, and yet here she was fawning over a total interloper in their lives.

"Don't tell me your ability to charm the females of the world extends to cats," she said.

"What can I say, ladies love me." He scooped up Honeypot and placed her on the floor—a move that would have gotten Felicia slashed—before getting up and walking over to the box of pastries on the kitchen counter. "Bear claw or chocolate croissant?" He popped open the box top and looked in. "They threw in more, too. I think that's a quiche Lorraine, and there's a cherry danish among other things."

He looked up. "I wasn't sure what you drank, either, so I brought a green tea, an iced coffee, a hazelnut latte, and a black coffee."

How did the saying go? Never trust a rich guy bearing gifts. Okay, that wasn't *quite* it, but it was close enough. She sniffed a trap of some sort, she just didn't know what exactly. "What is this?"

His smile was anything but comforting. "A test date to determine what I'm working with."

He crossed his arms over his broad chest and gave her an appraising look that went from the top of her head, where her more-than-damp hair was stuck to her skull, down past her T-shirt—that had her wishing she'd taken the time to put on a bra, skimmed past her yoga pants with the bleach stain spanning one thigh from a recent laundry accident, and down to her unpainted toenails. Tyler had known her since she had braces and zits, so the fact that she wasn't a glamor girl wouldn't be a surprise to him. That didn't mean she wasn't prepared to do a little...freshening of her look. Animals did it all the time to attract a mate, as Hudson rightly pointed out the other day.

Resigned to Hudson's answer before she even put it out there, she asked, "Does that mean you want me to go get dolled up?"

"That's just the glaze on the pottery." Keeping his gaze on her, he reached into the pastry box and pulled out a bear claw before nudging the container across the counter to her. "I want to see the good stuff."

Okay, she had no idea how to take that. She turned it over in her mind while she grabbed the chocolate croissant that was still warm. "You mean like conversation?"

Oh God, please say no. She hated small talk. It frazzled her brain and then her nerves kicked in and all that came out of her mouth was about ants.

"Sure, let's start there." He grinned and took a giant bite of the pastry. "Go ahead. Wow me."

"Okay." Her brain blanked, and her pulse kicked up a notch or twenty. She talked to people all the time. She had friends. She wasn't a complete social dork. However, the pressure of being "on" had her palms sweaty as she grabbed the tea. "Um…. How was your day?"

He cocked an eyebrow. "Well, even though it's hours earlier than I normally get up on a Saturday, and I'm not a morning person, it's going okay. How about you?"

"I've been up since five." She took a bite of the croissant and managed to bite back her moan of pleasure as the buttery, flaky, chocolate goodness melted on her tongue.

"Why?" he asked, before demolishing the rest of his bear claw in one bite.

She savored her next bite and tried to come up with the words to explain that nothing-can-touch-me feeling she got in the mornings. It was like the world was full of possibility and all she had to do was reach out and grab it. It was as close to fitting in with the world that she ever got.

"I like the city when it's quiet," A police siren blared outside the window. "Well, quieter. I have breakfast, read the paper, catch up on the latest journal articles and go for a run."

"Every Saturday?" he asked.

She nodded.

He grimaced. "That sounds horrible."

"Not at all. It's my favorite part of every week." She sipped the green tea and then took a deep inhale of the hint of jasmine wafting out of the cardboard to-go cup as she did so, her gaze tripped on the early birthday card from her mom that she had stuck to the fridge with an ant magnet. That was the point of all this, not sugary carb goodness. For Tyler, she could push past her natural shyness and take a few steps outside of her comfort zone. That meant staying focused.

"We need to get down to it. The clock is ticking, and I don't need help talking to Tyler, I need to make him jealous. I did a lot of thinking last night about what you said."

"But not the kiss," Hudson said, his focus dropping to her mouth.

Hot spots blazed high on her cheeks. "And in the animal kingdom, creatures do have superficial, visual ways to attract a mate. An example is the Long-Tailed Widowbird."

He gave her a blank look.

Okay, time to dial down the nerd a bit or at least translate it into regular English. "They're these gorgeous jet-black birds in Africa with orange and white shoulders, a blue-tinted bill, and nearly two-feet long tails. The tails make them much more visible to predators, but it is the key to attracting a mate."

"So, you want a longer tail?" he asked, swiping her cup and taking a quick drink of tea. His face twisted the moment the liquid must have hit his tongue. "Ugh. That stuff is awful."

"It's an acquired taste," she retorted, taking back her tea. "What I'm saying is that I am prepared to go through some sort of superficial makeover to get Tyler."

"Okay, that's a start," he said, resting his forearms on the counter and leaning forward—close enough that she couldn't miss the musky tease of his cologne.

She couldn't place the scent, but it made her eyes flutter just a bit and her thighs clench. *Fucking pheromones.*

"However," he continued, "there's more to catching Tyler than just looking the part."

"Oh, I know." She nodded her head in agreement, relieved that he was seeing the brilliance of her plan. She may not have a ton of confidence in human interaction, but when it came to arranging an experiment, she had absolute faith. "That's why you're going to be there making him jealous."

"I don't know about that." He reached out and took a

strand of still damp hair, winding it around his finger.

"It's perfect." Gaining inner sass from some place she hadn't even been aware of, she smacked his hand away, freeing herself, and took a step back from the counter. Having the two feet of granite between them suddenly didn't seem like enough. "You don't even want to know the number of studies I found last night that delved into the effect of what wanting what someone else has on mate selection in humans."

"There are studies on that?"

"Lots of them." Her initial Google search had pulled up more than fourteen million hits.

He pushed back from the counter, taking one of the to-go cups with him. "It'll never work."

The look of know-it-all smarm on his handsome face as he took a drink, watching her over the rim of his lid, was enough to make her want to march right over to him and—ohhhhhh! He almost got her that time. He just wanted to rile her up. Her brothers had loved to do the same thing. They'd push right past her natural shyness until she reacted. She'd learned to avoid getting drawn in with them, she sure wasn't going to fall for it with Hudson. She inhaled a long breath through her nose and held it for the count of three before releasing. There, much better.

"It will," she said, her voice as firm as her resolve. "I've done the research."

He rounded the counter to her side, stopping just short of where she stood, too stubborn to give up ground in her own apartment for the sake of her crazy libido. His gaze dipped down to her mouth, then to her hard nipples poking against the T-shirt—obviously she was cold with her hair being wet like it was. For five nerve-wracking seconds she just stood there, anticipation crawling across her skin as he dragged his gaze back to her lips. She didn't want another kiss. She didn't. But her tongue darted out and wet her lips of its own volition anyway.

"And if it doesn't work?" he asked, a rough grit to his voice that hadn't been there a moment ago.

The words were out before she'd thought them through. "Then, we do things your way."

"No matter what?" He took another step forward.

"Within reason," she said, her voice shaky.

She could feel his body heat, see the way his pupils had dilated, and her fingers twitched with the need to reach out to touch him.

"Fair enough," he said.

He reached out.

Her breath caught.

He moved his hand past her, leaving a trail of almost-coulda-been behind him and took a cherry danish out of the box behind her. Air filled her lungs with a *whoosh* as she watched him take a bite.

"One for the road," he said with a grin, his voice back to its normal teasing tone. "I'll be back at seven. Wear something boring-business-dinner-hell appropriate."

She blinked, trying to catch up with the jump the conversation had taken. "What for?"

"Carlyle Enterprises client dinner," he said as he backtracked to the chair, put on his shoes, and then moved toward the door, Honeypot curling between his legs in a figure eight as he did so. "Tyler will be there. It'll be the perfect little test environment for your theory."

Hustling to the door, she picked up the cat, refusing the flinch when the ingrate sank her claws into her forearm. "I'm right."

He gave her an indulgent smile and opened the door. "Of course you are."

The man may not have many brain cells—at least not ones he'd admit to—but he was smart enough to get out and close the door behind him before she could formulate an appropriately scathing remark. And she would. It would just take a few hours—and even if he was still around, she probably wouldn't be able to get it out. Honeypot hopped up onto the counter and then the windowsill, where she started wailing. That man. He'd pushed his way into her life, made her cat fall in love with him, and was questioning her tactics. Well, Mr. Hot and Rich was about to learn just how *very* wrong he was.

Chapter Six

Wearing her go-to little black dress wasn't going to work for this, since Felicia had just worn it at a few nights ago at the fundraiser. Staring into her tiny closet—organized to utilize every inch of its nearly nonexistent size—she came up with two options. One, the navy blue pantsuit was all business. Two, the gunmetal gray sheath dress that covered her from neck to knee. On most people, the dress would have been a miniskirt, but Felicia would have to shop in the kids' department to find something that fit her that way—not that she did. Neither outfit got her particularly excited, but they'd work. She just couldn't decide which one. Done with trying to figure it out on her own, she grabbed her phone and hit up the second person on her help-a-sister-out list.

Felicia: *One or two?*

Frankie: *Context.*

Felicia: *Trying to pick an outfit.*

Frankie: *???*

Felicia: *It's Fallon's Vegas weekend.*

Frankie: *So I become ur go-to for clothes?*

Felicia: *You want to know the underwear options, too?*

Frankie: *Fuck no! UR my sister.*

Felicia: *Pants or skirt? One or two?*

Frankie: *You can't ever tell anyone.*

She clicked a quick picture of the outfits laid out on her bed and sent it.

Frankie: *Two.*

Felicia: *xoxo*

Frankie: *I'm serious. Not. One. Word.*

Felicia: *Only the guys at your firehouse.*

Frankie: *…*

Felicia: *And Ford's buddies at the cop bar.*

Frankie: *…*

Felicia: *Chill. Secret's safe.*

Frankie: *Better be. Hot date?*

Felicia: *Night, bro.*

Frankie: *Come on, Ant Lady. Spill.*

Felicia: *No way. U gossip like mom.*

Frankie: *Let me know if I need to knock this guy's head loose.*

Felicia: *xoxo*

After that little bit of brotherly love disguised as a promise to beat up her fake date, she barely had time to throw on the dress, put on her standard black dress shoes with the half-inch heel, grab her purse, and smooth her hair into a bun before Honeypot went on full Hudson alert. Striding through the apartment, she shushed the cat to no avail. The fur ball's one eye was only for the man knocking on her door. Angling her body to block the cat's probable escape attempt, she opened the door and squeezed out, quickly shutting the door behind her.

Hudson stood next to her as she locked the two deadbolts. "I think that cat loves me."

"Something like that," she said, not wanting to feed his ego, and then dropped her keys in her purse and headed up the stairs as Honeypot yowled from her spot on the windowsill.

Thank God Honeypot would stop as soon as she lost sight of them or else her neighbors would put a hit out on her.

"So, what's the plan," he asked when they hit the sidewalk.

"Isn't that what you should be laying out, Professor Higgins?" she asked, finally getting used to being around Hudson enough to bust his chops a little.

"Uh-uh." He shook his head and opened the back door to a black town car idling at the curb in front of her apartment. "Tonight is your experiment. I'm just along for the ride."

She slid inside, not liking how he'd phrased that, as if he expected her hypothesis to get blown to bits. Hudson got in after her, closing the door and making the roomy interior seem crazy tight.

"Straight to the Kobe Grill?" the driver asked from his spot behind the wheel.

Hudson grimaced. "How late are we, Linus?"

"I dropped off Sawyer and Clover thirty minutes ago."

Hudson sighed. "Think they're done talking business yet?"

"Doubtful," Linus replied, pulling out into traffic.

She couldn't see the driver's face from her position, but she couldn't miss the smile lines crinkling around his eyes reflected in the rearview mirror. Again, Hudson surprised her. The easy relationship between him and someone who was obviously an employee was as genuine as it was unexpected. She shifted in her seat, the guilt of her preconceived notions about him taking up the little bit of space between their bodies and crowding her even more.

"I suppose we can't avoid it any longer," Hudson said. "Off to the seventh level of hell. At least there'll be alcohol."

Hudson winked at her, but there was no hiding the tightness around his usually smiling mouth. He was up to something. Again. She just had to figure out what—and she would, she didn't have a choice. With an analytical brain like hers, variables just meant more questions and she had to have answers. She mulled the problem in silence for the next ten blocks as they made their way to one of Harbor City's hot new neighborhoods, but couldn't come up with a solution. By the time Linus double-parked in front of the restaurant, she was as frustrated as that time she was seven and had yet to solve the old Rubik's cube of her parents she'd found boxed up in the garage.

"You're not planning on sabotage?" she asked as soon as Linus got out.

"No way." There was that teasing grin that did funny things to her stomach even though she should be immune—after all, she knew the real reason behind this outing. "I'm totally hooked on you. Have been since I set eyes on you at the fundraiser."

If she'd have rolled her eyes any harder, they would have fallen out of their sockets. "No need to go overboard. No one's going to believe love at first sight. I'm more of an acquired taste. That's what we need to go with here."

He quick pivoted in his seat to face her. The move brought his knee in contact with hers and sent a jolt of awareness that made her entire leg tingle all the way up to her core. Reflexively, she clenched her thighs together. His gaze dropped to her lap. Shit. She really needed to get replacement batteries for her vibrator because that was the *only* explanation for her body's reaction. That it always seemed to happen around Hudson was correlation, *not* causation.

The passenger door opened from the outside, but she couldn't tear her attention away from Hudson's dark smolder.

Finally, he dragged his gaze up to her face. "You don't think anyone would believe I'd fall for you at first sight?"

"I *know* so," she said, white knuckling that bit of truth and the bravado she'd need to make it through the night. "Now let's go inside and you do what you do best—flirt your ass off."

• • •

If there was a *Misery*-style super fan with a sledgehammer ready to swing down on Hudson's leg and he was forced to pick who was shocked more when he and Felicia arrived at the table, he'd go with his sister-in-law Clover. Sawyer and Tyler were too busy doing the tough-guy-glaring-because-I-can't-whip-out-my-dick-and-tape-measure thing to take notice of his and Felicia's arrival.

"Hudson," Clover exclaimed, elbowing his older brother—who happened to be her new husband—in the ribs. "You made it."

He shrugged. "Mom keeps telling me I need to take more

of an interest in the family business, so here I am."

"Thank God. Maybe you can talk some sense into him," Sawyer grumbled.

"Not likely since there is absolutely nothing of that proposal that works for my client," Tyler shot back.

Sawyer snorted. "What a load of absolute bullshit."

"Find a room already, would you two," Hudson said. "Now, how about we pretend to be civilized people so as to not scare off my date."

"Your date?" Clover asked, the glimmer in her eyes reminding him way too much of the one his mom used to level at his brother during Operation: Marry Off Sawyer.

While part of him wanted to get up and run from even the idea of getting married, he had to play it smart. Clover could unintentionally help him get exactly what he needed out of this dinner: a temporary ceasefire between Sawyer and Tyler by distracting them both into wondering exactly what was going on with himself and Felicia. Of course, driving Tyler nuts with some kind of lust-powered Felicia-related jealousy wasn't gonna happen tonight. Oh, he wasn't going to do anything to harm her efforts that way, but she'd done it already to herself. She looked like a very unsexy librarian and kept giving Tyler the same look a dog gave a T-bone steak.

"Let me introduce Felicia Hartigan. She's an entomologist at the Harbor City National History Museum with a specialty in myrmecology. Also, she has a one-eyed cat that's in love with me. Felicia, you know Tyler. This is my brother Sawyer—don't take offense, he's permanently grumpy—and his wife, Clover, who obviously has a fetish for that type of thing along with an addiction to DIY."

Hudson pulled out a chair for Felicia next to Tyler and took the free chair on her other side. The move gave him a front row seat to observe her flirting skills.

"Myrmecology?" Sawyer asked.

"I study honeypot ants," she said.

"Whatever you do, don't ask her how they got that name before we eat dinner," Hudson said. "Trust me."

"Regurgitation, or allowing others to drain you of food to feed others isn't that unusual in the animal world," she said before taking one of the dark brown rye rolls in the middle of the table that were already on everyone else's bread plates. "Anyway, if you had to choose between eating that or starving, I know which one you'd pick."

"Starvation," the men at the table said, practically in unison.

"Ignore them. They're all lying," Clover said. "Tell me more."

And that's how the night went. Clover and Felicia talked ants, travel, and food he'd never heard of while he nodded in the right places and took every opportunity to touch Felicia—an arm draped around her shoulders, tucking one of the tendrils that had escaped her bun behind her ear, and even feeding her a forkful of his garlic mashed potatoes because she'd ordered the sweet potatoes. It wasn't over the top, but you couldn't miss the message about Felicia that Hudson was sending—unless you were Tyler, it seemed. The man glanced over, occasionally giving him a slightly confused but nowhere near jealous look before deep diving back into talks with Sawyer about business and the latest Harbor City Giants game. For her part, Felicia barely said two words to the man. In fact, except for the borderline stalker way she looked at Tyler when she thought no one was watching, it was as if she wasn't able to communicate with him in any way visible to the naked eye. She had no flirting game. None. And it didn't help that she melted against him and then squirmed away every time he touched her. For a woman who wanted to make another man jealous, she sure wasn't acting the part.

"If I give you two tickets to the next Giants game, will

you please stop talking baseball?"

Sawyer and Tyler both turned to him, mouths' hanging open in shock.

"Don't tease, Hudson," Clover laughed. "Those playoff tickets are crazy hard to get. You don't even want to know how much money he's offered up for a pair."

Hard? Try impossible. The man he'd gotten them from had paid an arm and a leg for them. All Hudson had had to do was paint an arm and a leg and voila the tickets were his. "I have two tickets behind home plate."

"You don't even like baseball," Sawyer said.

"Let's just say I have my ways." Sadly, a way that no one in his family knew about—or could know about unless he wanted to disappoint them and insult his dead father's memory beyond repair. "They're for game three next week. You want them or not?"

Sawyer had that look, the one that said he was still trying to work out how his baseball-hating little brother had two of the most sought-after tickets in sports. "But—"

"Stop interrogating him and say yes, Carlyle," Tyler interrupted. "You never did know when to let something go."

"That's hilarious coming from you," Sawyer shot back. "You are the king of grudge holders. Do you remember our sophomore year in prep school when…"

And the two men were off, reliving high school memories and planning for their night at Giants Field. Hudson relaxed back in his seat, satisfied that at least one of the missions he'd had for tonight was working out. When Arthur Graves had offered to trade him the two tickets for one of Hughston's most famous paintings, Hudson had known immediately that it was the perfect way to get his brother and Tyler to spend some time together. That Hudson was handing off the first critically acclaimed paintings that he had ever completed under his alter ego's name was a small price to pay.

"Up to your old tricks again?" Clover asked, putting all the details together in an instant the way she always did.

She'd been one of the first people to realize that Hudson had been finagling to get her and Sawyer together from the get-go. It had been the perfect solution to keeping everyone in the Carlyle family happy after his father's death had left everyone mourning in their own way. Sawyer's obsession with work had dialed up to two hundred and their mom had thrown herself into Operation: Marry Off Sawyer, scared out of her mind that her eldest son was going to go through life alone and die too young of a heart attack like their father.

"Just pawning off some tickets I didn't want," he said, curling some of Felicia's hair that had escaped her bun around his finger. The silky strands soothing the jagged rip that appeared inside him when he thought about his father. "There's nothing more to it than that. You know me."

"Exactly." The speculative gleam in Clover's eyes confirming that she was on to him.

"I feel like I'm missing something," Felicia said, looking from him to Clover and back again.

"Clover just likes to think of me as one of her fixer upper projects," he said.

"You're a diamond hiding in plain sight, and you know it."

"Everyone in Harbor City knows I'm handsome, rich, and fun." He lifted his wine glass in a sardonic toast to himself. "If that's hiding, then I am fantastic at it."

Clover laughed and Sawyer pulled her into his conversation with Tyler—something about Australia—and Hudson turned to Felicia. She was chewing her bottom lip as if she hadn't just had a fabulous steak dinner, and her black framed glasses did nothing to hide the worry making a V between her eyes as she stared at Tyler.

"I don't understand why it isn't working," she whispered.

Because A plus B didn't always equal C, a fact that had to drive a logical, linear thinking person like herself way past the point of frustration.

"I do." He leaned his head in close to hers, inhaling the scent of that fruity shampoo she always used. "Are you ready to do things my way from now on?"

A delicate shiver shook her shoulders. "Am I going to regret it?"

"It'll only hurt a little," he teased.

"We'll talk about it later," she huffed and nudged him back into his own personal space.

That they definitely would.

Chapter Seven

Hours later, questions and second-guesses whirled around inside Felicia's head as she paced barefoot from the edge of her small kitchen to the opposite side of her living room. Hudson watched, an amused expression on his face. The ass. He shouldn't be allowed to look all sexy smug with her cat purring up a storm at his feet while she tried to unwind what went wrong tonight in her head.

She hated being wrong, but she'd obviously missed something because otherwise Tyler would have at least looked at her twice tonight. Instead, it had been all baseball and business. Oh, he hadn't been rude and they'd talked a bit, but it hadn't been anything more than the normal friendly chitchat, except this time surrounded by the Carlyles.

She jerked to a stop next to the low storage ottoman that did double duty as her coffee table. *That was it. The variable that had messed things up.* Having Hudson there to make her seem more desirable to Tyler was one thing, but having Sawyer and Clover—as nice as they were—changed the dynamics of her experiment. All she had to do was repeat the dinner minus two Carlyles and *bam!* Success.

"We have to do it again, but this time no Clover or Sawyer," she said, calm settling in her belly as she realized that her plan just needed a small tweak not a total start over. Nothing was worse to a bulldog like her than having to switch plans mid-experiment; once she knew what she wanted, she went for it in a straight line, no curves, no alterations. "If it was just the three of us, then my plan to make Tyler jealous would totally work."

"That's not happening, Matches," Hudson said, crossing over to her. "You agreed that if your plan didn't work, then we'd do things my way."

He was close enough that she had to tilt her head way back to give him a proper glare. The flinty look did nothing but make him grin down at her. That was annoying, but it was his follow-up wink that sent her right over to somebody-hold-my-earrings territory. Anger always made her stomach get all fluttery and her breath come faster. So that must be the reason why she could hear her pulse pounding in her ears. It had to be. The only other logical answer for why she was so hyped up and super-aware of the musky scent of his cologne and the way his muscular chest filled almost her entire view was that she wanted to rip his clothes off and climb him like a tree—and that was totally unacceptable. This was good old fight or flight, nothing more.

Refusing to give him the satisfaction of looking away, even though her neck was starting to get a crick, she stood her ground—literally and figuratively. "We need to give it one more try."

"We will." He brushed back his longish light brown hair that had fallen in front of his eyes. "But it's gonna happen my way."

"And what does that entail besides a makeover?" It wasn't the best comeback. Hell, it wasn't *even* a comeback, but it was hard to think with him looming over her like he was all brawn, sex appeal, and cocksure confidence.

"You're focusing on the wrong thing again, Matches. It's not how you look that will hook him," he said, his gaze traveling over her as tangible as a touch. "You're amazingly hot already, if the idiot would just take a look."

Her cheeks flamed at the compliment, even if it was a bunch of hooey. She knew very well where she fell on the cute scale and it wasn't anywhere near amazingly hot.

"I presume you're going to enlighten me how that's going to happen," she managed to get out in an almost completely normal voice.

"You can't force attraction." His gaze dropped to her mouth, making her lips tingle with only a look. "Just like you can't ignore an attraction that's already there."

Her focus skittered away from him before she used every last bit of determination she had to force it back. "There is no attraction."

"Uh-huh." He nodded and reach out, his hands coming to rest on her hips with only a hint of pressure. "So, if I leaned down and kissed you right now, you wouldn't feel a thing?"

Her heart made a break for it, hammering against her ribs. "Nope."

He made an uh-huh sound as his grip rose to her waist and tightened. "And if I unzipped that dress that covers up every dip and curve of your body?"

She gulped and ignored the throb growing between her thighs. "Nothing."

If she'd been wearing pants, they would so be on fire, but there was no going back once she'd decided on a path of action.

"So, when you start making those sweet, soft, needy moans again, that's just my imagination and not actual attraction on your part?" he asked as he lifted her and set her on top of the ottoman.

Now it was *her* staring down at *him*. Sure, it was only by a few inches, but she'd take it. The new perspective gave her a different view, letting her better see the flecks of green in his brown eyes and the faded scar above his left eyebrow.

"Matches," he said, sliding his palms down until his large hands covered her hips, with the tips of his fingers grazing the rise of her ass. "Is it really all just in my head?"

"Totally," she said, her voice only registering at a breathy whisper.

SOS warning sirens blaring in her head had absolutely no effect on the reaction being this close to him was having on her body. Her skin prickled with awareness. Her bra had suddenly become tighter. A slick warmth of desire gathered between her thighs. And Hudson's hands hadn't even moved nor had he taken a single step closer. It was just the thought, *the idea*, of him kissing her, stripping her, touching her that had her ready to explode—and judging from the seductive promise in his eyes, he knew it.

"You're a lousy liar," he said, his hot, intense gaze zeroed in on her mouth. "You really want to make Tyler notice you?"

Answering was beyond her at that moment. The best she could do was nod.

The muscles in his jaw tensed as he clenched his teeth together and something determined, dangerous, and delicious sparked in the air around them. Her heart hiccupped, and she went totally still, more than a little bit desperate for what would happen next. But instead of tugging her closer and drawing her mouth down onto his, he exhaled a tortured breath and briefly closed his eyes.

"Then use the attraction between us to your advantage, so the clueless fuck begins to see you as more than just that girl who has spent most of her life mooning after him."

Ouch. That hit smack dab right in the middle of her most

vulnerable parts. "I haven't been moon—"

He shook his head, stopping her words, before going on. "What you have or haven't done up until now doesn't matter anymore because from this moment on, everything is going to be different. You just have to trust me to show you how to charm Captain Clueless right out of his preconceived notions of you because you, Matches, shouldn't have to moon after anyone."

His hands were still on her hips, anchoring her to him, but she had no idea what to say, what to do...until she did. The idea had barely formed before she dipped her head lower and brought her mouth down to his. Kissing Hudson was like diving off a cliff into the ocean—exhilarating and totally nuts. She shouldn't be doing this. The thought fought its way to the surface, but before she could act on it, his tongue swept into her mouth, teasing and tempting and making her forget everything else but how damn good he made her feel. Everything had gone electric. The moans sounding soft against her ears, they were her—and every time one escaped, he pulled her closer against him, his fingers gripping her tight. Just when it seemed she was either going to implode or explode from the intensity of it, he broke the kiss, his hungry lips tracing the line of her jaw.

"That is the hottest sound I've ever heard." His words were gruff, muffled as they were against her skin as he kissed and nibbled his way toward her ear. "Someday, I'm going to turn that sound into a painting that I'll never sell."

Too turned on and needy to make sense of his words, Felicia let them flow over her as she gripped his strong shoulders and gave in to to the desire sweeping through her. This man. Hudson. He was infuriating and manipulative and the most amazing kisser she'd ever met. So distracting were his lips on her throat that she didn't even realize he was inching up her skirt until she felt air on her thighs.

"Spread your legs as wide as you can for me," he said, raising her skirt until it was bunched near the top of her legs.

She stilled, doubt holding her hostage. "I can't."

"Why?"

Her mind was a jumble of words and phrases, none of which made sense at the moment.

"I don't want to do anything you don't want," he said. "Never think you have to."

Want? *Want?* She wanted it all. Despite knowing that a man like Hudson Carlyle wasn't for a girl like her—and that the man who was right for her was sitting in his apartment on the other side of Harbor City—she did want. Badly. So she relaxed her grip on his shoulders and spread her legs as far as the ottoman would let her. The moment she did, he rewarded her by gliding his hands lower over her bare skin and slipping underneath her dress hem.

His sharp intake of breath matched her own the moment his thumb slid over the bare, desire-swollen flesh at the apex of her thighs. "No panties?"

She groaned as he glided his thumb closer to where she wanted him to go. "Oh God...hate them."

"I will happily burn every single pair from every single store in Harbor City if you want."

That grin of his, it was more smolder now than straight smile. It made her core tighten with enough force that another small moan escaped. She couldn't take it—not any longer.

"All I want," she said, breathing hard and adjusting her stance to give him better access, "is you...touching me."

He inched his thumb over, caressing her outer lips. "You need it, huh?"

"God yes," she said, letting her head fall back.

He pulled his hand back far enough that he wasn't touching her but not so much that she lost the sense of just how close he was to her most sensitive spot. "How bad?"

"Is this your idea of teasing me?" she asked, squeezing her eyes shut as frustrations of all varieties mounted.

"No, this is me turning you on." He nipped at the pulse point at the base of her throat before kissing it better. "I see the way the pulse in your neck speeds up every time I drag things out, every time I start talking dirty."

"This isn't talking dirty." *A little face saving while she all but begged a man who made her irrational to make her come? Sure. That's a great plan, Hartigan.*

"Oh yeah, care to take the lead?"

"Only if you promise to leave me speechless," she said, pulling from a sass reserve buried deep in her subconscious.

He froze and she worried she'd said too much, then he raised his mouth from the sensitive spot where her neck met her shoulder and brought it close to her ear. "Done."

"Make me come."

Before she could say anything else, the pad of his thumb grazed her hard clit, circling over the top of it, and she lost the ability to do anything but react because he was right. She was already on the edge from his teasing denial. It did make her thighs shake in anticipation of all the things this man could do between them. And he was. First one finger than another sliding between her wet folds and circling her sensitive opening as he strummed her clit with his thumb. It was too much and not even slightly close enough. Then he slipped both fingers inside her, filling her up so much better than her battery-operated boyfriend ever could. The sensation of fullness took her breath away, and she moved her hips to the rhythm he'd started.

"That's it, Matches, ride my hand and get yourself off on me so that later tonight I'll be able to smell your sweetness right before I wrap my hands around my hard cock and jerk off to the memory of the way you look right now."

Something about the gravel in his tone as he pumped his

thick fingers inside her, twisting and curling them to hit every sensitive spot she had made her thighs quake as her body climbed higher and higher. She was close, so damn close. Just a little bit longer.

"Damn, you squeeze my fingers so tight. I can't wait to feel how it feels around my cock when I've got you spread eagle on the bed, and I'm fucking you so deep that my balls are bouncing off your ass."

The mental image of him over her, his hair falling low over his forehead as he pounded into her was all it took to push her over the edge. She barely recognized the strangled cry ripped from her throat as her voice broke and her back arched and the best climax ever rushed through her like a tsunami.

When she finally opened her eyes again, the raw, smoldering heat in his gaze caught her unaware. "Fuck. That was something to see," he said on a shaky breath, gently pulling her skirt back down and lifting her off the ottoman.

"I can stand," she said, almost believing it as the world around her slowly came back into focus. Thankfully, he didn't believe her and lifted her up into his strong arms.

"I know you can," he said, nuzzling her hair. "But I've got you."

He carried her over to the blue chair and lowered her into it. Then, he took a few steps back, fisting and relaxing his hands as if whatever it was he wanted to do with them, he couldn't anymore. She racked her brain trying to come up with some weird kinky shit she'd say no to, but after that orgasm, she came up blank. Whatever it was, she couldn't imagine Hudson wouldn't be able to make it feel good.

"You're not totally wrong," he said, taking another few steps away from her and closer to her apartment's front door. "Making Tyler jealous isn't a bad plan. But it won't work until we can show Tyler the Felicia he needs to see. That look on your face, the one you have right now, with your lips swollen from kisses and your cheeks pink from a wake-up-the-neighbors orgasm? That's the Felicia he has to see if he's going to buy that we're a couple, and realize what a complete clueless douche he's been about you for all these years. Although, how he's managed to miss it up until now, I have no idea."

It took a second, but the ice-cold splash of realization finally hit her like a two-by-four to the right temple. The humiliated burn on her cheeks was matched only by the angry burn searing her insides. "So that was to prove a point?"

"Consider it your second lesson in seduction," he said, his tone light but a thin thread of bittersweet ran through it. "It's all about making people feel good."

Even she had to admit he'd accomplished that—for all of about forty-two seconds before reminding her of exactly where they stood with each other and why he was even in her apartment at all tonight. What had just happened hadn't been real. Like everything else about Hudson, it was all about the show. Embarrassed that she'd ever forgotten that, she bolted out of the chair, ready to shove him out the door if that's what it took to make him go before the lump growing in her throat choked off her words.

She glared at him as she marched toward him. "You're such an ass."

"True, but no one will believe you." He stopped in front of the front door. "Everyone knows that I'm the charming Carlyle, the ass is my brother."

Man, when people got it wrong, they *really* got it wrong. "How do you ever manage to pull that off?"

His hand froze almost to her deadbolt, and his jaw tensed. It lasted just long enough for a nugget of guilt to form in her stomach before he flipped open the deadbolts and turned to her with his signature—if, she was beginning to believe, false—roguish grin.

"Let's tackle your Tyler problem first," he answered. "And then, maybe, I'll let you in on my secret." He opened the door and was halfway out when he stopped and turned back toward her. "See you soon."

An exaggerated wink and he was gone, pulling the door shut behind himself, leaving her to stare at it, wondering when she'd lost control of her normally tightly-restrained life and, for the first time, whether it would be worth it if she got the man she'd always wanted in the end.

Chapter Eight

The company cafeteria at Carlyle Enterprises was on the sixth floor of Carlyle Tower and, like the rest of the building, it had a modern, sleek design and was run with ruthless efficiency by a benevolent dictator determined to make it something extraordinary. Although Sawyer ran the rest of the corporation, the sixth floor belonged to Mrs.—first name unknown—Esposito. Short, round, and just shy of seventy, she ran a kitchen that fed the hundreds of Carlyle employees with an iron spoon. Until Hudson had met Felicia, Mrs. Esposito had been his hardest case. It had taken him a whole week to win her over.

It was at least half an hour since the last of the lunch rush had gone back to their offices when he strolled up to the nearly deserted cafeteria counter. Mrs. Esposito stood behind it in her pristine white apron and trademark black long sleeve shirt and pants. The digital menu above her head announced today's special was manicotti, steamed carrots, and a baguette, plus an oatmeal raisin cookie.

"You again." She looked him up and down, the early

afternoon sunlight pouring in through the floor-to-ceiling windows, making her gray hair gleam like steel under her hairnet. "You're still too skinny. I'm putting extra cookies on your plate, but no touching them until your steamed carrots are gone."

"No time for lunch today, Mrs. Esposito," he said, giving the cookies inside the glass display case a hard look. "I'll take the cookies, though."

"A shocking development," she said, reaching for a pair of tongs with one hand as she opened the display case with the other. "I'll alert the media."

He watched her slip two cookies into a paper sleeve branded with the Carlyle Enterprise logo. "If I didn't know any better, I'd say you were sweet on me."

Up went one penciled-in, jet-black eyebrow as she held onto the cookies. "How goes the plan to reunite Sawyer with his former best friend?"

What the—?

How he managed to not let his jaw drop to the floor he wasn't sure. He shouldn't be shocked. The woman was more plugged into the goings on at Carlyle Tower—and the people who worked inside it—than just about anyone else.

"Is there anything you don't know?" he asked.

"The winning Lotto numbers. Other than that?" She pulled a face and shrugged her shoulders. "No. Plus your mother came in for a non-fat, soy milk latte Friday morning."

And there was the answer to that question. Mom and Mrs. Esposito must have been doing a little complimentary intelligence gathering. The secrets those two could crack if they ever teamed up on a professional basis would be astounding—and as scary as shit. He snagged the bag of cookies from her, took one out, and broke it in half—handing one part to her. She accepted it as her due and poured two small glasses of milk, pushing one across the counter to him.

He dunked his cookie and took a bite. "So, you spent the weekend wondering how much progress I'd made in two short days?"

"It was something to do while I scrubbed my shower grout," she said before taking a bite of the cookie.

"I know Sawyer has a cleaning crew over to your apartment once a week," he said, not liking the idea of her working in slippery conditions. He and Sawyer had already all but ensured that her work in the Carlyle Tower cafeteria was supervisory only. "You don't have to do that."

She made a noncommittal snort and took another bite of the cookie. "Myron says I don't have to work anymore, either, to cover our bills, and yet here I am."

"The place wouldn't be the same without you," he said, turning on the full wattage of the Carlyle charm.

"Enough pretty talk," she said, even as her she seemed to grow another inch taller. "Give me the update."

He thought about telling her the version of the plan his mom thought he was following, but in the end, he just couldn't lie to her—or he needed a confidante. He wasn't sure which. So he gave her the quick summary of his genius plan to get Tyler to want her so she'd be free to choose a better man for herself—leaving out the part about hoping she'd choose him for however brief a time it took to work her out of his system and onto his canvas—including his deal with Felicia and dinner last night. What happened after dinner—and the fact that it had kept him up most of the night and weekend—he kept to himself.

Mrs. Esposito brushed the cookie crumbs into her hand and dropped them into a nearby trash can before adding their empty glasses to the dirty dish bucket on a rolling cart that one of her kitchen minions would deliver to the dishwasher. Once her dominion was set back to rights, she turned to him, a considering look on her face that had him wondering what in the hell he'd missed or if he'd said more than he'd intended.

"I see. So how does helping this Felicia woman decide she doesn't want Tyler make things better between him and your brother exactly?" she asked.

"Oh, it doesn't exactly. But she's not right for him. Never would be. But there *is* a woman I think is perfect for him," If anyone could handle someone like Tyler, it was Everly. "And this might be just the thing to spur her into seeing what's right in front of *her* eyes, too. Love makes people do crazy things, right?" It was the reason why wars were fought, painters picked up the brush, and the world turned.

Up went that penciled-in eyebrow. "You know this from personal experience, huh?"

"Not when you keep turning down my marriage proposals," he said, returning to the teasing tone he always used to deflect in these situations when the real him had started to poke through the Hudson Carlyle facade.

"I'm a married woman," she said, chuckling. "And even if I wasn't, you couldn't handle me."

"True enough, Mrs. Esposito." He gave her a wink and grabbed his remaining cookie. "Now off I go up to Sawyer's office to see how making plans to use those tickets has greased the wheels of progress."

"Do you need directions?" she teased. "I could draw a map."

"You're killing me, Mrs. Esposito." He laughed as he walked away. "Thanks for the cookies."

He snarfed down the second cookie in the elevator on the way up to Sawyer's office on the sixty-third floor, appeasing the dread monster shredding his stomach with every floor number that lit up showing his rise. God, he hated this building. No. It wasn't the building, it was the expectations that came with it. Sawyer had been playing with blocks and crayon spreadsheets from birth. Hudson had ignored the blocks and used the crayons to color the walls. All his life, he'd known two things with absolute certainty. One, his family loved him. Two, there was no career path for him except one that led to Carlyle Tower. Oh, he'd fought against it, but the last name Carlyle came at a price—one that eventually led to him lying to the very people who deserved the truth. So that's how he'd ended up with an office on the same floor as Sawyer that he visited once a quarter. He spent his time between trips to his secret painting studio at the cabin wining and dining clients—more often entertaining the spouses so Sawyer could negotiate the business end of things—and counting down the hours until he could get a paint brush back in his hands.

The elevator doors opened and he stuffed that thought to the back and let his shoulders relax as he sauntered out. Sawyer's executive assistant, Amara Grant, sat behind her desk.

"Afternoon, Hudson," she said, her fingers not missing a beat as they flew across the keyboard.

If multitasking was an Olympic sport, Amara would be the world record holding gold medalist.

"Hey there," he said, walking out into the open space that served as Amara's kingdom. "How are the kids?"

"Jaden just made varsity basketball and all-county honor roll," she said, continuing to clack away on the keyboard. "Kai brought home a Tae Kwon Do championship trophy and decided she'll be the youngest African American woman elected president."

"So, they're slacking off as usual."

She laughed. "You here for your brother? He's in with Clover, and the door's unlocked so it should be safe."

He groaned, definitely not wanting his brain to go there. "I do not need that mental image."

Amara's fingers stopped, and she looked up at him with an evil grin. "Why do you think I told you?"

Her chuckle and the clicking of the keys followed him through the big double doors behind Amara's desk and into Sawyer's office. His brother and Clover were seated next to each other at the conference table with spreadsheets and piles of research and estimates spread out around them.

"Making another pitch for total world domination?" he asked.

Clover looked up over her shoulder, a smile on her face. "Why think small? Try total universe domination."

"All we need is for you to dazzle a few aliens," Sawyer said.

"Consider it done." He pulled out the Giants tickets from the inside pocket of his jacket. "I brought these for you and Tyler."

His brother's face lit up, and he accepted the tickets as if they were mini Rembrandts. "How did you manage to get these," he asked. "I couldn't get ahold of them no matter how much I offered."

"I have my ways." The kind he wasn't about to tell his brother.

Not after what happened last time Hudson had started to bring up his secret painting at a family event. If it hadn't have been for his father's supposed clean bill of health, maybe they would have realized his shortness of breath and the tingling in his hand had been the first symptoms of potential heart trouble. Six months and one massive heart attack later and Michael Carlyle was gone.

"Thanks, man." Sawyer strode to his desk and put the tickets into the top drawer.

"There is a catch," he said, settling down onto the guest chair on the other side of Sawyer's desk. "You have to take Tyler."

His brother glowered at him and pulled out one of the tickets. "Here. Take the extra ticket back."

"Nope." Hudson shook his head. He'd given up one of his favorite painting for those tickets, and he wasn't going to let a little victory slip through his fingers because of his brother's stubbornness. So he turned and did a little spin work. "Tyler has made connections all over Asia and is consulting with some of the biggest companies over there. That's Carlyle Enterprises' biggest target area for growth right now, and we can't afford to continue this little middle school feud you two have going."

The grimace slid off his brother's face, replaced by a smarmy grin. "Mom will be so proud. Is the prodigal son finally coming home to the family business?" He turned to Clover, shaking his head. "You know, he tried to walk away from it all in college." Then turned back to Hudson. "What was it? Painting? Photography?"

Something sharp slashed his stomach lining, but he managed not to flinch. "Painting."

"That's right," Sawyer said. "Your talents for schmoozing would have been highly missed."

"Especially if Sawyer had to be in charge of it," Clover said, teasing her husband with the truth and then turning her notices-everything-attention on Hudson. "I didn't know you are a painter."

"Was," Sawyer said, relieving Hudson from having to do anything but pretend it didn't matter. "He stopped in college after dad almost lost his mind about it."

"Why?" she asked.

Now wasn't that the question he'd never been able to find a good answer for. So instead of fighting, he developed an alter-ego one that was starting to weigh on him. The urge to tell them the truth built up pressure inside him until it physically hurt. The words, admitting the truth, were pushing against his lips when he realized that Clover had gone white and was pressing her lips together hard.

"Are you okay?" he asked, all thoughts of revealing he was Hughston pushed to the side again.

"I'm fine. It's just I'm fighting some nasty morning sickness," she said, her hand rubbing circles over her belly. "It'll pass. It always does."

"You're pregnant?"

Sawyer laughed as he pulled out a chair for his wife. "Come on. I suck with details, and even I would have connected morning sickness and pregnancy without having to ask."

"We just found out, and we're waiting a few more weeks before sharing the news. I'm a little cautious on making it public because I know so many people who've had miscarriages."

His brain took a second to catch up with the announcement. "Is there anything I can do?"

"Say congratulations," she said, color coming back into her face as she smiled.

"And wish for a calm and stressless pregnancy," Sawyer said, looking down at his wife with so much emotion on his face it was uncomfortable to see.

Shit. Poking old family scars by revealing he was Hughston sure wouldn't give Clover the stress-free environment the happy couple wanted. He vowed then and there to keep his mouth shut. Their news was better anyway. Who didn't love welcoming a new generation into the family?

"Congratulations," he said, hugging Clover and high fiving his brother. "This is great news."

"Just promise us one thing," she said, her voice muffled by Hudson's shoulder. "We wanted to tell Helene ourselves, but not for a few more weeks."

"Your secret's safe with me," Hudson promised, figuring his mom had probably already guessed anyway, the buzzing of his phone saving him from saying any more. "Sorry, I need to check this."

He pulled his phone out of his front pocket and swiped his thumb across the lock screen.

Felicia: *OMG, Tyler just asked me out. You are officially wrong about last night.*

He read the text again. It didn't make any more sense on the second reading.

Hudson: *What kind of date?*

Felicia: *Coffee*

Sawyer and Clover had gone back to the papers spread out on the conference table, but his sister-in-law kept sneaking looks over at him. Ignoring her penetrating gaze as best he could, he kept his attention on his phone.

Hudson: *Where? When?*

Felicia: *A place close by. Soon.*

What are you hiding, Matches?

Hudson: *?*

Felicia: *OK fine. It's at the museum coffee shop in 30.*

Loving that she was finally starting to get comfortable enough around him to let her secret fiery side out, he could actually hear her huff at the end of the text.

Hudson: *Did he use the term date?*

Felicia: *He said he wanted a quick chat.*

Nice try, but no fire, Matches. The tightness in his chest eased.

Hudson: *1. I'm not wrong. 2. It's not a date, but that doesn't mean you can't flirt. Just don't go all meme stalker girl on him. 3. Remember the other night's lesson: seduction can't be forced.*

He stared at his phone waiting for the dot-dot-dot bubble announcing her answer was incoming but none came. No doubt she was glaring at her phone and calling him every name in the book right about now for bringing up her screaming orgasm. That was okay. He could take it. Preferably in person again.

"Whatever that was," Clover said, drawing his attention up from his phone. "It sure did put a smile on your face."

Out of habit, he flipped his phone over to keep the truth hidden. "Just a little project I'm working on."

"Another secret one?" Sawyer asked.

He shrugged and offered up a lazy grin. "Is there any other kind with me?"

His phone vibrated in his hand and he looked down, wondering what insult she'd finally come up with.

Felicia: *You're infuriating.*

He added insults to the lessons-for-Felicia list because for the youngest of seven, she was horrible at it.

Hudson: *Kisses right back, Matches.*

Standing, he slipped his phone back in his front pocket, ready to face down the questions that were surely coming next. His family was nothing if not nosy and interfering—not that he was an exception to that rule.

"Was it the woman from the other night? Felicia?" Clover asked, obviously taking to the Carlyle creed. "I liked her."

So did he. He especially liked the way she'd come so hard around his fingers the other night that his dick had been jealous for days. That wanton look on her face as she bit her bottom lip and just let go, spreading her legs wider so he could get a better angle, had haunted him over the weekend, and he'd jerked off more times than he'd thought possible for a thirty-year-old man with a healthy and full sex life up until a week ago.

"It's not serious," Hudson said. "It never is with me, remember?"

After all, she was about to have coffee with that douche-canoe, Tyler Jacobson. The guy she was probably thinking about when Hudson had made her come last night. He gritted his teeth as a tight knot formed in his stomach, the kind made of electrified barbed wire and poisoned lead—not because he gave a shit. No. Felicia was just someone he was helping, a project—one that wasn't ready for a public debut yet. She was still untreated canvas. That's all it was.

"Too bad," Clover said, her tone a little too neutral to be believable.

"Don't worry about me, I'll manage." On guard because she seemed to always see a little bit more of the truth about him than either his mom or brother, Hudson gave Clover his patented don't-hate-the-player grin before turning back to his brother. "Now, Sawyer, can you be trusted not to fuck up an evening at the ballpark with Tyler or do I have to find a third ticket so Clover can supervise you?"

"Oh no," she sputtered, her hands up in protest. "You're not getting me near the two of them. My ears were bleeding last night from all the baseball talk."

"Looks like you're on your own, bro."

"Great," Sawyer muttered. "This'll be as much fun as going to the flea market."

"Hey," Clover squawked, her love of all things refurbished

and refinished had become legendary after she'd out-negotiated Sawyer—something that was unheard of in their family. "You *like* going there now."

"No," Sawyer said with a suggestive grin. "I like watching your ass as you strut around looking for deals."

Clover rolled her eyes and shook her head, glancing over at Hudson. "Can you do something about your brother?"

He shrugged. "I've been trying my entire life and failing miserably."

Sawyer crumpled up a piece of paper from the conference table and launched it at Hudson, who dodged it with ease. Then, his brother leaned down and whispered something in Clover's ear that made her eyes go wide and her cheeks turn pink. Deciding that his mission here was complete, Hudson got out of the office and into the elevator before those two got any more sickening. He made it all the way to the fiftieth floor before he pulled out his phone and texted Felicia for an update.

Chapter Nine

Felicia took a sip of tea from her ANTS DO IT TO THE DEATH mug and tucked the stray strands of hair that had slipped out of her ponytail behind her ears and looked at the clock on her phone for the fiftieth time in the past thirty-five seconds. Her bottom lip was starting to throb from her nervous nibbling, and if her heart went any faster, she'd be worried about passing out on the walk down to the coffee shop. Worst of all, she had to wait five more minutes before she could go down.

According to Hudson, she shouldn't show up early. On time was fine, but early at a table with both of their drinks already ordered and delivered was a no-go. While that seemed like efficiency to her, he called it—she scrolled through the texts from the past ten minutes—"a stalker's delight."

Why was he so obsessed with that description? She wasn't being all creepy and stalkery. Of course she knew Tyler's drink order. They'd literally known each other for more than fifteen years. That most of that time had been with him visiting the Hartigan house and her butting into her brother Frankie's room to say hi and try, unsuccessfully, to hang out with them didn't matter. Oh, forget it, she wasn't doing it Hudson's way. He'd never know anyway. She got up from her chair, grabbed her phone, and began walking out of her cubicle. Her cell buzzed in her hand.

Hudson: *Don't do it.*

She froze and looked around for his hulking frame. No Hudson. No hidden cameras. Nothing. How did he know?

Felicia: *Do what?*

Hudson: *You're already in the coffee shop aren't you.*

Ha! He was guessing.

Felicia: *No, I'm in my cubicle.*

Technically true.

Hudson: *Sitting down?*

She looked around again. Still nothing but the itchy feeling that he'd bugged the ant lab somehow. She sighed and admitted the truth.

Felicia: *Standing in the doorway.*

Hudson: *Caught you!*

Despite everything, one side of her mouth turned upward. He was incorrigible.

Felicia: *You need a keeper.*

Hudson: *And you need to follow directions better.*

Felicia: *I'm a scientist. We're naturally inquisitive.*

Hudson: *What are you wearing?*

She looked down to fill the blanks.

Felicia: *Jeans and a T-shirt.*

Hudson: *Lab coat?*

Felicia: *Hanging on the back of my chair.*

Hudson: *Underwear?*

She typed out T-H-O-N before stopping herself. *Damn it.*

Felicia: *None of your business.*

Hudson: *Same as the other night?*

Heat flamed against her cheeks, and she ducked back into her cubical before anyone noticed. The other night. Yeah, that was one way to describe her totally losing her mind and her inhibitions to the point that she'd orgasmed standing up while on an ottoman in the middle of her living room. If life were fair, she would have been able to put it out of her mind completely and pretend it had never happened. But the truth was that she hadn't stopped thinking about it, or wanting it to happen again. Obviously, her body's reaction to Hudson was just transference. Whatever attraction she felt toward him would all work itself out as soon as she got Tyler to really notice her.

Hudson: *I bet you're cute and commando. That's the mental picture I have right now. It's hot.*

She clenched her thighs together and forced her fingers to type something other than the status of her now damp panties.

Felicia: *I'm not answering that.*

Hudson: *I can come over and investigate. Hanging around a scientist has made me more curious about my world and more appreciative of the scientific method of discovery.*

As if.

Felicia: *You're full of shit.*

Hudson: *And you're not as nervous now.*

Her hand went up to her bottom lip. It wasn't nearly as tender as it had been before and her hands had stopped twitching. *How had he...* Before she could finish the thought, her phone vibrated in her palm.

Hudson: *Time to go. Have fun with Captain Clueless.*

Okay, she had to hand it to him. Hudson Carlyle was a total pain in her ass, but he was good to have around occasionally. She dashed off a quick bye text and hustled down three flights on the staff-only staircase to the bottom floor. Visitors were thick between the hanging great white shark display and the museum coffee shop, but she still spotted Tyler who stood tall above the crowd. Of course, his inky black hair, intense blue eyes, and confident stance would make him stand out in any crowd.

It wasn't until she swerved around a gaggle of kindergartners walking hand-in-hand in a giant swirling line that she realized his hair was mussed, and he had the distracted air of someone whose brain was miles away.

"Everything okay?" she asked when she finally made it to his side.

"Just another run-in with the world's most annoying upstairs neighbor," he said as they made their way to the back of the long line leading to the harried baristas. "The woman wears heels twenty-four-seven as she stomps around her apartment, and she has wood floors. It's like living below a herd of stiletto wearing elephants."

Thank God Mrs. Blankenship in the apartment above her only made tons of noise during her Saturday morning cleaning extravaganzas. "Sounds like fun."

"That's one word for it," he grumbled, shoving his fingers through his hair and leaving a straight up mess in their wake. "I'm working on a plan, though."

"You always were a schemer." The words were out of her mouth before her brain had a chance to realize he might take that as an insult. God, why didn't her high IQ help with social situations *at all*? "I don't mean it in a bad way."

"Nah, you're right. A man's gotta have a plan, and I've got a ton of them," he said as they got to the front of the line. "Come on, let's get that coffee. I need to run some stuff past you."

One green tea (her) and an extra-large coffee (him) order later, and her phone buzzed against her ass as they stood in another line waiting for their order. She should ignore it. Tyler stood next to her checking his own phone. She had it out and in her hand a second later. So much for willpower when curiosity was involved.

Hudson: *What's going on?*

Felicia: *In line for coffee.*

Hudson: *Perfect. Now about that underwear…*

Her pulse rocketed.

Felicia: *Ignoring you.*

She shoved it back into her back pocket, determined to ignore him—at least until she got back up to her cubicle.

The barista called out their order, and they retrieved their drinks, and Tyler headed off to a table in the corner blessedly away from the shouts and whines of the child-sized weekday museum crowd. She followed behind, her self-satisfied smile growing with each step. That was a good sign. It had to be. Why ask for a coffee date and sit at the most private table there unless he'd had an epiphany about them? Her plan the other night had worked. All Tyler had needed was a little nudge in the right direction.

As she sat down in front of him, she couldn't help but notice the way he fiddled with the cardboard sleeve around his hot coffee and the noticeable muscle tic in his jaw. He was nervous. Of being with her? Of what he was about to tell her?

Finally, he looked up, his blue eyes staring directly into her. "I don't even know where to begin with this."

Her pulse went into double-time. "Start anywhere."

"Okay," he said, nodding his head with firm determination. "I need help with something a little sketchy, but I promise it's not illegal."

Not exactly a will-you-go-out-with-me answer.

The sip of green tea in her mouth lost its taste, and she forced herself to swallow past the disappointment blocking her throat. "That's comforting because I look like crap in orange."

He toasted her with a slight tip of his coffee to-go cup and a half-hearted smile, but it was obvious his mind wasn't on her but on whatever plan he was working on this time to make the world bend to his will. "I need some information about one of the museum's patrons."

"What kind of information?" she asked, the green tea sloshing around in her stomach as it knotted itself.

"If they're still donating, and if so, if their donations have changed over the past year."

Okay, not exactly public information but not the nuclear

codes, either. Still, she knew Tyler. There was more to this than idle curiosity. "What's this all about?"

He shrugged. "I'm just filling in some blanks on a financial profile I'm putting together."

Uh-huh. Right. "So why not ask the client yourself?"

"Not possible."

That was it. No explanation. No cajoling. No Hudson-like teasing that had Team Annoyance and Team Anticipation facing off against each other inside her. Just an unspoken black and white, will you or won't you, hanging in the air between them.

"I don't even have access to that information," she said, sounding wishy-washy even to herself.

He leaned forward, intensity burning in his blue eyes. "But you could get it."

"Maybe." Okay, yeah, she could get it. Her boss would love for her to take a greater interest in pumping the museum's patrons for money. But to reveal private information about a donor… That was iffy territory.

"Come on, someone in the business office has to owe you a favor or need one," he said. "Whatever it is, I'll make it happen."

"It's that important?"

He nodded. "I believe someone is lying about their finances and could end up harming thousands of employees if it's true."

Shit. This was definitely *not* where she thought this conversation was going to go. If she had, she sure as hell wouldn't have told Hudson about it. The very last thing she wanted was to hear him laugh at her misreading of the social cues—again. Tyler looked at her expectantly.

Her phone buzzed against her ass. Relieved at the interruption, she pulled it out of her back pocket.

Hudson: *What do you call two teenage ants running to Vegas? Antelope.*

"Important text?" Tyler asked.

"No," she said, putting her phone down on the table next to her tea just as another message flashed across the screen.

Hudson: *What's the difference between writing your will and owning an ant farm? One is a legacy, and the other is a sea of legs.*

That was awful. Horrible. She didn't know what dark corner of the internet he'd found that so-called joke, but he needed to back away. Fast. Still, she was smiling, and her gut had stopped churning her tea. By the time she looked up at Tyler again, her logical brain was back in the driver's seat.

"Are you sure?" Snoop that he was, Tyler glanced down at her phone as he asked.

Now it was her turn to shrug as if it wasn't important. "It's just Hudson."

He straightened in his seat, his broad shoulders going stiff. "Hudson Carlyle?"

She nodded.

"What's going on with you two?" he asked, his gaze narrowed in on her. "I was surprised to see you at dinner with him."

Okay, this was her opening. She had to take it. "Why, don't you think I date?"

That would have sounded a whole lot more convincing if the last word hadn't come out in a squeak.

"No, because of him," Tyler said. "He doesn't seem like your type. He's got a certain kind of reputation and, anyway, let's just say I have a history with the Carlyle family."

Not wanting to go anywhere near what she imagined to be Hudson's reputation, she swapped topics. "Want to talk about it?"

"Sorry, that touchy feely crap isn't for me. I'm more of a man of action." He slid a piece of paper with a single name scrawled on it toward her.

Oh yes. The whole reason for this coffee date. Not because he saw her as date potential, but to ask a favor of a friend. "And of schemes."

"Exactly." Tyler twisted the end of an imaginary mustache. "So, you'll do it?"

She took the piece of paper and nodded.

"Thanks, Felicia," he said as he pushed his chair back and stood. "I hate to ask a favor and dash, but I'm late for a client meeting."

Pushing back her disappointment—after all, she was well-practiced at it when it came to Tyler—she smiled. "No problem."

"Thanks again. I knew you'd help."

And he was gone, lost in the sea of tourists and Harbor City regulars gathered under the great white shark hanging from the ceiling. Well, so much for a date. This was more like a dead drop. She glanced down at the name. Gregori Sirko. Beyond a name in the financial section of the Harbor City Journal, it meant nothing to her.

Gathering up her tea and phone, she stood up and then made her way through the throng of people and back up the employee stairs to her office. Her phone vibrated the moment she sat down in her chair. Damn. It really was like he had her office bugged.

Hudson: *How's it going?*

Felicia: *It's gone.*

Hudson: *And...*

Felicia: *No change.*

That was putting it mildly. Oh sure, she had some kind of don't-tell-anyone spy mission, but that didn't change the fact that Tyler still didn't see her for anything beyond his friend's nerdy kid sister who he'd known forever.

Hudson: *Don't worry. We'll make it happen.*

She sat her phone aside without responding. What could she say? All of her predictions had proved wrong. A few minutes later, she was analyzing the data from her latest field report and trying not to think about the Tyler situation when her phone buzzed.

Hudson: *So, what color underwear? I've been distracting myself with ant jokes, but the internet is out of them.*

She laughed despite herself. He didn't give up; she had to give Hudson that.

Felicia: *Red cotton with little white hearts.*

Hudson: *Can't wait to see them.*

Her legs clenched against the tingle of anticipation, making her pulse sky rocket. She set her phone down, her hand a little shakier this time. Fighting to ignore the way her body had gone into overdrive at his text, she tried to work it out logically.

1. She was attracted to Hudson in some kind of cruel transference joke of fate.

2. She had to spend time with Hudson in order to get Tyler to finally notice her.

3. She needed to learn how to seduce Tyler and Hudson was obviously willing to teach her.

4. Orgasms relieved stress, and she was feeling very tense right about now.

Nothing about her body's reaction to Hudson changed her plans or her goal. It just meant that her lessons with Harbor City's Professor Higgins had the potential to be a little more orgasmic than expected. Nothing to worry about there at all.

• • •

Well, it could have been more orgasmic if Felicia had actually gotten to see Hudson. Annoyed that four days and almost four nights had gone by without a peep from her professor, she tossed aside the journal she'd been reading in bed and grabbed her phone.

Felicia: *Where are you?*

A reply came almost instantly.

Hudson: *Miss me?*

Felicia: *You're supposed to be helping me.*

Hudson: *I am. I'm teaching you patience and anticipation.*

Felicia: *If you could see my face right now you'd know what I think of that.*

Hudson: *Show me.*

Selfies weren't her thing. Especially not selfies when she was in a raggedy old sleep T-shirt with her hair in a messy bun.

Hudson: *Chicken?*

"Fine," she grumbled to Honeypot, who was curled up on the corner of the bed completely ignoring her, held up her phone and snapped a quick picture of her glaring at the phone, sending it before she could change her mind.

There was nothing for almost a full minute, then her phone vibrated.

Hudson: *I've missed you, too, Matches.*

She stared at the text, unable to unravel the meaning. She must have missed something. Scrolling up in the text stream so she could reread, her thumb hit the photo she'd sent, enlarging it. Her stomach dropped. *Oh shit.* Half her face took up the top quarter of the photo, but that wasn't what had her cheeks burning. The white cotton of her T-shirt was thinner than she'd realized. There was no missing the dark shadows of her nipples against the threadbare material, and the stretched-out V-neck dipped at just the right angle to show off the upper swells of her breasts.

Felicia: *I didn't mean to send that.*

Hudson: *I don't know, a lesson in sexting is good.*

Felicia: *I don't know how to do that.*

Hudson: *Matches, you most certainly do. I'm so hard I could pound nails with my dick.*

Her breath caught, and her nipples puckered against her shirt, and it wasn't because of a chill. It was October outside but the dog days of August in her room. In a flash, her skin was flush, sensitive, hot, and needy. It was too much. Falling into the moment, in the name of this experiment with Hudson, was one thing. Doing it while he was God knew where with God knew who—a lead weight pulled her stomach down to her toes at *that* thought—and doing God knew what was not gonna happen. She shot off one last text to end the conversation.

Felecia: *I have to go now.*

Hudson: *Chicken. ;)*

Nope. That wasn't going to work a second time. She all but flung her phone across her bed. It landed with a thud by Honeypot, who jolted up with a hiss and flew off the bed. If only she could get away from the way Hudson made her feel as easily as her cat stalked across the room.

• • •

A week spent painting at the cabin usually went by in a rush, but not this time. A certain pocket-sized ant researcher kept turning up in Hudson's paintings, which wasn't going to do him any good if he was going to make the deadline for his next gallery show. He sat down on the porch, a crunchy peanut butter and grape jelly sandwich held in his paint-stained fingers, and checked his texts. Nothing from Felicia—not since that wet dream of a photo two nights ago. Anyone else and he would have assumed the shot had been staged and one of fifty taken before a final picture was filtered and sent. Not with Felicia, though.

Unable to take the radio silence anymore, he put down the sandwich and started a text.

Hudson: *Still in that T-shirt?*

Two minutes later, his phone dinged.

Felicia: *It's noon, and I'm at the ant lab working on my article for the premiere journal in my specialty.*

Hudson: *That's not an answer.*

After five minutes with no response, he poked her again.

Hudson: *I have a mission for you.*

This time, he got an immediate response.

Felicia: *?*

Hudson: *You need to get three date dresses.*

Felicia: *Payday's next week.*

Hudson: *I'll talk to my personal shopper at Dylan's Department store. She'll be expecting you after work today. Sixth floor. Ask for Jacqui. Everything's my treat.*

Felicia: *You have a personal shopper?*

Hudson: *Focus, Matches.*

Felicia: *Does your mom still cut your food, too?*

He let out a bark of a laugh and smiled. *There* was his sassy girl.

Hudson: *I'll let you do it for me if you wear that T-shirt from the other night and nothing else.*

Felicia: *I threw out the shirt.*

He wasn't above going through her trash to get it back. Honeypot would stand guard.

Hudson: *That's just mean.*

There was a pause, and then a photo popped into the text stream. In it, Felicia was at work, her hair in a ponytail, wearing her glasses and a blue crewneck sweater. He assumed there were pants to her outfit, but he couldn't get visual confirmation, so his imagination at least got that much of a treat. Her very kissable pink lips were smooshed into an exaggerated pout, and she was tracing an imaginary tear down her cheek. She was mocking him. His dick didn't care. The sight of those lips and the big guy was ready for action.

Felicia: *Life is pain.*

And near constant hard-ons. He needed to get back to Harbor City. Now.

Chapter Ten

Felicia trudged across the street, one block from her house, clutching half a month's rent in the form of three dresses in a garment bag close to her chest. There was no way in hell Felicia could actually wear the dresses Jacqui had talked her into buying.

She'd take them back after work tomorrow. They were too expensive. Sure, Hudson could afford it, but her pride couldn't. They were too short, too clingy, and too far out of her comfort zone. Worst of all? Patterns. Every petite girl knew that patterns did nothing but engulf small body types until there was nothing left of the person. Of course, she'd been totally on board with every purchase right up until she hit Forty-Ninth Street. That's when she crossed the street behind a beautiful, tall, model-type woman and watched as every man she passed did a double—and sometimes triple—look. When Felicia had gotten there? Not even a glance. *That* woman was the kind who could get away with short, clingy, pattern dresses. By the time Felicia had gotten three blocks from home, she'd mentally listed every reason why she wasn't that type of woman. That is why she had to work harder—and a little sneakier, if she was going to be honest with herself—to make Tyler notice her. And to do that she didn't need dresses, she needed Hudson, but he was AWOL. The big jerk.

Honeypot's yowling sounded as soon as Felicia turned the corner. She was too far away for the cat to have spotted her. Excitement thrummed through her even before she spotted her own Henry Higgins lounging against the banister around the entrance to her walk down apartment. The October wind had rearranged his longish hair, but instead of looking a mess, it just made him look like a woman had just ran her fingers through it after he'd given her the best orgasm of her life.

Projecting? Maybe a little bit.

His long legs ate up the half a block between them in two heartbeats, and he took the garment bag from her, slinging it over one shoulder. Grinning down at her, his other hand came to rest on the small of her back. The heat from his touch seared through her fall jacket and through the lightweight sweater she'd pulled on this morning, sending a jolt of awareness that made it feel like she had too many layers on.

"Glad to see the shopping trip was a success," he said as they started walking toward her apartment.

Ha. Was that what people called it? "They're going back."

"Why?"

"Because they are." Firm. No argument could sway her.

He leaned over, bringing his mouth within a hairsbreadth of the shell of her ear. "I bet they look hot."

Blushing as an older couple strolled by, the woman giving her a knowing smile, Felicia decided it was the evening chill that had her nipples puckering and pushing against the lace of her bra. "Not hardly."

"I'll be the judge of that," he said, his breath dancing against the sensitive skin of her ear before he straightened up and let his hand drop an inch lower as they walked. "Anyway, anything's better than that black dress you wore to the fundraiser."

What? She jerked to a stop. "That was a brand-new dress. A classic, black dress that everyone looks good in."

He snorted. "And it belongs in the donation bin."

The man was crazy. She'd just bought that and had been lucky to find it in the 70 percent off rack in the junior's section at Dylan's. She scrambled to match his long stride, ready to defend her birthday dress to the last stitch.

"It's the perfect little black dress," she said. "It works for funerals and parties."

"There is nothing right about what you just said," he said, stopping at the top of the stairs leading down to her apartment door.

Honeypot was caterwauling, but he didn't even glance in the lovelorn cat's direction. His attention was completely centered on her, so much so that Felicia could practically feel the touch of his gaze. The sounds of the city faded away until the horns from the cars inching their way through rush hour traffic barely made a beep, and the throngs of people rushing home as the sun dropped lower and lower in the sky melted into the background. It was thrilling...a little bit scary...a total rush...and something she should *not* be feeling with Hudson Carlyle. Transference was one thing. Getting lost in the pretend world he offered up on a silver platter was something else, something dangerous to any woman who wanted to keep her wits about her and not forget the real reason why one of Harbor City's most eligible bachelors was carrying the new dresses he bought for her. He delivered Tyler Jacobson to her, and she helped Hudson reforge the bromance bond between his older brother and her lifelong crush. That's all. Nothing else.

Well, and she'd agreed to pose for him in a painting. Not nude, of course. It was strange he'd not mentioned the painting since that first night. Maybe he couldn't even paint, and art was just a pickup line for him—one he no longer needed since she'd straddled her ottoman.

"Did you ever consider that you spend a little bit too much time thinking about my clothes?"

What Hudson did with his mouth wasn't smirk or a grin. It was a full-on sex smolder that could turn brainiacs like her stupid if they weren't careful.

"Matches, I spend a lot more time thinking about you out of them," he said, a gruff edge to his words—the kind that reverberated down her spine. "Trust me."

Heat hit her with the force of a Mack truck. *Shit.* She had *no* idea what to do with that. Out of some desperate corner of her mind came a feeble whispered shout: Tyler.

Yes. Tyler.

She shifted her focus so that she was looking past his left ear instead of at his face. "I could have used your help this week."

"What happened?"

"Tyler called, and I tried flirting but ended up giving him a fifteen-minute lecture about how male ants die after sex." God. Just saying it out loud was like reliving her latest humiliation all over again. It had been mortifying, but she hadn't been able to keep her trap shut.

"And this didn't make him fall to his knees and beg you to go out on a date with him?"

"No, you ass." She walked down the steps, past where Honeypot sat in the window plaintively meowing, to her front door and started digging through her cross-body bag for her keys.

"So," Hudson said, following her down—his massive ego coming along for the ride. "You're saying you need me."

She stopped mid-search and glared at him. "Fine. Yes. I need you."

"Then let's go inside." He held up the garment bag with Dylan's Department store's logo on it. "We can come up with some conversational go-tos while you try on the dresses for me."

"No way." That was *not* going to happen. Even the idea of it had her searching her bag for her keys with greater urgency.

Hudson came to a stop next to her, leaning one shoulder against her doorframe. "If you'd rather stand around in your underwear, I'm good with that, too."

A week ago, that comment would have thrown her, but she was onto him now. Thanks to all their text exchanges and conversations, she'd cracked the Hudson code. This was how he exerted control, he teased and flirted and charmed his way into having the upper hand. Call it Small Woman's Syndrome, but she couldn't help herself from jumping into the fray and letting him know, he didn't have control of her.

Looking up at him, she took in the confident bordering on cocky way he stood with one finger hooked around the hanger of the Dylan's garment bag that was tossed over his shoulder. The light from the streetlamps highlighted the strands of blond in his light brown hair and added in some shadows that made him look more angular and dangerous than he did in the daylight. The sight called out to some part of herself she didn't recognize. Still, she couldn't back down. The idea struck the second she wrapped her fingers around her keys and pulled them from her bag. This was, after all, lessons in seduction and were part of the bargain they'd struck.

Emboldened, she slid the keys into the deadbolt before turning so her back was to the door and her front to him. "Hudson, sweet boy, what makes you think I'm even wearing panties?"

One side of his mouth curled up, but with something a lot more intense than humor. "Sweet boy?" he asked, his brown eyes going dark with desire, his free arm extended over her shoulder with his hand pressed firm against the door. "Are you taunting or flirting?"

"Is it working?" she brazened.

Another step and there was nothing between them but too many layers of clothes. "Yes."

"Then it doesn't matter, does it?" What should have been a cool retort came out breathy.

"Of course it does." He traced a single finger down the side of her face and along her jaw, leaving a line of fire in its wake. "Taunting is just for show. Flirting is for results."

"What kind of results?" The question popped out before she could stop it.

He glided his finger across the seam of her slightly parted lips, so butterfly soft that it was almost cruel. "The kind where you end up naked, sweaty, and satisfied. What will you be doing with Tyler?" His hand fell from her mouth and the gruff edge to his voice turned demanding and hard. "Do you plan on taunting or flirting?"

Tyler? Who in the hell was Tyler? She fought to pull back from the edge of the abyss and succeeded enough to sorta remember the only goal left she had left to accomplish on her before-I-turn-thirty list.

"Flirting," she said, her voice sounding small and far away.

He growled low in his throat and dipped his head lower. "Then you should practice."

"On you?" It came out more of a plea than a question, but she was too far gone into the moment to care.

"Or under, your choice."

"I thought flirting was verbal," she said, the words slipping out powered by nerves and an electric anticipation.

He was so close that heat from his body seeped into hers, scattering every last survival instinct she had. Still, he didn't cross that final inch separating their mouths. She wanted to scream. She wanted to plea. She wanted to do whatever it took to make sure it didn't end.

"Matches," he said, the nickname a whispered promise against her lips. "You have a lot to learn."

Then his mouth crashed down onto hers, and her last thought before her body's reactions drowned out everything else but Hudson was that she had never been more glad that she'd always been an excellent student.

• • •

This is exactly what Hudson had been thinking about during every mile of the trip back to Harbor City. Felicia's soft, full lips parting under his as she made that sweet, little moan that went straight to his dick. Fuck. Kissing her was beyond good. Her lips parted beneath his, and he slid his tongue inside, tasting and teasing her into response—and *did* she respond. Licks. Nibbles. Her hands skimming over his chest. Felicia pressed close to him, her arms going around his neck as she drew herself up on her tiptoes, making her body glide across his hard cock until it nestled against her belly. Being this close to her, with her clinging to him like he was the last solid thing in a shifting world, felt good, but it sure as hell wasn't where he wanted his dick right now.

He broke the kiss, his prick shouting in protest as he did so. "We need to get inside."

"Why?" she asked, looking up at him with lust-fogged eyes.

"Because if we don't. I'm going to fuck you against your front door while half of Harbor City walks by." With anyone else it would have been an idol threat, but not with Felicia. If she'd been wearing one of the dresses in the damn bag he was holding instead of jeans, he couldn't guarantee he wouldn't have it pulled up to her hips already.

Her eyes widened, but she turned and opened the door. Honeypot rushed forward, but they hurried inside, and he slammed the door shut before the beast could escape. The last thing he wanted was to chase a one-eyed cat down the street with his dick as hard as an iron spike. Honeypot took one look at them, lifted her tail in disgust, and stalked over to her spot on the windowsill to hiss at the people walking by.

He locked both deadbolts while Felicia watched, still clutching her keys in her hand. Nervous energy and jittery sexual frustration surrounded her like steam—any minute now she was going to blow.

"Are you hungry?" she asked, not moving an inch toward the kitchen. "Did you know honeypot ants gorge themselves on desert flowers for the sugary nectar during the rainy seasons?"

Refusing to let his mind go there when he had other—sexier—things to consider rather than the eating habits of ants, he held out the garment bag to her. "Go try on a dress."

She blinked. "You want a fashion show?"

No, he wanted to bend her over that blue chair, yank down her pants, shove her panties aside, and drive his dick into her until she came so hard she milked his cock dry, but that wasn't going to happen—at least not yet. This was still a lesson, and what better way to show the value of driving someone to the edge of sanity with lust than to actually experience it.

"One dress."

"I thought you wanted..." Her words trailed off as she scrunched up her nose and started trying to work through what she must see as an illogical construct.

Not giving himself time to change his mind, he unzipped the garment bag and pulled out a dress, not bothering to look at it. "Go change."

"You can't order me around," she huffed but took the dress.

"I just did." He spun her around and gave her a light shove toward her bedroom door. "Now go do what the professor says."

It took all of thirty-six seconds after she shut her bedroom door before he decided waiting and drawing out the pleasure was a stupid idea invented by sadists. To pass the time, he flipped through a scientific journal about ants and made it fourteen pages before giving up. Next, he checked the contents of her fridge, which was as barren as his own. After that, Honeypot hissed him away from coming any closer, her tail twitching in annoyance. Finally, he heard the click of the bedroom door opening.

He turned and then the world stopped spinning. Felicia was wearing an electric blue dress that stopped just shy of her knees that was made out of some kind of fabric that hugged her curves with a V-neck deep enough to highlight everything underneath. And just to make everything better and worse, the whole thing looked to be held together by a length of fabric tied into a bow at her waist.

"It's all wrong, I know, but Jacqui was so convincing in the store," she said, brushing her hands over her hips and already backing up toward her bedroom. "It'll take me just a second to get out of it."

"Don't you dare." The only person untying that bow was going to be him.

She gulped. "What?"

"You look amazing," he said, searching for a better word to describe the effect she was having and coming up empty. "Even Captain Clueless won't be able to miss that after he sees you in this."

And it was going to take Hudson everything he had not to punch the idiot out for never doing so before. Because whether she was in this dress or one of her ridiculous ant shirts or the world's ugliest little black dress, Felicia Hartigan was impossible not to notice.

She tugged at the hem. "It's too short."

He started toward her, and she gulped, her hands flying like nervous birds around her as she fiddled with the dress.

"It's too tight." Again, she smoothed her hands over the material, skimming her palms over her hips.

Stopping within arm's reach, he gave her a slow up and down perusal, taking in all that she'd been hiding under the baggy T-shirts and boy-cut jeans. Her whole look before practically screamed don't look at me. Now? There was no looking away.

An aroused flush had started in the valley between her tits and stretched north. "It's not me."

"Matches, it may not be your go-to style, but this is all you," he said. "Every gorgeous bit."

"Stop saying that," she said, the pulse point in her neck jackhammering. "I'm well aware of my limitations. I'm too short. Too flat chested. Too—"

Before she could finish with whatever bullshit she was continuing to offer up, he silenced her with a kiss—if that's what it could be called. It was more like a dam breaking. Their hands and mouths were everywhere, tasting and nipping and kissing from one patch of exposed skin to another. His balls ached with the need not just to touch her but to see her.

He tugged at the bow designed to look like it was holding the entire dress together. "Take it off."

"You first," she said, straightening her glasses that had gone cockeyed, determination taking her chin a couple of degrees higher. "This is a lesson after all. I should see how the master does it."

"A lesson," he repeated, wishing not all of his blood had gone straight south from his brain, because it took longer than it should have to translate that. Once he did, there was no missing the laughing gleam in her blue eyes. So, someone thought they could take the upper hand? That wasn't going to happen. "I'm happy to demonstrate. Take a seat."

The closest one was the ottoman she'd stood on when she'd come all over his fingers the other night. She must have made the same connection because her lips parted on a quick inhale before she sat down, her legs crossed at the ankles and her knees held tight together. To top off the prim look, she rested her clasped hands in her lap and straightened her spine until even an old timey finishing school principal would have been impressed by her posture.

He shrugged out of his jacket and reached for the top button of his shirt. "Ready?"

"Yes, sir," she said with a shy smile he didn't believe for an instant.

She may not crave to be the center of attention but, once she was there, she flourished with a sassy attitude that made him even harder. He couldn't wait to discover whatever other surprises she was hiding under that veneer of nerdy girl next door.

"So, you want to start slow." He slipped the top button free. "One thing at a time while maintaining eye contact."

Not that he could look away from her and miss seeing how into this little strip tease she was. While her face remained impassive, by the time he'd finished unbuttoning his shirt and dropped it to the floor, she'd inched forward on the ottoman until her ass was probably barely on it. His hand went to the top button of his jeans, the pad of his thumb flicking it but not enough to pop it open. Her hands separated, and she clutched the edge of the ottoman. Her thighs clenched and flexed before relaxing again. Oh yeah, she was *definitely* enjoying this.

"There's a fine line between teasing and taunting, you

have to learn to walk it even as your body is screaming at you to move faster," he said, dropping his hands from his jeans, the top button still in place.

She groaned and bit down on her bottom lip, watching with big eyes as he reached behind his head and grabbed his white undershirt, pulling it off over his head.

"And is your body telling you to speed it up?" she asked as the undershirt slid from his grasp and floated to the floor.

Telling? More like demanding and threatening total and complete revolt. That part was bad, but the look in her eyes is what really did him in. He strode forward until he stood directly in front of her, his iron hard cock pushing against his jeans only inches from her face. When her pink tongue slipped out and wet her lips as she stared at that bulge, he almost nutted right there and then.

Gritting his teeth, he sucked in a breath through his nose and let it back out slow, willing his body to get with the fucking program. "Why don't you observe and enter the data in your field report?"

Breaking the no-touching rule, he took one of her hands and pressed her palm to where his dick strained against the denim. Her soft touch was bad enough, but when she encircled him as best she could and let out a sound that was a mix between a sigh and a moan, he could only close his eyes and start naming every shade on the color wheel while praying to regain control before he went over the edge and came in his jeans.

"Unbutton me," he said, holding on so tight to the last vestiges of his control that his tone fell somewhere between sandpaper and razor wire.

Felicia looked up at him with those big eyes, her mouth parted and full bottom lip glistening. "Are you sure?"

Fuck, no. "You have to learn to take and to give."

Her fingertips skimmed over his bare abs, making his

muscles jump, and he fisted his hands to keep from cupping her head and urging her closer. If she noticed, it didn't show. Instead, she stayed focused on tracing the happy trail of hair that went from his lower abdomen to his jeans, her fingers finally landing on the button that was fast becoming the center of his existence.

She stilled her hands, but leaned forward, her hot breath brushing against his skin, and looked up at him. "What was that you said about a fine line between teasing and taunting?"

Hell. Why did he always have to fucking talk so much? "You're right on it, Matches."

"Does that mean you're hot and bothered?" she asked, taking off her glasses and tossing them onto the nearby chair.

"More like hard and demanding." And closer to dying than a thirty-year-old who just got a clean bill of health should be.

"What do you want?" She flicked open the button of his jeans.

Shit. That list was as long as he was. "Those perfect lips of yours wrapped around my dick."

"Oh." She licked her lips. "Is that all?"

"Matches, that's just the beginning."

Tugging her lip between her teeth, she inched down the zipper of his jeans, pulled his cock out from the confines of his boxers and gave him a saucy wink before leaning forward and taking him in her hot mouth, making him totally forget about lessons, Captain Clueless, or anything else except the magic she was performing with her wicked little tongue.

Chapter Eleven

This kind of control could be addicting. There was just something about watching Hudson forget to be Mr. Charming and instead let the real him—the demanding, determined him—come out that made her wet and aching. Instead of easing that ache with her own fingers as she sucked him deeper, she reached out and took his hands, bringing them to her head. His hard exhale as he threaded his fingers through her hair and guided her mouth on a torturous, slow journey up and down on him elicited a shiver deep in her core. Also, it left her hands free to wander, and they did—over his thick, muscular thighs and up to his hard ass so tense from holding back.

"Look at me," he ordered.

She did, losing her sense of rhythm for a second at the sight. His eyes had gone dark and intense with the promise of what was to come, and she wanted it, she wanted it all. A hot wave of desire settled low in her belly, and she cupped his ass, pulling him closer until he filled her mouth completely and went farther until he hit the back of her throat. He let out a harsh groan that sent a delicious shiver down her spine. She stayed there, dancing on the edge of just enough and too much, loving every breathless second of it. And then she swallowed.

"Fuck, I can feel that throat of yours working me." His fingers tightened in her hair as he arched his hips, going deeper. "That's it."

He eased back before continuing with a slow thrust forward that brought her lips down to the very base. Once. Twice. Three times. Then, he pulled out completely, stepping away from her and leaving her sucking in breaths and desperate for more. Judging by the fierce look on his face, she wasn't alone. He had what remained of his clothes stripped off in a heartbeat. God, he was phenomenal. Long, strong legs. Broad shoulders. Defined abs. A dusting of light brown hair across his chest and a happy trail over his six-pack abs that led straight to the rock-hard length of him that she was standing and reaching for before she even realized it.

He evaded her touch with a step back. "Patience is definitely not one of your virtues."

"Not even close." Especially not now with evidence of her desire soaking the cotton center of her panties.

"Good." He picked her up, tossed her over his shoulder so her top half hung upside down, and started marching to her bedroom. "Because I'm done flirting."

Normally, this position would have pissed her off. However, because it gave her the perfect view of his ass and allowed her hands to roam freely across his sinewy back, she wasn't complaining. No. She was exploring every inch of him she could touch, lick, and smack. Too soon, he put her down so her feet sank into the plush rug in front of her bed.

"Your turn," he said as he sat down on her bed, a lone male island in the girly, ruffled powder blue sea of her bedroom.

"So, let me see if I got this lesson right." Her fingers went to the sash helping to hold her dress closed, but instead of pulling it open, she toyed with the soft material. "The key is to go slow." She tugged at the sash. "But not too slow." The material slipped free, but a button kept the dress from opening completely. "To tease." She drew her fingers up over her hip to the button. "But not to taunt." She slipped the button free, but held onto the material, allowing only a few inches of bare flesh to show. "To pull the anticipation tight." She took two steps so she stood between his legs, loving the battle to stay in control playing out on his face. "Until something snaps."

She let go, and her dress fell open. He'd never seen her this close to naked before. The other night she'd been still wearing her dress when he'd made her come. Not now. Tonight, she was exposed, vulnerable, unprotected by her usual roomy clothes. When he didn't move, didn't even say anything, the voices she'd managed to stay silent up until now started up, detailing all her faults and chipping away at her until she was reaching for the dress edges to wrap the material around her.

"Don't you dare." He covered her hands with his, keeping them by her sides. "You're fucking beautiful."

• • •

Something snapped all right. His control.

She was wearing canary yellow panties and a matching bra with a little white bow that nestled right between her tits. And she was showing it all *to him*. The high, round curves of her breasts. The triangle of freckles on the rise of her hip. The smooth line of her thighs leading straight to her panty covered center. He hadn't been so entranced by a woman in her underwear since Mary Katherine McMurray had stripped down to hers before they went night swimming at the beach during summer break from prep school. He'd been sixteen and a virgin then. Now, he was thirty with almost as many notches on his bedpost as people assumed. Still, he wasn't sure if his dick realized the difference because he was about to fucking blow. Meanwhile, she was gnawing on her bottom lip and staring over his shoulder.

He let go of her hands and forced his own, palms flat, on the couch. "Let the dress drop."

Her gaze skittered back to his face. Nerves. Bravado. Desire. "Bossy, aren't you?"

"Don't make me say it again."

She didn't. The dress fell to the floor. Her lips, wet from her tongue, were parted and she took in an unsteady breath, which emphasized the hard points of her nipples straining against her bra. He let his attention drop to the scrap of material covering her pussy, and there was no missing the dampness turning it a darker shade.

"Matches, you are so turned on right now."

She stayed stubbornly quiet—not admitting to it and not asking for relief or for him to leave. Someone sure had that whole cut-off-your-nose-to-spite-your-face thing down. What she didn't realize was that this wasn't about showing her how to seduce Captain Clueless—Hudson had no fucks to give about that idiot's turn-ons—this was about Felicia focusing on what turned *her* on. Going with the flow when you were giving pleasure was so much easier than figuring out what got you off, but she deserved more.

He traced his fingertips down her side, following her curves as they ebbed and flowed. "If you don't know what you want that's going to make you scream with pleasure and when you want it, you can't ever give that kind of experience to anyone else." He paused and looked up from her creamy flesh to her face, once again knocked sideways by how beautiful she was. "So, tell me, how turned on are you right now?"

"Very," she said, her voice barely above a whisper.

"Good." He hooked his fingers in the elastic band of her panties and pulled her closer until the creamy flesh of her stomach was only inches from his mouth. "What do you want?"

Her cheeks turned a deeper pink. "You know."

"I need you to say it."

When she remained silent, no doubt trying to find a loophole in his demand, he dipped his head lower and licked a long, slow line across skin right above her panties. She shivered against him and slid her fingers into his hair, pushing his head lower—or at least she tried to.

"Words." He easily resisted her efforts to move him and kissed her hip. "There's nothing more seductive."

Her fingers in his hair tightened, and she tugged his head back. "I need you to lick me."

"Here?" he asked and swiped his tongue from the center of her panties to her belly button.

She let out a little moan. "My clit."

He pulled her panties down over her hips. "Just your clit?"

"No." She shook her head, her gaze fuzzy. "All of it."

"Just my tongue?" He shoved her panties the rest of the way down, baring her completely and giving him a first look at her swollen, glistening lips.

"Fingers, tongue, lips, whatever the hell you want to use, I just need to come."

That was all he needed to hear. "Then do it."

She hesitated for half a second before releasing his hair and pushing hard against his shoulder so he fell back on the bed. The gleam was back in her eyes—the one she'd had before she sucked his cock deep in her hot mouth—but she didn't say anything. Instead, she crawled up his body, kissing and licking her way northward until she straddled his head. Again, her hands went to his head, threading through his hair, holding him in place.

"I want this," she said, her voice husky with need, and lowered her slick folds to his mouth and rocked against him. It was the hottest thing a woman had ever done to him.

Wet and soft, he couldn't get enough of her. Using just enough pressure to push her to the edge but not drive her over, he slicked his tongue up one side, slow and easy, before circling her clit and making his way down the other side at a steady, unhurried pace. He watched as she tossed back her head, lost in the chase for her orgasm, and began rotating her hips, pressing herself against his mouth with more urgency. Being between her legs, tasting, teasing, and taking her higher, it was the only place in the world he wanted to be because watching her let go like this was fucking amazing. He clamped his hands on her rounded hips, urging her to press against him as he laved his tongue over her. When he sucked her clit into his mouth, her back bowed, and she went rigid on top of him.

"Holy shit, do that again," she begged.

He did, raising his head to change the angle for better contact. Her thighs trembled on either side of his head as she tightened her grip on his hair.

"Right there," she cried out with primal desperation as she yanked on his hair. "Hudson!"

She came against his lips in a sweet rush with enough force that her fingers in his hair just might have left him with a couple of bald patches but was totally worth it. Taking a few more leisurely licks, he watched as she eased down from her high, loving the flush in her cheeks and the wicked gleam still sparkling in her blue eyes.

"If you don't have a condom, I'm going to be so pissed," she said, rolling off him and laying on her back in the bed, looking every bit like a well-satisfied woman who still wanted more.

Without a word, he got off the bed, grabbed his jeans from the floor, fished out his wallet from the back pocket, took out a condom, and rolled it on with world-record speed. Then, he leaned over the bed, hooked an arm underneath her knees and yanked her to the edge. Too far past the point to make a flirty lesson out of this, he almost lost it there as his balls tucked up tight against him. He released her legs, arranging it so they were spread as wide as possible. In tune with where he was going with this, she lifted her hips, giving him a teasing little wink that didn't do a damn thing to calm the storm brewing in him.

He grabbed hold of her hips, lifting them so only her shoulders and feet touched the bed. The move brought her wet opening in line with the swollen tip of his cock. "I'm not going to be able to go slow and sweet."

"Who said that's how I wanted it?" she asked in a throaty purr. "Give me everything you've got."

Against the laws of physics, her declaration made his dick even harder, and he slid home between her legs in one long thrust that sucked all the breath out of his lungs and took away his sight. All he could do was feel her around him, holding him fast.

"Damn, you're tight," he managed to get out as he withdrew to the tip before pushing forward again, harder.

She met his thrusts, her hands gripping the comforter as an anchor, offering up a litany of demands and pleas all along the line of "more," "now," and "oh God." He pushed another few inches in. God, she felt good wrapped around his dick. Fuck that. Good didn't begin to cover it.

"Yes," she moaned.

He jerked her toward him at the same time as he slammed his hips forward, burying himself balls deep in her hot, wet pussy. She clenched around him, squeezing him tight. Christ. He wasn't going to make it much longer. It was too much. *She* was too much.

"You like me filling you up," he said, looking down at where their bodies joined, watching his dick disappearing inside her as she met each and every one of his thrusts.

"God, yes," she cried.

He pumped into her again and again, the vibrations building at the base of his spine. "You want more of this cock?"

She turned her face to the side as she moved her hips in a figure eight, so intent on rubbing her juicy clit against him that her words came out muffled. Oh no. She wasn't getting away with that now. Not after she'd finally got that dirty mouth of hers to tell him exactly what she wanted, what would make her feel good and take her as high as she wanted.

"You've gotta say it, Matches." He started to pull out of her, inching out his cock as she gripped him as if trying to keep him in place. "Tell me or this goes away."

Empty threat? Meet Hudson.

"Fuck me," she said, panting. "Make me come all over that big dick."

Thank fucking God.

He plunged into her—forcefully, relentlessly—as she met his every move and groaned in protest each time he withdrew. The electric vibrations zipping through him gathered in his balls. He was close, and she was coming with him if he had to spell the names of his favorite painters backward to continue long enough to get her there. He slid one hand that had been on her hip around to the small of her back to help her stay up and then brought his other hand to her slick folds, strumming her clit. Again and again, he pushed into her until his balls tightened and he knew his time was up. He squeezed her clit between his finger and thumb just as he buried himself as deep inside her as he could. She cried out, her pussy clamping down on his dick as she came. That was all it took. Hudson went over the edge with her, straight into oblivion that seemed to last for days.

Darkness tugged at the edges of his vision, but he couldn't give in—not even if, judging by her eyelids being at half mast, Felicia was feeling the same. Gently, he lowered her to the bed. She scooted over, giving him plenty of room after he got rid of the used condom in the trash can by her nightstand. By the time he got under the covers and pulled her close, she was already breathing deep. Yeah. He knew how that went. So instead of fighting it, he drew her tight to his chest and followed her lead.

. . .

Felicia woke up in increments. Her room was dark. Something solid against her back. Soft brushes of air warmed her neck. A solid weight around her waist. It took a few seconds for her normally agile brain to connect the dots. Hudson. In her bed. Naked.

Every moment came rushing back to her. The way she'd rode his mouth, her hands buried in his hair. How he'd looked at her with pure lust as he'd filled her up. The mind-melting orgasm that had nearly broken her in two. This should be awkward. It wasn't, and that made her scooch away from him, it was only an inch—enough room to break the skin-to-skin contact of her back plastered against his front—but it was almost enough.

"You snore," he said, his voice all rumbly and sleep roughened.

Indignation shot through her, and she jerked up into a sitting position, clutching the sheet to her less-than-impressive chest. "I do not."

"No." He grinned, his hooded gaze going to where she'd covered herself. "But it's fun seeing you get defensive about it."

Her nipples went hard under the weight of his gaze. *Damn it.* She did not need to be reacting to him like this. It was annoying. "Is that lesson number four? Post-coital embarrassment? Is that what I should do to Tyler after we fuck?"

Something that looked a lot like anger skittered across his face before Hudson smoothed his expression out into practiced nonchalance. The professor was back in place. "That wouldn't be my recommendation."

For some reason, that ticked her off more than the fact that she couldn't stop sneaking peeks at the wide, muscular expanse of his chest or the ripple of his ab muscles as he sat up. Not that she should care that he'd slipped back into character. What was it to her? He was a means to an end for her just as much as she was for him. The reminder had her sucking in a shaky breath as she fought to contain her temper and her body's reaction to the man in her bed. Fighting wasn't going to get either of them closer to their goals—and that's all that mattered.

Remember your list, Felicia.

"Sorry. I wake up grumpy," she said, going for a cool-and-collected scientist in action vibe. "Let's start over with a debrief. Any notes?"

He raised an eyebrow. "Notes?"

"Areas I can improve on for Tyler." Now that wasn't awkward or anything considering she was naked and in bed with Hudson.

She wasn't a virgin by any means, but sleeping with one man in an effort to land another was vastly uncharted territory for her. *That way be dragons. And orgasms. Shut up, horny Felicia.* A nervous giggle bubbled up and escaped her tightly clenched lips.

"For Tyler," he said, each word coming out with an edgy slowness. His jaw tightened. It was almost imperceptible, but she caught it.

"Yes, my technique," she continued as Team What-The-Fuck-Are-You-Doing buzzed in her stomach but she couldn't seem to stop herself from pushing him farther away. "The slow burn. The whole, flirting and teasing but not taunting thing."

He let out a dry bark of a laugh. "I think you have it down pat." He rolled out of the bed and grabbed his jeans from the floor. "You can't go wrong with any of the moves I taught you."

"You're that good?" As if she didn't know and if the sore muscles in her thighs wouldn't be telling her all day long.

He turned around, his jeans still unbuttoned, his chest bare, and a wicked smile on his face. Her mouth went dry as fast as other parts of her got wet.

"Matches, we both know I am."

Some of the tension leaked out of her, and she chuckled. This man. He was something else. "Your ego needs its own zip code."

He shrugged. "Never said it didn't."

"So, what's next?" She asked fighting the screaming demands of her body to jump him here and now. "Am I ready for a date?"

"Is that what you want?" he asked, his tone neutral.

Her stomach flipped and then flopped before landing like an anvil in her abdomen. "Isn't that why last night happened?"

He paused, staring at her like he could see all the secrets she had, including that time in ninth grade when she'd tried to kiss Tyler and ended up making out with his collarbone. Long story. Long, embarrassing story of an awkward short girl and her first beer.

"I'll see what I can work out," he said. "You need to walk before you run."

Ignoring the inexplicable nugget of disappointment poking her chest, she grabbed ahold of the reason why all this was happening. Because she wasn't ready? Because he was still trying to help her land another man? They both had skin in the game. "And when I do, everyone will be happy—your brother, too. I don't know what I can do to help there, but I'm a quick learner."

There went that panty-melting, if practiced, smolder of his. "That you are."

Hudson snapped his jeans closed and then leaned across and brushed his lips across her forehead. The brief touch was as frustrating as it was a relief. Really. It *was* a relief. She didn't want more. Lesson time was over.

Without another word, he strolled out of her bedroom, and a minute later she heard her front door click shut followed by a plaintive meow from Honeypot. Meanwhile, she couldn't look away from the blue dress lying on the floor next to her bed as she realized that Hudson had—again—left her with no clue what was going to happen next and what exactly he meant by learning to walk.

Chapter Twelve

Hudson was restless. Itchy. Growly. Normally that meant he needed a brush in his hand and a blank canvas in his sights. Since he had both of those things at the moment, he grumbled to himself and picked up his phone—the one he'd been eyeballing constantly since he left Felicia's the night before last. His fingers worked as fast on the keyboard as they had on his cock every time he thought about the face she'd made when she'd come apart on his dick.

Hudson: *Name three interesting facts about yourself.*

He stared at the phone, willing her to answer. As soon as the three little dots appeared on his screen, his shoulders relaxed.

Felicia: *Why?*

He grinned. Persnickety little Matches.

Hudson: *It's called conversation.*

Felicia: *?*

Hudson: *It's the thing humans do so they don't babble about ant sex on dates.*

Felicia: *You're an ass.*

She wasn't wrong; it was just most people didn't see it.

Hudson: *That's interesting fact number one about me. Your turn.*

Felicia: *I graduated top of my class in high school and college.*

And water was wet.

Hudson: *I never doubted it. Next?*

Felicia: *Nope. You're up.*

His brain went blank, and he scanned the cabin looking for something—anything—to tell her about himself. The temptation to share his secret was there, chomping away on the back of his brain like a dog with a bone, but he shook off the urge. Only one person knew about his double life—and Everly Ribinski, gallery owner and professional badass Harbor Cityite, wasn't about to tell anyone. So neither was he.

Hudson: *My dick is pierced.*

Felicia: *Liar. You forget, I've seen your dick.*

Seen it? His cock thickened against his thigh at the memory of how she'd more than just *seen* it.

Hudson: *And sucked it.*

Felicia: *Stop trying to fluster me. I know your tricks. You're up.*

Hudson: *As is the case whenever I talk to you.*

Felicia: *Waiting...*

She was just stubborn enough to stay silent. It was a challenge he couldn't back away from, not that he was going quietly.

Hudson: *Fine. I did not graduate at the top of my class in either prep school or college.*

Felicia: *Lame factoid. I want something good.*

Hudson: *Then you have to give it.*

Felicia: *Lesson number four-hundred-eighty-two?*

He was really starting to hate these stupid "lesson" conversations. They were fun until she'd mentioned fucking Tyler last time. That comment still had screwed with him hardcore.

Hudson: *Yep. Another lesson.*

Sure it was. Just another day in his double life as The Dude Whisperer. God. He shouldn't even think that. His balls actually shriveled a little bit. Not that modern-day Henry Higgins sounded any better. *Focus, Carlyle.* Felicia thought she was his protégé and he was just texting her so she'd learn the art of flirty conversation and land Tyler. Not for any other reason.

Felicia: *Fine. I can double knot a cherry stem.*

Hudson: *I'm assuming there's more.*

Felicia: *With my tongue.*

Hudson: *Impressive.*

And his prick—the one that she'd used her talented tongue on the other night—nudged the back of his zipper.

Felicia: *Batter up.*

Shit. This give-and-take thing was easier with the socialites who were never really listening. He glanced down at his bare feet.

Hudson: *My first toe (second toe?) is longer than my big toe.*

Felicia: *That's Morton's Toe! The Greeks were totally hot for it. They used it in sculpture, as did the Romans. The Statue of Liberty has Morton's Toe, too.*

He snorted out a chuckle.

Hudson: *And you just made it weird.*

Felicia: *No. I made it awesome.*

To quote one of Sawyer's favorite movies, that word did not mean what she thought it meant—but she was close.

Hudson: *Time for number three.*

Felicia: *I'm saving up for an original Hughston painting.*

Fuck his giant ego because it had him thumb typing before he could stop himself.

Hudson: *Which one?*

Felicia: *Daybreak. It makes me feel the same way I do on Saturday mornings.*

"It's my favorite part of every week." That's what she'd said. And his painting made her feel that way. Not that she knew it was him. And that little factoid was enough to pop the bubble on whatever had taken over his body and erased his earlier irritation because suddenly her not knowing his secret made the barbed-wire itchy feeling return. And that didn't make any fucking sense.

Felicia: *You still there?*

He stared at the words on the screen, unable to come up with a fittingly reply.

Felicia: *It's your turn, don't wimp out.*

The barbwire started piercing his skin, leaving invisible holes in his flesh.

Felicia: *Hudson.*

Desperate to end this conversation that he hadn't been able to wait to begin, he fell back into old habits and changed the conversation.

Hudson: *Sorry, Matches. Duty calls.*

Felicia: *You hardly ever go into the office.*

That's where she was wrong. It's just his office was a cabin with amazing natural light and an abundance of privacy so he could keep his secret from everyone.

Felicia: *Still there?*

Yeah, he was. He never seemed to be moving. That wasn't

a conversation he wanted to have with himself let alone the hot ant scientist with a lifelong crush on his brother's best friend. Speaking of which…

> Hudson: *Pick you up at seven tomorrow night. Wear one of the new dresses. The Carlyle brothers have another business meeting with your future boyfriend. See you then.*

Then, he turned his phone off and went back to glaring at the blank canvas in front of him.

• • •

Felicia smoothed her hands over the red dress dotted with the tiny navy flowers for the eleventy-billionth time and forced herself not to look at the clock.

"Hudson will be here when he gets here and not a moment sooner," she muttered to herself.

Great. Now she was talking to herself. Another ten minutes and she'd change again. Dresses littered her bed. The ones that Hudson had paid for and the few she already had. The only dress that remained in her closet was the blue wrap dress she'd worn the night she and Hudson had…well, they had a lesson she wasn't going to forget. Ever. It had been radio silence until yesterday. *Which is exactly how it should be.* She yanked her hair back into a high ponytail, wrapping a ponytail holder around it, using more force than necessary. Anything more than that mindset and the whole Eliza Doolittle/Henry Higgins, Jedi/Yoda thing could get thrown out of whack. They were two people with a common goal and compatible sex drives. That was that. There was no reason to muck it up with anything else. Her rubber band broke, snapping her fingers with a wicked smack, just as Honeypot began to yowl.

"Perfect timing," she grumbled, letting her hair fall to her shoulders as she marched to the door.

She scooped up the cat and yanked it open, ignoring Honeypot's sharp clawed protest.

"Hey there," Hudson said, wearing a navy-blue suit that had him looking every bit like the millions of dollars in his bank account. "I see my girl couldn't wait to see me."

Felicia's synapses sizzled to a crisp. *His girl?* Heat rushed to her cheeks. Then he reached out and scratched Honeypot behind the ear. Oh yeah. *That* girl. The furry one who was now purring like a race car engine. Felicia's face turned shades of the sun hot. Good. That was *exactly* who she'd been hoping he meant.

Liar.

She shoved the cat into Hudson's arms, hoping in the petty part of her heart that Honeypot would choose that moment to puke up a fur ball. "I need to go get another ponytail holder."

"No way." He strode in like he owned the joint and put Honeypot down on the blue chair.

She jolted to a stop only a few steps short of her bedroom and whirled around. "What?"

"Remember? We're doing this my way." He closed the distance between them in a few strides. Yes, her apartment was tiny, but it still wasn't fair. He was too tall. Too close. Too confusing. "You've got great hair. Leave it down."

"I suppose I should chuck the glasses, too?" she asked, the question coming out more brittle than she meant.

Why in the hell was she being like this?

"Hell no. Those are hot as fuck," he said with total sincerity and a little leering, but in a non-creepy way. "Totally reminds me of my math tutor."

Her panties, a thong because of the dress's body con fit, tried to wriggle their way off her body while her brain kept a tight grip on the lacy fabric. She fucking swore they did. It was insanity. That's what happened when you slept with the Henry Higgins of Harbor City while trying to land another guy. It discombobulated a person.

"Whatever," she said, not meaning to huff but unable to stop herself.

He cocked his head, making some of his light brown hair fall over his forehead before he swept it back with his long fingers. "What's wrong?"

Pull it together, Felicia.

"Nothing."

He didn't look like he believed her. "Nervous about Tyler?"

The simple and pure logic of the question was like an epiphany. That had to be it. Not the whole transference, animated panties thing, but nerves.

"That must be it," she said. "Sorry, I'm out of sorts."

"You'll do awesome." He gave her a wink. "Just follow my lead, and you'll be fine."

"I have an entire lecture on ant colony interactions all ready to go." The look of horror on his face finally made her shoulders ease down a couple of inches. "Relax, I'm kidding."

"Don't hide your brain, Matches. It's one of the sexiest parts about you," he said. "Just keep the gross ant facts to a minimum."

The compliment—even with the ant comment—settled like warm honey in her belly, and for once she didn't try to unwind it like a riddle. She just allowed herself the luxury of accepting it, grabbed her purse, and walked out the door, leaving a mewling Honeypot behind.

The Crane and Berry was the kind of restaurant with a waiting list that went into the years. As the hostess in her head-to-toe black led them back to the table, all of that calm was washed away by the sight of Tyler sitting next to Sawyer at a corner table with guarded expressions on their faces. They each had a closed menu and a half-filled glass of scotch in front of them. The nerves bubbled back to the surface, then Hudson's strong fingers slid across the expanse of her lower back and he leaned down.

"I'm betting on black lace with little ribbons tonight," he whispered in her ear half a heartbeat before he straightened and pulled out a chair for her at the table—the one right next to Tyler. Then he took his seat on the other side of her and shook his head at the two men. "I presume the bloodletting hasn't started yet."

"No, we've got all the details just about worked out for the office complex in Singapore," Sawyer said, his tone tight. "It's just getting him to give his blessing to Mr. Lim that we've got it down."

"Sounds like things have changed a little bit since you and Frankie had your lawn mowing business," she said, reaching for the goblet of water above her plate. "Didn't you get everyone to sign off on using you two exclusively for the entire summer in exchange for a ten percent discount?"

"Sounds like you," Sawyer grumbled, even as his lips were starting to curl into a smile.

"Damn straight," Tyler said before turning to Felicia and giving her a curious look. "Something's different. Do you have new glasses or is it your hair? I don't think I've ever seen it down before."

She grew at least two inches while Hudson stiffened beside her. Of course, he would have known exactly what was different even if he hadn't been the one helping her to make that transition, but Tyler was different. He had *never* noticed how she'd looked before. This was progress, even if it was ham-fisted.

"Yeah," she said, her face managing not to turn beet red as she reached up and smoothed the long strands tickling her shoulders that were exposed in the sleeveless dress. "Trying something different."

"I like it," Tyler said, his gaze traveling down from her hair to the scoop neck of her dress, looking at her in just the way she had been hoping for years he would. "It suits you."

While the comment didn't set off the swarm of butterflies in her belly, Felicia held onto the triumph of that moment, sailing on the high of it, for the rest of dinner. There was some talk about the office complex Carlyle Enterprises hoped to build for Tyler's client, but things relaxed after the food was served—especially after Sawyer got a notification on his phone that the Giants' star slugger had hit a grand slam. That led to the two men clinking glasses and from that point on the conversation went from stories about their days at prep school and college to Tyler's high heel wearing upstairs neighbor.

"So she walks around in her apartment. What do you want her to do? Float?" she asked with a chuckle.

"It's not that," he said, his face animated and his blue eyes glimmering with excitement. He always was drawn to a challenge. "She complained to the building management that I was annoying her."

Sawyer snorted. "Aren't you the building management?"

"Yeah." Tyler nodded. "I own the place, but none of the tenants know that."

Okay. That made little to no sense. "Why not?"

Tyler grinned at her. "I have my reasons."

"And you're not sharing?" Of course he wasn't. That wasn't how Tyler operated. Ever.

He gave her a wink. "You know I always have something up my sleeve."

"Truer words have never been spoken," Sawyer said before turning the conversation back to the Giants and the upcoming playoff game they were both going to.

By the time the bill came, Tyler and Sawyer did the whole

manly fighting-over-the-bill thing before Hudson—who'd been weirdly quiet for most of dinner—swiped it off the table and took care of it without more than a mumbled, "I've got it."

It was weird, but she shoved the thought aside, instead relishing the way Tyler's gaze kept traveling back to her. That was what she had been after for years. She kept waiting for the thrill of anticipation to skitter across her skin or for the spike of awareness to find its way right to her core, but it never came. Not when Tyler draped his arm across the back of her chair. Not when he toyed with the ends of her hair as it lay on top of her shoulders. Not when he leaned in close and whispered that she looked great tonight. That she didn't get all freaked out—which usually meant blushing her way through an adrenaline rush—but that didn't mean anything. She was just focused on her goal, and she couldn't afford to let down her guard and enjoy the moment. That would come later. She just knew it would.

She stood, and they said their good-byes. The brush of Tyler's lips across her cheek was a win, but her reaction must have been delayed because it wasn't until Hudson pressed his hand to the small of her back as they walked through the restaurant that the telltale heat of blood rushing to her cheeks hit her. Of course, it was just a slow reaction to a successful night. And instead of focusing on it, she'd start planning the next stage in this experiment because that's what she did. She kept her attention solely focused on the goal—dating Tyler Jacobson before she turned thirty in less than two weeks.

• • •

The night had gone so perfectly that Hudson had an overwhelming urge to punch someone—anyone—square in the face as he sat in the back of the Uber with Felicia on the way back to her apartment. Captain Clueless hadn't missed a single opportunity to touch Felicia. Which was great. Really. Fucking. Great. Everything was happening just as he'd planned. Tyler and Sawyer had been giving each other shit over dessert—as they should be since they'd been friends since the dawn of time—and that asshole Tyler had finally started to notice what had been in front of him for most of his life. And Felicia had lapped it all up. *Not* what he'd had planned—or at least not what he wanted he could admit to himself.

Felicia turned in the seat next to him in the Uber, a little V of confusion appearing behind the bridge of her glasses. "What's wrong?"

"What makes you think something's wrong?" His hands balled into fists at his side? The fact that his molars were now a thing of the past?

She gnawed on her bottom lip for a second before answering. "You barely talked at dinner."

"It was hard to get a word in with Captain Clueless rambling on and on." And touching her.

Jesus. Pull yourself together, Carlyle. You fucked her, just like you've fucked plenty of other women in your life. Caveman is not a good look for you.

"He has a name," she said, her eyes narrowing and her chin tilting up in a stance he knew far too well. "Say it."

There was nothing in her tone to make him think she'd give up, so he schooled his features into a teasing smile and slipped on the mask that had always fit him so well up to now. "Tyler. The love of your life's name is Tyler Jacobson."

"And he liked the dress." She glided her palms across the clingy fabric covering her thighs, the ones with a few freckles spanning each one.

"More like he liked the woman in it."

"And isn't that why we're doing this?" she asked, looking

out the window as the bright lights of Harbor City flew by instead of at him.

"Exactly." Which did nothing to explain the iron ball in the pit of his stomach. He knew better than to order scallops on a Saturday night. Everyone knew the fresh fish came in on Monday. Obviously, The Crane and Berry had served him shitty scallops.

"So I should call him tomorrow," she said, reaching for her purse as the Uber turned the corner onto her street.

"No." It came out hard and fast, a verbal reaction more than a thought.

"Why not?"

Why not? Because of a million reasons that Hudson didn't even understand. "Because."

She straightened in her seat, ready for battle. "You'll need to do better than that."

"Because you have to make him work for it." Yeah, that sounded good. Maybe.

"Is this really your advice or is this because of the other night?" There was no missing the vulnerability in her tone.

"That was just a lesson." *Keep telling yourself that, chump.* "And this is another one. You need to let him stew for a bit." God knew the idiot deserved it. The car slowed as it approached her block and the streetlights glimmer caught in her hair and realization struck him right between the eyes. The delay wasn't for the moron, it was for him. The *other* moron. "You never want something as bad as when you can't have it."

She fiddled with a tendril of hair. "I don't know…"

"I know just how to make this work." He had no fucking clue how to make this work. He just knew he wasn't ready for her to see Captain Clueless again. He had to get her away from Harbor City. The car stopped in front of her apartment. "Pack an overnight bag. I'll pick you up tomorrow morning."

"Where are we going?"

"You'll find out tomorrow." And so would he, because he had no fucking clue where he could hide her for a few days.

She started to open the car door and get out and then hesitated, looking at him as if she was waiting for more, wanting more. He sure as hell did, too, but they didn't want the same thing—not really. Then the tip of her pink tongue snuck out, wetting her bottom lip and dragging his attention to one of the many cock-hardening parts of her. How many times had he pictured those lips wrapped around him like they had been the other night? Too fucking many. Not nearly enough.

Don't kiss her. Don't do it. Shove her out of the car and tell the driver not to stop until your brain takes back over for your prick.

It was good advice. The best advice. Too bad his dick was such a...well...dick in every sense of the word. Her hand was still on the door handle and one foot on the pavement when he threaded his fingers through the silk of her brown hair. The move was perfect for tugging her back against him, but he didn't need to—she came on her own, tumbling back against him, her eyes already hooded and her glossy lips parted.

He barely heard her mumble something about transference over the blood rushing through his ears on its journey to his cock as his lips crashed down against hers. She tasted of red wine and temptation—two things that had fast become his very fucking favorite—then he swept his tongue inside her sweet mouth. Her tongue met his, twisting and teasing him in strokes that sent a jolt of electricity straight to his cock. God, this woman. How the hell Captain Clueless had missed this for all these years was beyond him. He couldn't get enough of her, of the way she moved against him and moaned into his mouth. His fingers tightened in her hair, pulled her head back and let him deepen the kiss. Every bit of testosterone in him demanded he lay claim to her now, make her his. Tonight. Now. But that couldn't be. The realization was enough to make him ease back even as his body fought against it, and she moaned her disapproval until the only parts of them still touching were their foreheads and his fingers in her hair as they fought to regain their breath.

He needed to get her out of his system. Take her someplace where no one would know to look. The idea hit him with the subtlety of the F-Train headed uptown and just as surprisingly. He couldn't take her there. He never took *anyone* there. His gaze dropped to her kiss-swollen lips. It was the only place he wanted to go with her.

Forcing himself, he sat back and let her hair slip between his fingers. "See you tomorrow at eight, Matches."

She blinked, questions brewing in her blue eyes, but instead of bulldogging the point, she just nodded and stepped out of the Uber, closing the door behind her and leaving him to wonder if he'd totally lost his mind. The answer, obviously, was fuck yes.

Chapter Thirteen

When her cell rang the next morning, Felicia was still dripping wet from the shower. It was only seven. There was only one person who'd call her this early on a Saturday. A quick glance at Caller ID confirmed it.

She hit the speaker button, propped the phone on the counter and continued to dry off. "Hey, sis. Ready to *finally* spill all the gossip from your girls' weekend in Vegas? You're not allowed to go on a trip and then work back to back shifts at the hospital ever again. I need my gossip."

"Why do you sound weird?" Her older sister said, straddling that line between curious, suspicious, and concerned that every emergency room nurse seemed to get after their first year on the job.

Felicia wrapped her hair in the towel and tucked in the ends. "You're on speaker, and I'm in the bathroom."

"Do *not* tell me what you're doing."

"Relax, I just got out of the shower—I'm not on the toilet."

"Thank God because that's just nasty. Do you know how much bacteria is on your phone already. Why would you add more?"

"Everybody poops," Felicia said, slipping on a spa-weight robe that helped keep her warm in the draft coming through the opaque window in her bathroom despite it being shut tight—or at least as tight as it could be (thank you, extra thick wooden dowel jammed inside the frame to keep it from opening any farther).

"But they shouldn't use the bathroom while on the phone," Fallon said.

Felicia couldn't argue with her sister there. "Duly noted, Queen of Etiquette."

"So, what's this I hear about you calling Frankie for outfit advice," she said, taking full advantage of the thirteen months age difference between them (hello, Irish twins) to launch an interrogation. "Who's the dude? Please tell me it's not Tyler Jacobson."

"What if it is?" she asked, her voice doing that thing it always did whenever she felt cornered and out of place. "What if he's naked and sprawled out on my bed right now?"

Fallon wasn't impressed by her bravado. "If there was a hot, naked man in your bed then there's no way you'd be answering the phone."

Of course, she immediately singled in on a mental image of Hudson with the sheet wrapped around his bare hips, and her body warmed way more than was acceptable considering she was talking to her sister. "Probably not."

"Oh, that sigh sounded hopeful."

Okay, this was going to go nowhere good, way too fast if she didn't distract her sister. "What's wrong? No hot guys in Vegas so you have to imagine them in my apartment?"

"Don't even ask," she huffed. "There were shots so I can't confirm or deny any of that beyond the fact that I met one giant jackass."

"Please don't ever say that to Frankie or he'll freak." As

the oldest of the Hartigan kids, Francis James Hartigan was as bossy as he was tall, broad, and determined to keep all of his siblings out of trouble as much as he got into it. "Speaking of which, how did you know he helped me out the other night?"

"Our big brother has an even bigger mouth."

That was so the truth. "What did he say?"

"Only that he'd steal my nursing clogs if I told that he'd helped you pick out a date night outfit."

"That's your fault for giving your extra keys to a firefighter with a history of being an overbearing pain in the ass."

"Fair enough," Fallon said. "So who's the dude?"

"Just a friend who's helping me out with a project." Not totally a lie, so she managed to keep her tone steady. Mostly. God, she sucked at lying.

"You've got an ant man, huh?"

She flashed on the look of horror on Hudson's face when she'd explained how the honeypot ant had gotten its name. "More like the opposite."

"And you're not gonna tell me more?"

"Nothing to tell." How could a person even begin to explain this crazy ass situation? They couldn't—especially not her latest lesson that had left her screaming her release as she rode Hudson's face.

"I can practically see the blush from my living room across the river in Waterbury. You always were the worst liar."

"Seriously, Fallon, there's nothing to tell." Nothing she *could* tell, that was for sure.

"So meet me for lunch and don't tell me all about it."

Felicia glanced at the clock. Hudson would be here soon and she was still wet and naked, in a totally different way than the last time he'd been inside her apartment. "I can't."

"How come?"

"I'm going out of town."

"Promise to tell me all the details when you get back, and I won't tell Frankie you're headed off for a weekend of amazing hot monkey sex."

"I'm not having sex." Lessons. She'd be having lessons and that was totally different. Her core clenched. *Totally. Different.*

"Then why haven't you asked me for advice on packing if you aren't planning on leaving everything in the overnight bag?" Fallon said with all the superiority an older sister could muster.

"I'm hanging up now," she said, never more glad that Fallon hadn't FaceTimed her and been able to see the five-alarm blush burning her cheeks right now. "Oh, but first, can you feed my cat while I'm away?"

"Yes. And love you, too, sis." Fallon made a kissy noise and disconnected the call.

Felicia left her phone on the counter and crossed into her bedroom, the overnight bag sat in the middle of her already made bed. Team Anticipation and Team Annoyance were back duking it out in her belly, making her lungs tight. Just looking at a bag shouldn't do this to her insides. But it did. What's worse is that it wasn't the sight of the bag that made her nipples pucker against the soft material of her robe. It was the hope that Fallon was right and that she'd never unpack.

· · ·

Hudson had been up since dawn—a freak occurrence of epic proportions—double guessing his plan to make Felicia the first person to step foot inside the cabin since he inherited it at eighteen. He'd been staring at his penthouse's pristine ceiling for hours by the time he finally gave in and picked up the phone. He didn't need to look up the number. He'd known it by heart since his first day of school.

"What's wrong," his mother answered.

"Why would something be wrong?" he asked as he paced from one end of the bright white room shot through with slashes of indigo, amber, and ebony, the hardwood floor cold on the soles of his feet.

"Because it's before noon on a Saturday and you initiated the call," Helene said with all the subtlety of a cop in an interview room with a phonebook and a pipe.

He strolled out the door and headed straight for the kitchen and the coffeemaker. "I call you all the time."

"Not this early in the morning. What's wrong?"

Okay, this had been a mistake but the only other person he knew that got up this early was Sawyer, and he'd learned the hard way that his brother and Clover were the kind who got naked, sweaty, and orgasmic first thing in the morning. He only made that mistake once.

Popping the coffee pod in the machine, he tried to think up something—anything—that would explain this call to his mom besides the truth, that he hadn't been able to stop thinking about Felicia. She was his project not a potential date, as far as his mom was knew.

"Are you still there?" his mom asked, concern thick in her tone.

Shit. The last thing he wanted was to freak her out. She'd finally stepped out of a three-year mourning and, while she was emotionally stronger than when he'd watched *My Fair Lady* practically on repeat with her, she wasn't the same woman she'd been before his dad's heart had unexpectedly given out on him.

"I'm here." He hit the brew button. "I just wanted to let you know that I'm going out to the cabin this weekend."

"What is it that you do all the time out there? Wait, don't tell me," she said, the words rushing out. "A mother shouldn't know those things."

"It's true, I'm having orgies at the cabin I inherited from grandpa. I figured he'd appreciate it."

"The man never appreciated anything," Helene grumbled. "God rest his soul, but he didn't—especially not the son he'd ignored."

Hudson may not have been able to tell his dad, Michael, about his art after the massive blowout they'd had his senior year in college, but that had been the only—if major—blip in their relationship. Otherwise, it was all baseball games, family vacations, and smack talk during boys-only poker nights. That hadn't been the case with his dad and his grandfather. Those two had barely been able to be in the same room without an arctic blast freezing the whole place.

"What ever happened between them?" he asked.

Helene mumbled something under her breath before speaking, "Just the regular pigheaded Carlyle man no-one-knows-what's-right-but-me thing."

"I resent that," he said, speaking up for the men in the family.

"No," she shot back. "You resemble it. Now, what's this I hear about you bringing the same someone to two client dinners."

Sawyer sure had a big mouth when he wanted to. "Just trying to help Felicia hook Tyler like you asked me to. Nothing makes a man notice another woman as much as another man noticing the same woman." Yeah, that was as fucked up as it sounded.

He picked up his now full cup of coffee and walked out to the balcony to enjoy his view of the park. It was a sight that always relaxed him, especially this time of year when the leaves had gone from deep green to a mix of orange, red, and gold.

"That's it? Clover made it seem like more."

"Why would Clover think that?" Crap. That wasn't a

good sign. While Sawyer was all big picture, his wife noticed every detail—even the ones Hudson always tried to hide. Time to spin this away from the woman he couldn't stop thinking about and toward one of his mom's favorite pet projects. "Did she also mention that Sawyer and Tyler are hanging out again? And that they were able to meet for a client dinner without Clover being there as a buffer?"

"It is a job she's proven herself to be quite good at, and on that note—how is your little mission going?"

That's it. Spin that conversation like you get paid for it. "I think Operation: Bromance is going well."

Better than expected really, and he hadn't even gotten Tyler to fall for Felicia yet. He could have but he was going slow—for her sake, of course. No matter what kind of list Captain Clueless had been at the top of for her, the man was a grade A dipshit and didn't deserve a woman like Felicia.

"How about that side assignment I gave you to find someone of your own to bring to charity events?" his mom asked, interrupting his internal rant.

"And break the hearts of women across Harbor City?" He fell back into character. "Why, Mother, I can't do something like that."

"That may be, but you are hereby under orders to bring a date to the Dixon Library masked ball fundraiser Wednesday night."

He knew that tone of voice. She'd used it on Sawyer before she started dragging single women along with her to every family function in her mission to get her oldest son to stop focusing only on business and to actually take the time to appreciate the really important little things, like love. Not that Hudson needed to worry about that. He had years in front of him. Decades even. He'd find someone, someday, but he wasn't looking for it now. His double life gave him more than enough to juggle. An image of Felicia popped into his head, calling him a liar.

"I'll be fine going by myself," he said. "I'm sure I'll meet someone there."

Yes. That's just what he needed. Some no-strings-attached and no-ants-discussed hot sex with a woman who didn't make him forget that she didn't want him. He was just a man with a willing dick who could help her get exactly what she wanted—even if what she wanted was a douchebag. He refused to acknowledge his dick had no interest in anyone but Felicia right now. The traitor.

"I suppose I could make that work," Helene's voice came through the kind of extra calm way that every child—small or grown—knew meant shit was about to go down. "I do still have contact information for all of the ladies that Sawyer couldn't run away from fast enough."

"I'll probably bring Felicia." Now, where had that come from?

"Wonderful," his mom said too quickly, and the skin on his neck started to itch.

"Has there ever been a day you couldn't bend a Carlyle man to your will?"

His mom sighed, all the gamesmanship leaking out on that sad sound. "Just once and it almost broke my heart, but that's neither here nor there." Her tone changed to her more natural, take charge one. "I'll see you Wednesday, please bring Felicia by the penthouse first. I'm holding a low-key cocktail party Tuesday night. I think I'll send an invitation to Tyler as well and do my part to push things along."

"Mom, if you ever decided to use your powers for evil, we'd all be doomed."

"I don't doubt it," she said with a chuckle. "I love you, darling."

"Love you, too, Mom." And he did. The woman was bossy, demanding, and a force to be reckoned with, and one of his most favorite women in the world even if she was wrong. The last complication he needed in his life right now was a date—especially not with his own personal Eliza Doolittle who was still in love with the wrong man.

Chapter Fourteen

When Hudson double parked his Alfa Romeo 4C Spider in front of Felicia's apartment, he found her waiting out front, a small overnight bag at her feet, and a wary expression on her face. The woman would never make it as a poker player, but she'd kick ass as a mime. With Honeypot's wail blaring out of the apartment, he got out, popped the trunk, and grabbed her bag off the sidewalk.

"Wondering if I'm taking you away to kill you in my cabin in the woods?"

She followed him to the back of the car, her ponytail swaying from side to side along with her hips. "Is that where we're going?"

He dropped her bag in the trunk, using the motion as an excuse to lean down enough to inhale the fruity scent of her shampoo. *That's it.* He had become a creepy freak. He jerked back a step and reminded himself for the billionth time that she was in love with someone else. "That's what you want to know about, not the killing part?"

"I trust you," she said, strolling to the passenger's side

and opening it before he could reach the handle. "At least not to kill me."

"Well, don't you take all the fun out of things."

She got into the car, and he shut the door behind her, giving him the entire walk around the front—ignoring the asshole in the sedan honking his horn as if no one ever double parked in Harbor City—to repeat all the reasons he could think of as to why taking Felicia to the cabin was a good idea. He came up with pretty much jack shit. Still, he got behind the wheel, pulled into traffic, and headed north out of the city.

The drive took two hours, and for most of it they played a game called "find the shittiest song on the radio." Okay, really, she was playing without realizing it, but she looked so damn happy singing along that he kept forgetting to tell her that the driver gets to pick the music. In between highway karaoke, they talked art, ants, and architecture—agreeing on next to nothing, right up until they both decided that if anyone deserved a monument created in their likeness it was the Harbor City leprechaun, a fifty-year-old man who dressed up all in green everywhere he went and told everyone, "Top of the morning."

The conversation dragged once he pulled off the highway, drove the three miles down a county road to an electrified security gate (grandpa liked his privacy), and punched in the code that only he had. He couldn't blame her. At this time of year, the trip up the driveway was spectacular with the sun fighting through the clouds to hit the fall leaves just so they shined brilliantly in the afternoon light. It was magic—and it always made him want to haul out a canvas and paint so he could get it all down. Finally, two miles in from the gate, he parked the car next to the ten thousand square foot, two-story log cabin with its stained-glass front door and wraparound porch.

"This," she said, her eyes round. "Is what you call a cabin?"

Okay, it was more of a lodge, but considering the place in Vail, it was on the small side. "It is by Carlyle standards."

"Those are some standards." She turned and looked a little slack jawed at him.

He supposed they were, but unlike the rest of the Carlyle empire, this was just his and it showed as soon as he walked through the door. His gut tightened. That he could see the oak and colored glass from where he stood at the bottom of the steps leading up to the porch meant he was really here, really doing this. After they walked through the door there was no going back, no hiding who he really was.

Shoving his fingers through his hair, he wrapped his fingers around her forearm stopping her from going up the steps. "Before we go in, I have to swear you to secrecy."

She grinned up at him and pushed up her glasses, stray hairs that had slipped her ponytail dancing around her face in the breeze. "Is this where you're going to off me?"

"Worse," he said, covering up his nerves with a slathering of teasing and leering. "This is where I'm going to paint you."

"Please tell me you're not going to stick one eye here and the other one over there somewhere."

"I'm more of a realist."

This was it. The moment when he could change his mind, keep his secret, and drive them both back to the city. But just seeing her here in this light made him crave a paint brush and a blank canvas like a chocoholic joneses for a candy bar. It wasn't all-consuming, but it was damn close. That's why he was doing this—because he'd known from the first moment he'd spotted her at that fundraiser that he needed to get her on canvas. That was the reason. *Not anything else.* He could just shove any lingering doubts about that to the dark corner of his brain. Helping her was all part of Operation: Bromance because as soon as Tyler realized all he'd been missing with Felicia, he'd start wondering about everything else and then all the little moves Hudson had made to get Tyler and Sawyer together as friends again would pay off. And what did he get out of this? He got to paint Felicia. Sure, he'd hoped for maybe more, but this was enough. It had to be because as he well knew, no matter how close they became, Henry Higgins and Eliza Doolittle didn't walk hand and hand into happily ever after at the end of *My Fair Lady*. They went their separate ways, just like he and Felicia would because fakers like him didn't end up with women like her. So, all of this would have to end, but not today, not yet.

Stop being such a chickenshit, Carlyle, and take her inside.

He did, the sense of being home rolling over him as soon as he opened the door. There was a reason why he'd set up shop at the cabin besides the privacy—the floor to ceiling windows on three of the four sides of the open concept main floor that provided ideal light at nearly every hour of the day. Canvases for his upcoming show at Everly's gallery covered the space. Each one showed the faces of the Harbor City residents he encountered in random trips around the city. Old. Young. Stock brokers. Cabbies. Kindergarten teachers. Those who worked overnight shifts. Those who'd retired decades ago. Those who were decades away from their first job. Each one of whom helped to tell the story of Harbor City. A card detailing each subject's story would accompany each painting as it hung in the gallery. The project had taken more than a year to come together and the faces—nervous, excited, grumpy, and even combative—that greeted him from the canvases were like old friends at this point.

Felicia went from painting to painting, respecting the ones still covered by sheets and inspecting the finished works on display. Each step she took, each closer look she leaned in for, squeezed his lungs tighter. He'd watched hundreds, thousands, of people check out his work. It hadn't ever made him as nervous as he was now as he tried to read her face and figure out what she thought. For once, he couldn't tell. It was making him edgy enough that he was about to chew a hole through his cheek.

Finally, she turned away from the portrait of the bodega owner with a smile as wide as the horizon and cocked her head to one side. "These look familiar, but I know I haven't seen them before. They almost look like…"

"Hughston," he filled in for her.

She nodded, walking to his side. "You're a big fan?"

"I *am* Hughston." He didn't even hesitate. He should have. "No one knows, so you can't tell anyone."

Whatever he'd been expecting—and he really wasn't sure—it wasn't for her to laugh. A big laugh. Like a Santa Claus kind of belly full of jelly laugh. The kind that made her wrap her hands around her middle and toss her head back with what looked like absolute shock and joy. The breath he hadn't meant to keep locked up eased out of him, and he found himself laughing along.

"But why the big secret?" she asked.

"It's a long story." One he sure as hell didn't want to get into now—or ever, really. He poured his emotions out onto the canvas not out in the world. "Besides." He leaned down, slipping on his charmer personality like a well-worn pair of jeans that didn't fit nearly as well as they'd used to, and traced a finger down the exposed length of her neck. "You haven't told me what color your panties are today."

Her blush and stubborn silence on the topic lasted for as long as it took to give her a quick tour of the place as the wind changed from a gust to a howl outside the cabin. By the time they strolled into the guest bedroom, the sky was nearly as black as his mood. It was the last place he wanted her to spend the night, but she'd been more than upfront with him about her goal. Tyler Jacobson. Captain Clueless. Mr. Shit for Brains. Sir Luckier Than He Had a Right to Be. It wasn't that *Hudson* wanted to date her—after all he didn't date, he slept around, everyone in Harbor City knew it—but Felicia deserved someone who wasn't totally oblivious. Besides, he'd already accepted a long time ago that any woman worth her salt, when she found out why he'd kept this part of his life hidden from his family, would realize he really wasn't a keeper. Shame and guilt gnawed at him every day of his life but luckily no one ever bothered to look beyond the charming façade. Until Clover. And now Felicia.

Annoyed all of a sudden, Hudson dropped her bag like it was a steaming hot french fry fresh out of the deep fat fryer at Vito's. It landed with a *thunk* that was eclipsed a moment later by the near-deafening crack of thunder that boomed outside the windows. Felicia let out a yelp of surprise right before the lights went out and they were plunged in darkness.

• • •

Felicia didn't hate the dark, but it sure wasn't her best friend. She was the kind of person who left a tiny light on in the bathroom—for Honeypot, of course—and quick-stepped it from the light switch to her bed at night. So when Hudson took her hand in his and led her down the stairs, as the entire main floor lit up in giant flashes of white light followed by loud crashes of thunder, it made the iron hand fisting her lungs loosen its grip a bit. Together they made it to the kitchen where he grabbed a large lantern-like flashlight from under the sink and placed it on the island. The light provided a soft yellow oasis for them while the sudden storm battered the trees outside.

"The utility lines are above ground so the wind knocks

out the power whenever a storm comes up like this," Hudson said, looking out the huge windows at the trees dancing back and forth while still holding her hand. "They'll get it back on soon."

Obviously, her body trusted his pronouncement, since her stomach picked that moment to let out a loud growl. "Sorry. I'm a nervous eater."

"Don't like the dark?"

"Only if my eyes are open." Shit. She didn't mean to say that. With her size, it was hard enough to get people to take her seriously. Admitting she got nervous in the pitch black wasn't something she did. *But you just did.*

Hudson didn't tease her like Frankie would have or roll his eyes at her like Fallon usually did. Instead, he kept hold of her hand as they walked around the lit safety zone and gathered two bowls, a box of cereal—the kind with clover-shaped marshmallows, bonus!—and milk from the dark but still cold fridge. Half a bowl later, her stomach and taste buds in a sugar-induced chill pattern, she tried to reconcile her mental image of Hughston with the man in a dark-blue sweater eating Lucky Charms with her while the storm thundered outside. Maybe she should have doubted him, but she didn't. It made sense in a way. There was such a sense of joy edged with a bittersweet yearning underlining Hughston's work that it fit with the Hudson she'd come to know. So when he'd made his declaration, the pieces fit together perfectly logically in her mind.

"So why the big secret? I'd think your family would be proud of you." The words rushed out before her brain had a chance to stop them.

"Proud?" He snorted and shook his head. "Not likely."

She'd met his brother and mother. They weren't as gregarious as the Hartigan clan, but there was no doubting they loved Hudson. The disconnect made her brain itch.

"Why?"

He took another bite of cereal. "When did you know you liked ants?"

"The first time my parents took us to a church picnic. I watched the ants marching away with as many crumbs as they could carry, and I was hooked." She'd followed the little conga line of insects back to their nest, nearly decking a kid older than her who tried stomping the ants at the end of the line. If Frankie hadn't gotten to the kid first, she would've had her ass handed to her. As it was, it took her older brother, who was big for his age even at twelve, to shoot the jerky kid a dirty look and he scurried off.

Hudson nodded and took a deep breath, as though debating whether to share more. "That was me the first time I picked up a brush. It was all I wanted to do. In college, I took every art class I could fit in between business courses. It drove my dad nuts. He called painting a distraction from what I should really be doing—learning the family business. He was so driven, he made Sawyer look lazy."

What an ass. "Didn't he see how talented you were?"

His lips compressed as something dark flashed across his face, only to be replaced a half second later with that laissez-faire smile and a cool shrug of his broad shoulders. "He never saw any of my paintings."

Correction. What an epic ass of legendary proportions. "How's that possible?"

"When you're running a business the size of Carlyle Enterprises, it's easy not to be able to even think about anything else." The words came out practiced—hollow—as if he'd said them to himself too many times.

"Even his family?"

"He wasn't *that* bad, just focused. We did plenty as a family—baseball games, vacations, family movie nights—and I never doubted he wanted the best for me. But I wasn't like

Sawyer, and I know it drove him a little nuts. He never got the art part."

Old hurt etched lines around his eyes and she reached out, taking his hand in hers. The spark was there, sizzling along her skin, but there was something else, too. An understanding that hadn't been there before.

"My dad wanted to understand, I just don't think he could. Then, my grandfather passed away and my mom had a health scare. They thought it was cancer. I think the one-two punch of that made him worry that he wasn't doing a great job of raising the next generation of Carlyles—at least when it came to me. Finally, my senior year in college he gave me an ultimatum: give up painting and start learning the family business or he'd cut me off. I didn't give a shit about the money, but losing my family? It wasn't something I was willing to do."

She tried to imagine Hudson at twenty-one, forced to choose between family and his passion. That he picked his family both made her proud and broke her heart. "So how did you do it?"

"I gave my dad what he wanted, or at least the illusion of it. I kept painting, it's just I did it without telling anyone. At first, I figured it was just for me, but then my friend Everly saw them and she helped me come up with a plan. That's when I became Hughston. Everyone got what they wanted."

No wonder he slipped between the public version of charming Hudson and the real him so easily. He'd been doing it for years. It must have been exhausting. "Why not tell them now?"

"I was going to a few years ago, but my father had a sudden heart attack. His last words to me were about the family and finding my place in the world of Carlyle Enterprises. I promised him I'd try." He paused, pushing his half-eaten bowl of cereal to the middle of the island, and shoved his fingers through his hair. "Then, after he died, my mom was more than a little lost. Sawyer and I did everything we could to make her life as smooth as possible. I couldn't imagine telling her I was doing the one thing I'd sworn not to do. So instead I planted the idea that it was past time Sawyer got married. That gave Mom a mission with some unfortunate results so I had to figure out a way to find the perfect woman for Sawyer and luckily clover answered the ad for a buffer."

"But you're not being you." And it was hurting him, she could tell.

"I am," he said, slipping his hand free from hers. "I'm just giving them the me they want to see."

She should let it drop. It was his life. It's not like how Hudson chose to live it had anything to do with her. She shouldn't even care. But she did. And it wasn't fair—not to him or his family—and it was wearing him down. There was no missing it in the soft light of the lantern. How she'd failed to see it before, she had no idea.

"Don't they deserve the real you instead of the charming facade?" she asked.

He looked at her as if the question had never occurred to him before and opened his mouth, but before he could say anything the lights snapped back on in the rest of the house, taking away the intimacy of the moment. The kitchen lights must have been off before the outage, but the change was palpable and accompanied by the switch in Hudson as the mask she was beginning to hate slid into place.

Leaning in close enough to her ear that she felt the heat of him against her neck, he whispered, "So you never told me, what color are your panties tonight?"

There it was. That thing he did to put her off balance. But it wasn't going to work this time. She'd seen too much of the real Hudson. "You don't have distract me."

"Maybe," he said, tracing his finger down the column of

her neck, leaving a trail of desire in his wake, "I'm trying to distract myself."

Her breath came in fast as she squeezed her thighs together, trying to maintain some sense of the closeness they had before even as her body betrayed her because it wanted Hudson now. "With my panties?"

He nipped at her collarbone. "You could just show me."

The words sparked a realization. He needed Hughston to escape not just his family's expectations but of the world's, too. The name Carlyle really did come at a cost, and this place—this cabin in the middle of the woods—was the only place he could actually be himself. And he'd brought her here. *Her.*

Without another thought, she pushed him away and took a step backward, her hands going to the hem of her soft gray sweater, and she pulled it off. Her nipples were already hard, pushing against the lace of her bra. Desire, hot and demanding, heated her skin against the fall chill as she dropped her hands to the button of her jeans.

Hudson watched as she stripped off everything except her cherry red lacy bra and panty set, his eyes darkening with lust. "What are you doing?"

Powered by some kind of confidence that usually only came out in the field, she strutted over to him. "It's time for another lesson, except this time I'm teaching you."

"Oh yeah, what lesson is that, Matches?" he asked, the gravel in his voice making her core clench.

"To just let yourself be you in your own skin." She slipped her hands under his sweater, the sparse spattering of coarse hair on his chest tickling her palms. "It wasn't easy growing up as a quiet nerd in a big, loud Irish catholic family. I had to figure out how to let all of the joking about my height and my nose being always in a book wash over me."

He raised his arms without her even asking, and she

pushed the sweater higher, relishing the sight of his muscular chest revealed inch by inch as she raised it over his head and then let it drop to the floor. God, he was beautiful. He was all hard planes, solid muscle, and hunger—for her.

"And us getting naked," he said as he wrapped the fingers of one hand around her wrists, stopping her from unbuttoning his jeans. "What's that going to teach me?"

Lifting herself up on her tiptoes, she leaned against him, pressing her breasts against his chest as she cupped his hardness through his jeans and squeezed. "How to let go."

Chapter Fifteen

Hudson had seen the "Mona Lisa" up close. He'd spent hours in front of Botticelli's "Birth of Venus" and countless other paintings lauded for their beauty and sex appeal. None of it came close to seeing Felicia standing in her red lace bra and thong in the middle of the cabin's kitchen, lit only by the light from the emergency lantern.

"So you really think you can teach me something?" he asked, surprised he was even able to form words, as dry as his mouth had gone at the sight of her.

"I learned from the best," she said, trailing her fingertip across the line of his collarbone—a part of his anatomy he'd never considered a turn-on until now. "First, you want to flirt."

"Are you going to try an ant pickup line on me?"

"No." She dipped her head and lapped at his nipple, sending a shot of lust straight to his already hard dick. "I'm going to flirt without words."

"And…" The teasing comment he had lined up turned to chalk in his mouth when she climbed up on the foot rungs of the barstool before straddling him.

The move put her tits right in line with his mouth as she held on to the chair back behind him. Her puckered nipples pushing against the lace was more temptation than even a much better man than he could take. He drew the hard nub into his mouth, sucking hard through the lace and grazing the sensitive spot with his teeth. Her moan of appreciation was punctuated by the palm of her hand on his forehead pushing him away.

She made a *tsk-tsk* sound as she kissed her way down his neck. "I'll take questions and comments at the end of my presentation."

God. That wasn't fair. It was hot as hell, but not fair in the least. He didn't give a shit. If the world's sexiest woman wanted to torment him by turning him on, then so be it. "So, I'm in the strip club champagne room where there's no touching?"

"In an academic sense." She lowered herself to his lap and rocked her core against his cock. "No kissing. No licking. No sucking. And your hands should be on your chair."

He gripped the bar stool's seat, the edge of the metal underside digging into his palm he held on so tight. "I hope you remember the difference between flirting and taunting."

She ground herself against him with enough pressure to be both heaven and hell. "You should, because by the time I'm done with my skills presentation, you're going to be desperate."

She thought he wasn't already there? He had an almost completely naked woman—scratch that, a nearly naked Felicia—on his lap grinding on him, and he couldn't touch her. He did not want to play this game, touching her was pretty much all he thought about lately, but all it took was one look at the challenge in her blue eyes and he gave in. She must have sensed it because she took off her glasses and set them on the island.

Her hands went to the front clasp of her bra. "Close your eyes."

Every instinct in him screamed in protest. "But I want to watch you."

One side of mouth curled up in a sassy smirk. "Later."

Resigned to the fact that he'd created a sexy, teasing monster, he closed his eyes.

• • •

Having Hudson like this was as much of a power rush as that first blowjob. He sat still below her, his eyes closed as he breathed in a steady, controlled rate—but not for long.

She traced her fingers across the tops of his shoulders and down the outsides of his arms, relishing the feel of him as his biceps bunched with the effort it was obviously taking him not to let go of the stool. But he held on just like she knew he would—no matter what else anyone could say about Hudson Carlyle, he aimed to please. Tonight, though, was about him experiencing every touch and lick for himself just like he'd helped her that first night. Right now, it was time for the teacher to be the student.

"What do you want me to touch first?" she asked, giving in to temptation and kissing her way up the corded length of his neck.

"Is my dick out of the question?"

She rocked against the hard length of him. "Is that what you mean?"

"I'm a simple guy. I just want your sweet mouth on me."

She stepped down to the ground, standing between his splayed legs, dropped her fingers to the button of his jeans and popped it open. "Lift your hips."

"Just like that? You're not going to warm me up first?"

he teased.

Gripping his cock as best she could through his jeans and squeezed. "You feel pretty hot already."

He let out a tortured groan and lifted his hips above the chair, giving her just enough room to yank down his jeans and boxers. His cock sprung free. Thick and hard, it made her mouth water, and she wanted nothing more than to drop to her knees and wrap her lips around it. Instead, she waited, her hands at her sides.

"Are you trying to kill me, Matches?"

Looking at him from beneath her lashes, she took in the way his body had gone hard everywhere and the barely leashed predatory tension wafting from him. It was mesmerizing. "Maybe a little."

One side of his mouth curled up. "You want me to tell you what I want?"

"Sound familiar?" As if seeing him naked in front of her wasn't enough to make her slick with desire, the memory of that first night in her bed had her gripping his thighs to steady herself.

He took in a sharp intake of breath and let it out with a strangled groan. "It's not nice to use my own words against me, but if you're going to, I want you to kiss the tip. Make out with it."

She'd thought she'd been wet before. She was wrong. That one demand had her squeezing her thighs together to alleviate some of the pressure building up in her core.

"Open your eyes," she said, her voice husky with need.

He did and the primal lust she saw in them nearly made her forget her plan to make him lose control and drop the charmer facade. This was the real Hudson. The one who made her heart rate speed up and confess whatever color of panties she was wearing. He was passionate, demanding, and ready to lay her across the nearest flat surface and fuck her silly—but not yet. He was holding onto his self-control, but it was a battle. His every ragged breath and the tension in his forearms leaving his veins popping out showed just how much.

Lowering herself to her knees, she wrapped her fingers around the base, her fingers almost meeting, and kissed the head—slow, feathery soft, and with just enough suction to make him jerk against her lips.

"Fuck." He let out a harsh groan as he watched her, his focus zeroed in on her mouth making out with his cock. "That's good."

"How about this?" Maintaining eye contact she sucked him further in her mouth until he hit the back of her throat and she swallowed.

Judging by the stream of nonsensical words that came out of his mouth, his voice rough and desperate, he must have liked it a lot. His warm cock pulsed in her hand still wrapped around the base as she slid her mouth back up his shaft before stopping at the head to swirl her tongue around it and then repeating the process. She engulfed him a little bit more each time until her lips were flush with his balls. Tension kept him strung tight beneath her as she held herself there, longer than she thought she could, and reached out with the tip of her tongue to lap at his balls.

Suddenly, his fingers were in her hair, lifting her head up enough that he had room to withdraw and thrust inside her mouth, filling her up. This was it. This was what they both wanted—that moment when it wasn't about her needs or his wants, it was about their hunger. Primal in nature and focused on only taking each other higher, it sent a flash of pleasure through her that left her entire body trembling with desire. Pulling away from his fingers wrapped around her hair and letting his engorged cock go was not about to happen, though, she loved having him like this too much. So she slipped her hand beneath the elastic waistband of her panties and slid them between her needy folds, slick with lust.

"Yeah, that's it," Hudson said, his voice strained as he slowed his hips so that each stroke of his dick was as unhurried as it was deep. "Touch that clit."

She did, running her fingertip over it in measured strokes that matched the pace he was maintaining with his dick. Wet. She was so fucking wet and so turned on that even the slightest brush against her clit pushed her right to the edge of coming.

"I want to feel you come while my cock is in your mouth."

The words were such a turn-on but not as much as the tone—rough and tinged with desperation. This is what she wanted form him, for him, to be right on the edge with her.

"Look at how fast your fingers are moving underneath that lace." He released her hair and moved his hands so they cupped either side of her face. "So fucking hot."

Close. She was so close. The combination of his dick in her mouth, her fingers on her clit, and the dirty words coming out of his mouth had her toeing the edge of oblivion. The tightness in her body turned electric as she chased her climax, building and growing with every push of his hips and circle of her fingers. Her thighs trembled. Her core clenched and released in an ever-increasing rhythm. Her pulse rushing in her ears drowned out everything else but the sound of Hudson's voice.

"Touch that clit until you come, Felicia. I want to feel you moan around me."

He rocked forward, thrusting into her mouth right as her orgasm hit and she screamed, the sound muffled by his hard length before he withdrew. As she floated down from the high of her climax, he hooked his hands under her arms and lifted her to a standing position. It couldn't have taken a lot of effort on his part, she was so blissed out he could have walked her into the desert without sunscreen and she would have gone without a fight. The next thing she knew, her feet were dangling in the air as he lifted her up onto the kitchen island, pushing everything to the side. The coldness of the granite on her ass—thanks for the coverage, thong—brought her down to reality quickly.

"I would love to give you more time to recover from that hot as hell orgasm," he said, stepping between her legs. "But if you don't get the rest of your clothes off right now, I'm going to rip them off."

Still riding the rush, she put her hands behind her, palms flat on the island, and arched her back to push her breasts forward as far as possible. "And here I thought you only charmed women's panties off."

He hooked a finger into the waistband of her thong, setting off a shiver that made her core clench. "Last chance, Matches."

It was tempting, but it wasn't going to happen. She liked this intense, hungry version of Hudson, and she wasn't done teaching him a lesson.

She wagged a finger at him. "You weren't supposed to touch. Now we have to try the experiment all over again."

He got a look in his eyes that sent a thrill through her. "We're gonna do a lot of things tonight, but stopping me from touching you isn't one of them." He yanked hard against the lace of her thong, ripping it in two. "Don't say I didn't warn you."

Despite shredding her panties, he didn't start between her legs—or maybe it was because he'd torn them. The sexy bastard did love to torment her. Instead, it was her neck his mouth went to first—teasing kisses as his hands made quick work of her bra. Then, he took her nipples and rolled them to stiff peaks while trailing his mouth across her sensitive skin. He didn't have to tell her to close her eyes. It was impossible to keep them open. It felt too good. *He* felt too good, like they were meant to be like this and that the flirting and lessons and everything else had just been a way for the universe to get them here.

Jesus, girl, pull yourself together. You're a scientist not an English major.

That voice in her head didn't matter, though, not when he drew one of her nipples into his talented mouth and sucked. The rest of the world didn't matter. It was just them. The way it should be, and deep inside she knew it with a certainty that equaled her belief in the value of the scientific method. Electricity zipped across her skin, hot sensation that ricocheted through her until she thought she'd break—and that's when he moved lower, gliding his tongue over her stomach before taking a left to her hipbone.

She nearly screamed in frustration. "Hudson, please."

"What is it you want, Matches?" She could feel his grin against her hip.

"Your mouth on me."

"It is."

"Lick me. Suck my clit. Make me come."

"Greedy, aren't you?"

"You're just jealous that you only get to come once tonight."

"I don't know what kind of men you've been with, Matches, but they sure as hell weren't me," he said, his voice as cocky as a frat boy at a kegger. "I'm gonna expect a full-fledged mea culpa when I prove you wrong."

Finally, he dipped his head between her legs, moving his hands underneath her ass to lift her up higher. His tongue lapped at her clit in feather soft touches so light that it was absurd the heightened effect they had on her. Up and around he went, taking her so close only to pull back and start all over again. She bucked against his mouth, her hands seeking out his hair, and pushed herself more firmly against him. This is what she wanted. To have him everywhere. All at once. It was almost more than she could take. Then, he slid one hand off her ass and brought it between her legs, thrusting two fingers inside her and scissoring them so they stretched her entrance at the same time as the tips brushed against her G-spot.

"Don't stop. Don't you dare stop."

Thank God, he didn't. Hudson moved inside her with those magic fingers and changed the pace and pressure of his tongue on her clit. Harder. Faster. More intense. The sensations built until her orgasm crashed against her, washing away everything but the two of them.

• • •

Hudson loved the taste of her on his tongue almost as much as he loved being buried inside her or seeing her smile or hearing her talk about honeypot ants. Watching as her muscles relaxed after that orgasm, the hooded look in her eyes, he realized that he was in trouble—and had been since that first moment he'd seen her at the museum fundraiser—but he couldn't find it in himself to give a shit. All that mattered was that she was there, naked and spread on out the kitchen island, and he needed to be inside her as much as she wanted him to be there. He grabbed his jeans, pulled his wallet out from the back pocket, and took out a condom.

"You're so damn beautiful," he said as he rolled the condom over his straining cock.

Her lust hazy gaze never went higher than his waist. "You're not so bad yourself."

She tugged her bottom lip between her teeth, and he nearly lost it before he'd even started. "I'm not gonna last long."

"That's okay, I heard you come back for seconds."

"With you? I don't think there's a limit." He grabbed her hips and flipped her over so her tits were pressed against the island. "Hold on."

Unable to wait another second, he plunged inside her slick, tight core. He nearly went blind. So good. So fucking good. Tight. She was so fucking tight around him, the perfect fit. The last blood cells powering his brain fled south where all the fun was going on, and he switched into primal mode. He gripped her hips, lifting her and slamming her back down against him, hard and fast. The absolute rightness of it swept through him. Felicia might not be his, no matter how much he wished she was, but she was his for right now, and he was going to make sure she knew it.

"Oh my God, Hudson." She pushed back against him. "Yes. Fuck me. Fuck me hard."

"You want it hard?" he asked, dancing on the fine line of losing control.

"Please," she cried out.

Then that's just what she'd get. He plowed into her, hard and fast, just like they both wanted. Over and over again until the buzzing at the base of his spine grew with each stroke and he couldn't take it anymore. Back and forth, he rocked his hips, slamming into her as she pushed back against him, meeting him thrust for thrust, bordering on desperate, their bodies crashing together until she tossed her head back and came, screaming his name.

That's all it took. His balls tightened, and he pushed forward, his orgasm spilling into her harder than he'd ever come before.

It took everything he had not to collapse onto the floor in a puddle of satisfied male, but he couldn't do that to her. After disposing of the condom, he gathered Felicia up in his arms, picked up the lantern, and strode to his bedroom upstairs. She needed a bed and he needed to keep her close— at least for tonight. He'd deal with tomorrow in the morning, tonight she was his.

Chapter Sixteen

A scratching sound woke her up, but Felicia didn't want to open her eyes. Once she did, she had to face the fact that last night was different. Hudson Carlyle wasn't on her to-do-by-thirty list—but it was nice to pretend he was, at least for a little bit. There went the insistent scratching again. Curiosity made her a great scientist. Also, it made her a shitty pretends-to-be-asleep person. She cracked one eye open.

Hudson sat in a chair next to the bed with a sketchpad in his hands and wearing only his boxers. The ends of his hair brushed his cheekbones in some spots and stuck straight up in others, as if he'd run his hands through it repeatedly. So engrossed in what he was sketching, he didn't notice she'd woken up, which gave her an opportunity to observe him in his natural habitat. His charcoal pencil flew across the page, but he'd stop every few minutes to rub at the markings or use his nail to scratch at it. Then, he was off again, his pencil moving with a quick confidence and determination.

"I know you're awake," he said, not missing a stroke.

Busted. She glanced over at the two mugs on the

nightstand. One was dusted with dark black smudges. The other was still pristine. His and hers? She'd bet her ANT SEX IS A KILLER T-shirt on it.

"Please tell me there's tea in that mug."

One side of his mouth curled up, but his gaze stayed glued to the sketchpad. "What happened to little Miss Morning?"

What happened to her? A night of multiple orgasms that left her sore in places she'd never been aware of until she tried to stretch. "Someone kept me up past my bedtime. What are you drawing?"

That question got him to look up, and the cocky grin he shot her did things to her, good things, the kind of things that led to other things that led to her toes curling in the best possible way. "You."

The flush screamed up her chest to the hollow at the base of her neck. "Naked?" she asked, her voice an octave higher than normal as she yanked the covers up to her chin.

Hudson chuckled and used his free hand to tug at the comforter. "The human form is one of an artist's first inspirations."

"Now *that* sounds like a bad line." One she wasn't giving into. She kept a firm grip on the bedspread.

"Just sit back and let me sketch you." He didn't tug at the material again. He just waited for her to decide.

She should say no. It didn't matter if he was Hughston. She was still naked. Yeah. This was a total no-go. At least it was until she looked up at him because it wasn't Hughston sketching her. It was Hudson. And she did trust him.

"No face?" she asked, relaxing her hold.

"No face." He winked at her. "Just like a good cell phone nude."

A flare of jealousy went off like a firework in her chest, and she jolted up before she could stop herself, the comforter falling to her waist. "You get a lot of those?"

"Hold that pose," he said, suddenly all business. "I want to get you just like that."

For the next twenty minutes, she did just that—well, as best she could; she'd never realized what a fidgeter she was—and watched Hudson work. It was fascinating. He didn't flirt, didn't tease, didn't pull out any of his usual tricks. Instead, he was one hundred percent focused on his work. God, it was hot—especially since he was only in his boxers, giving her an eyeful of sinewy muscle. Of course, even with all she had to look at, her gaze kept going back to his forearm as he drew. Watching the thick muscles in that part of his arm move as he sketched was mesmerizing—and a total turn-on. Needing something to distract herself before she lunged across the bed and jumped him, she grabbed ahold of the first topic of conversation that popped into her mind.

"Have you ever thought about just telling your family about Hughston now that your mom's out of mourning?"

His pencil slowed down, but he kept sketching. "It's crossed my mind."

Oh no, he wasn't getting off that easily. "And?"

"It's been this way for so long." He paused, laying his charcoal pencil and the sketchpad down on the nightstand. "I should have… I should have said something years ago. But after what happened to my dad—and the fact that I'd basically lied to him for years—it feels like I'd be disrespecting his memory if they knew now."

The pain in his voice made her ache for him, but he wouldn't want to hear that. No doubt it would break some kind of guy code. So instead, she rolled onto her hands and knees and crawled across the bed to him. His hot gaze caressed her as she moved, gliding from her mouth to her dangling breasts to the hard tips of her nipples. His cock now strained against his blue boxers, and he pulled her closer as he sat, legs spread, hands white knuckling the arms of his chair, and a sexy smirk on his face. He knew just what he was doing to her because she was doing it to him. The little delay to draw out the anticipation got them both hot.

"So, you're telling me," she said, resting her hands on his strong thighs, inching them higher until the tips of her fingers were underneath the thin cotton, "the man who figured out how to finagle his workaholic brother into marrying, and how to distract his mom out of mourning by planting the idea that Sawyer should get married...*that man* can't figure out how to reveal he's the fabulously talented painter with an international following?" His eyes had gone dark, the pupils dilated with a lust equal to her own as she leaned toward him. "You're a man who's used to fixing things for everyone else and not for yourself. Sometimes you have to disregard your standing hypothesis and open yourself up to the possibilities. Maybe it's time you took something for yourself."

By the time she finished, her lips were practically touching his and her body was trembling with the effort not to close that distance between them. She wanted Hudson. Badly. But she needed him to hear what she was saying, too. Of course, if she'd been using the big brain in her head, she wouldn't be trying to have this conversation while naked and desperate to feel him filling her up and stretching her until he was imprinted on every part of her. What could she say? It was beyond impossible not to touch him when he was practically naked.

He released his grip on the chair's arms, but instead of giving in and touching her, he relaxed back with a cocky grin and cupped his dick through his boxers. "This has gotten way too serious of a conversation with a woman who has just-been-fucked-all-night-long hair."

Using every ounce of her willpower not to watch him stroke his hard length. If she did, she'd lose their unspoken war of wills. "Would you rather talk about the color of my panties?"

"You're not wearing any."

"Oops," she said, sitting back, spreading her legs wide, and slipping her fingers between her slick folds. "You caught me."

"Fuck," he groaned. "Get your feet up on the chair now."

She did, the move spreading her legs even farther as she continued to slide her fingers over herself, coming close to her clit but not touching it. If she did, she'd come before they even got started.

"That's it, Matches." He wrapped his hands around her ankles, his tight grip holding her in place. "Play with that pretty pink pussy. Does it feel good?"

"Yes." It did. So fucking good to have him watch her sink a finger inside, then a second.

"Does it taste good?"

Keeping her gaze on him, she lifted her glistening fingers to her mouth and slid them across her parted lips. "You tell me."

She didn't have to ask twice. He let out a curse under his breath and was out of the chair in a heartbeat, looming over her, his hands planted on the bed on either side of her shoulders but not touching. The look he gave her as he stared at her mouth almost undid her. Dominating. Possessive. Furious in its hunger. This wasn't a lesson. It was Hudson in all of his sexy, no-holds-barred glory. This wasn't the part of himself that he showed the rest of the world. This was for her. And just that fast she was on the edge, her body quivering as an electric ball tightened and grew inside her.

"Don't you dare stop stroking yourself," he ordered, every part of his body tight with the obvious effort not to touch her yet. "And you better not come—not until I say you can."

If he wanted her not to come, that was the very wrong

thing to say. "Why not?"

"Because I want to watch as your pussy clenches around your fingers so tight as you scream knowing that that is exactly what's going to happen a few minutes later when my dick is buried balls deep in you." Then, he licked the juices off her lips with slow, deliberate strokes before taking her mouth, claiming it in a short, rough kiss before shoving down his boxers and sitting back down in the chair.

Heart pounding, fingers slipping because she was so wet, she watched as he fucked his hand at a measured, deliberate pace. The head of his cock gleamed with pre-come, more with every lazy stroke.

"You like watching me."

"Yes." It came out more moan than word.

"I love watching you," he said, his voice strained. "In fact, I want a better view."

Leaving the chair, he lowered himself to his knees, his ass resting against his heels, so that his face was at the same level as her wet, glistening folds. "Look at how you take those fingers. Everything's so wet, so swollen. You're close, aren't you?"

She couldn't say anything, just mewl her answer as the vibrations in her thighs grew stronger. She couldn't look at him anymore. The stark want on his face was hotter than anything else, and she'd come if she didn't close her eyes.

"That's it. Just a little longer. Draw it out, Matches. Let me watch you."

Hot. So fucking hot. With her eyes squeezed shut, she tried to forestall the inevitable even as her body chased it. Then, she felt something new. Something decadent and delicious. The soft wetness of Hudson's tongue against her asshole as he flicked his tongue against the sensitive spot and circled to hit every nerve. She nearly came off the bed as pleasure ricocheted through her. She didn't know where it was coming from, it was just all encompassing and overwhelming.

"Hudson," she cried out, her orgasm so close it was as if her legs had gone electric.

The firm pressure of his thumb replaced his tongue, dipping inside her as she stroked her folds. "What do you need?"

"To come." Beads of sweat dotted her body. Desperate, so fucking desperate.

"Then do it." He punctuated his words by sliding his thumb inside her right as her fingertips grazed her swollen, needy clit.

It was as if the world stopped and then exploded around them in a billion neon pieces. Her orgasm didn't just curl her toes, it made her entire body seize with pleasure so rich, so intense that she lost the ability to hear or see or do anything else but feel. She'd just started to come down when Hudson grabbed her hips and flipped her over so she was on her belly.

"I want you just like that." He smacked her ass, the sting going straight to her clit.

Looking over her shoulder, she barely recognized the man behind her ripping open the condom wrapper as he climbed onto the bed behind her, his legs spread wide so he straddled her thighs. Any pretense at being Mr. Above-It-All-Charming was gone. There was a single-focused desperation in every taut line of his body, and it was all centered on her. He rolled on the condom with the efficiency of a man on the edge and grabbed her hips. He didn't yank her up and back, though. Instead, he pressed her hard into the mattress and slid his iron-hard cock inside her with one long thrust.

"Damn, you're so tight." He rocked back and then slammed forward. "I'm not going to last long. That show was too fucking good and totally worth it."

He wasn't going to last long? She was already on the edge again.

"Harder."

"That's how you want it?" He moved a hand from her hip to the small of her back, pressing her down and changing the angle so he hit just the right spot with every single hard stroke.

"Yes." She pushed back against him.

His hand on her back forced her back down, pinning her to the mattress. "Then you get it."

And she did. In and out. Forward and back. He fucked her until they were both covered in sweat and reduced to half speaking/half groaning dirty phrases that turned her on even more. She wasn't about to deny or delay her climax this time. As her body tightened around his pistoning cock, she chased that high, reaching for it with every breath until it broke over her and she screamed his name.

"That's it," he said, plunging into her with renewed frenzy. "Squeeze that cock, milk it."

Then, with one last hard thrust, he came, his body going still as it rolled over him. As he collapsed next to her, pulling her in close, she realized she hadn't thought of her mission to date Tyler once since she'd gotten in the car with Hudson. What exactly that meant, she'd figure out tomorrow when they got back to the city.

• • •

The elevator doors leading to Hudson's mom's penthouse closed after a young couple with a crying baby got off on the fifteenth floor, and he heaved a sigh of relief. If he had drunk anything alcoholic since he'd dropped off Felicia at her apartment last night, he'd blame the dull pounding in his head on a hangover. As tempting as it had been to go get drunk after Felicia had sent him packing—no doubt already planning her next play for Tyler. His hands curled into fists at the thought of her with the other man. She couldn't be his. He knew that. Understood it. That didn't mean he had to like it—especially since the entire point of hanging out with her was to help her catch Captain Clueless's attention. It was all she wanted, and the least he could do was not be a selfish bastard but make sure she got the stupid dickwad.

So instead of replaying every dirty thing they'd done over the weekend at the cabin—and the fact that she cut up her pancakes first and then poured the syrup (*Who does that?*), he'd ended up working on the less fun side of being Hughston. He'd spent most of the night and today working on the business of being an artist. Taxes. Bills. Interview requests. Scheduling a meeting with Everly to discuss the upcoming show. He may not have ever wanted to get his business degree, but he had to admit it came in damn handy.

The elevator binged as it stopped on the top floor, opening to a small lobby with two doors. One led to the penthouse of a retired actor who'd been in almost every action movie Hudson had loved growing up and the other door went to his mom's penthouse where she was holding court during her weekly family cocktail parties. They were called family cocktail parties, but Helene took an expansive view of the term. Though tempted to go knock on Hank Murphy's door to talk about the good old days when the old man had done every stunt himself, Hudson turned the other direction.

Helene opened the door before he had a chance to knock.

She gave him a quick air kiss and ushered him inside, hooking her arm through his. "I was beginning to think you were locked up in your cabin again."

"And miss out on the standing family cocktail hour?" he asked, giving her a teasing wink. "No way."

"You've missed plenty before, and this one isn't just family," she said leading him into the living room, which awkwardly enough had an original Hughston above the fireplace. "I invited Tyler and your new friend is already here."

His brain sped right past Tyler's name and jerked to a stop on the second part. "Friend?"

"There she is over there talking to Clover." Too well-bred to point, Helene nodded toward where Clover stood with Felicia near the grand piano covered with family pictures. "Last time I walked by, they were talking about ants that act as living refrigerators."

"The honeypot ant," he answered automatically.

If his brain had been working at all, he would have been disturbed that he'd offered up that bit of information voluntarily. As it was, all the blood in his body started speeding straight to his dick the moment he spotted Felicia. Her back was to him, and she was wearing a navy-blue dress that narrowed at her waist and flared out past her hips before stopping a good couple of inches above her knees. Her long brown hair was in her signature ponytail, but instead of slipping free at odd spots, it was all curled and bouncy. He wanted to hustle her into the closest room with a door just so he could wrap it around his fist as he fucked her.

"You know about it, too?" Helene asked, interrupting his very not safe for a family cocktail party thoughts. "I had to keep walking, so I wouldn't get drawn into conversation."

Pulling back from thoughts about Felicia, he led his mother a few feet closer to the piano because there was a waiter standing there with a tray full of champagne glasses. "I've never known you to be a delicate flower."

"I'm not, but that's not why I'm glad you decided to show tonight," she said. "You're on duty tonight."

"I am?"

"Yes." She pivoted them so they were facing Tyler and Sawyer, who were standing together and by the looks of it, all they were missing were their rulers. "They're here, but they're not talking. Again."

He did not want to go over there. Just looking at Captain Clueless had him curling his hands into fists. The last thing he wanted was to make that douchebag's life easier.

"You know, you can't just hit them over the head with a sledgehammer and force them to do what you want."

"I know. It's very annoying," Helene said with deadpan delivery. "Go work your magic."

Stubborn. Focused. Determined to bend the world to her image of it. At first, a stranger might think she was all Sawyer and no Hudson. The Hughston painting—the cosmos painted into a little girl's eye—told him different. If Sawyer was the hammer, then Hudson was the grease. Either way, they were both their mother's sons and always managed to get their way, they just went about it by different methods. After giving her a quick kiss on the cheek, he went in the exact opposite direction of where his dick wanted him to go and walked over to Tyler and Sawyer.

"How was the Giants game?" he asked.

"It just about killed me," Sawyer answered, going into insane amounts of detail about every hit, error, and RBI for the game that had gone twelve innings.

By the time he was done, the others had visibly relaxed, but not Hudson. Tyler had snuck too many looks over at Felicia for him to be calm. In fact, he was conjuring up a third possibility for how to not go to jail after he shoved the other man off the balcony when his brother asked him if he wanted another drink.

"Sure," he said. "Make it a double."

It took about fifteen seconds after Sawyer left for Tyler to start in. "Are you two seeing each other?"

Luckily, Hudson had had more than enough experience playing dumb for his response to sound natural. "Who?"

"Felicia," Tyler said, his attention going right past Hudson to the woman across the room.

He turned his gaze to the balcony. *You have enough money for good lawyers, Carlyle. You'd end up with fifteen years. Tops.*

Gritting his teeth, he forced himself to remember the determination and hope in Felicia's eyes when she'd told him why she'd had a lifelong crush on the idiot in front of him. It was enough—barely—to keep him from pushing the other man toward the balcony.

"Felicia?" he asked, managing not to include the non-verbal fuck you into his tone. "We're just friends. That's it."

Tyler the jackass's face lit up. "Because I don't want to elbow in if something's going on between you two."

Going on? Just orgasms. And pancakes. And a one-eyed cat. And the biggest secret of his life.

"With Felicia? No way. We're just working on a project together—something to pass the time." *Don't kill him. Don't punch him in the face. Tripping him so he falls into a tray of canapés was acceptable, though.* "She's not really my type."

He caught the movement of air behind him a second before the scent of fruity shampoo hit. Turning, he looked down at Felicia who gave him a flirty smile.

"I hope I'm not interrupting."

• • •

Felicia could do this. She could make it through a simple conversation even if all she could hear was the phrase "not my type" over and over in her head. She wasn't. She knew that. She'd always known that. And it wasn't like she wanted Tyler. Wait. She *did* want Tyler. It was Hudson she didn't want. She didn't.

How much longer are you going to lie to yourself? For a smart chick, you sure do act like your head's full of rocks sometimes.

She looked between the two men and it hit her like every stereotypical a-ha moment she'd ever heard about. While she'd been so focused on what she thought she'd wanted, she'd completely missed the fact that she wanted Hudson *not* Tyler and had since that first night at the museum fundraiser. Tyler hadn't been her ideal man, he'd been an idea. But Hudson? He was the flesh and blood man that she couldn't help but respond to. It had never been transference. It had always been Hudson. She was a total moron for not realizing it until now. It made perfect, frustrating, mind-boggling sense, and she'd just been too stubborn to look away from the goal she'd had for years to understand just why she couldn't get her "professor" off her mind. The question now was what was she going to do about it?

"Shit." The word was out before she could stop it.

Both men started.

"Everything okay?" Tyler asked.

"Sorry, just remembered something I needed to do for an article I'm putting together for the *Journal of Myrmecology*," she said, almost sounding like she wasn't lying through her teeth.

Hudson didn't look like he believed her, but Tyler ate up the bullshit line.

"You look gorgeous tonight," Tyler said.

"Thank you," she said, her mind still spinning.

She was saved from having to say anything else by his buzzing phone. "Sorry." He took it out and gave the text a quick read, his expression growing darker with every second. By the time he shoved his cell back in his inside suit jacket pocket, he was scowling.

"Trouble?" Hudson asked with a little more joy than the situation called for.

Tyler shot him a glare. "Just that annoying upstairs

neighbor of mine. She's called a tenant meeting."

Oh, that wasn't good. Even if he did own the building, if the tenants banded together about a quality of life issue within the building, then the Harbor City housing authority could get involved and there'd be nothing he could do about it. For a control freak like Tyler, there really wasn't a worse possible outcome than having someone else telling him what to do.

Felicia gave his forearm a comforting squeeze. "What did you do now?"

"What makes you think I did anything?" he said, not denying that he had.

Laughter bubbled out. "Because I've known you my whole life, Tyler Jacobson."

"Nothing that should have resulted in that she-devil busting my balls this much," he grumbled

Hudson smirked. "Not sure I believe that."

Before Tyler could get off a retort, his phone buzzed again. This time when he looked at it, though, he got a look on his face that she knew from years of observing him meant a whole lot of trouble for someone else.

"I hate to do this, but I have to go. Just had a little break on something I've been working on for years." He pocketed the phone and started to leave, but then turned back to Felicia as if he'd remembered a dinner casserole was in the oven. "Hey, I have tickets for the Dixon Library masked ball fundraiser tomorrow. I know it's short notice for a date, but would you like to go with me?"

"Sure," she said on autopilot, years of training for one goal had that effect on people. However, the excitement she would have felt a few weeks ago because of the invitation never appeared. "That sounds like fun."

"Great! I'll text later to work out the details." He gave her a quick kiss on the cheek and nodded at Hudson. "See ya, Carlyle."

Tyler hustled out of the penthouse, stopping only long enough to say what she figured was a thank you to Helene on his way out the door. Watching him go barely made a blip on her emotional radar. But even a sideways glance at Hudson made her heart speed up. God, she'd been so obsessed with her preconceived notions that she'd missed a six-foot-tall variable who was always asking about her underwear. What had he told her about the danger of assumptions? Yeah, she'd definitely made an ass out of herself when it came to Hudson.

God, what was her deal with wanting unobtainable men? Unless... She turned back to Hudson, taking in his uncharacteristic glower aimed squarely at Tyler's retreating back. It didn't take someone with years of observation experience to realize that Tyler wasn't on Hudson's list of favorite people. The past problems with Sawyer seemed to have disappeared so the only reason she could think of for Hudson to be glaring at Tyler was because of her. It was a biased hypothesis, but it made sense. The question was, how to test it?

"Congratulations," he said, turning his body to her but never quite looking *at* her. "Looks like you're finally going to get to cross that whole date Tyler thing off your to-do list."

"I think I'll wear the black dress. Your favorite from the museum fundraiser," she teased, wanting to gauge his reaction. "Or you could come with me tomorrow to pick something out. I'm sure you probably feel like you've spent enough time with me already..."

She let the opening for him to shut her down dangle in the air, her heart pounding against her ribs in anticipation and hope. Finally, he dropped his incendiary gaze to hers, and her breath caught in her lungs.

"Yes." The single word came out almost like a growl.

A flush of desire rushed up her body with enough heat to make her want to fan herself. He wanted her, that much was obvious, but did he *want* her like she was realizing she wanted him? "So you don't mind taking me shopping for another man?"

The idea of doing the same for him made her blood pressure skyrocket. Jealousy was a bitch that way.

"Why should I?" The same primal possessiveness from the other night flashed in his eyes, revealing the lie of his words—and he was lying there was no doubt about it. All those lessons hadn't been just lessons for him, either. "Remember, I'm Henry Higgins at your service."

Giving in to the urge to push him a little farther to see if he'd reveal the truth, she pressed her hand to his solid chest and rose up on her tiptoes so she could whisper in his ear. "Thank you."

Heat blazed in his eyes, but he didn't make a move. Stubborn man.

Knowing she had to go now or make a fool of herself in his mom's penthouse, she dropped back, her lips tingling as if she'd actually kissed him. She sucked in a deep breath and gave him a shaky smile before following Tyler's lead and, after offering her good-byes to Helene, strolled out of the penthouse, adding an extra little bit of sway to her hips.

He wanted her. He wanted her a lot. And she was betting he wanted her for more than just a quick fuck, otherwise he wouldn't look like he was ready to tear Tyler limb from limb. Right? Every good scientist knew when it was time to test out a new hypothesis and Felicia was very, very good at her job. She had the tools, thanks to Hudson's lessons, and now she was going to use them on him. It was time to become a honeypot of the non-ant variety.

She pressed the down button for the elevator and tried not to remember Hudson's words that she wasn't his type, because she was. The past month had shown that. Now all she had to do was get him to realize it like she had. "Just you wait, Henry Higgins, just you wait."

Chapter Seventeen

The dressing rooms on the private shopper floor of Dylan's Department Store were plush. Thick carpeting. Solid doors. Full length mirrors showing off three angles. Felicia felt way out of her comfort zone the next day, and that was before she stepped into the black, floor-length jersey gown with a low-cut back covered only by a few, barely-there crisscrossed straps. Once she was in it, and wearing the borrowed heels from the shoe department so she didn't trip over the hem, she took one last look in the mirror as she smoothed the clingy material over her hips.

"Flirt. Tease. Draw it out," she said, repeating the mantra she'd distilled Hudson's advice down to. "You can do this."

World's lamest pep talk complete, she stood as tall as possible—never discount the power of an extra inch—and tried to strut in too tall heels out to where Hudson sat in a trio of chairs directly outside the dressing room. Instead of looking out of place in the dainty chairs, they only emphasized his size and made him look like lord of the manor. It was enough to make a girl's knees weak and other parts of her soft and wet.

"So, what do you think?"

He looked up from his phone, and his jaw tightened.

Good sign? Bad sign? No sign? Time to add in another variable into this experiment in seduction. "I know it's a little conservative from the front."

He raised one eyebrow. "Conservative?"

"But then you see the back." She turned around, which meant she couldn't see his face, but she didn't need to in order to feel his gaze. It burned against her skin and yet he didn't make a move, didn't say a word. The butterflies were rioting inside her and her nipples were pointed peaks brushing against the soft jersey of the dress. This is what he did to her without even trying. It wasn't fair. Time to use his own logic against him. After all, he was the one who said you always want what you can't have. "I can just imagine how Tyler's hand will feel pressed up against the bare skin of my back as we dance."

"I'm not sure I can," he said, each word clipped short.

"Here," she said, turning and strutting on wobbly ankles over to him. "Let me show you what I mean."

Determined not to lose her courage, she jutted her chin a little higher and stood in front of him, arms held out in dance position. After a second's hesitation, he joined her, one hand on her hip and the other holding her hand close to his chest. Oxygen became something she didn't need anymore, which was a good thing because the moment she looked up at his handsome face set in hard, rigid lines so unlike the charmer she met or the real man she'd fallen for, she couldn't breathe. The air crackled around them with possibilities, all she had to do was get Hudson to realize the same thing she had—that plans sometimes needed to change and that even goal-oriented to-do lists had to be updated.

She took a tiny step forward, and his hand slid across the

bare expanse of her lower back, and he sucked in a hard breath and closed his eyes. If she were a more lacking observer, she'd have wondered if the twist to his lips meant he was in heaven or hell. Truth be told, she had one foot in both right now.

"Doesn't that feel good?" *And awful and not nearly enough?*

He mumbled something under his breath as he feathered the tips of his fingers lower until they rested just underneath the dress. With the piped in instrumental music to guide their steps, he pulled her closer until they touched from thigh to her cheek. There was no missing the hard length of him pressed against her belly. One step. Two steps. They moved together, saying everything without uttering a word.

He dipped his head lower. "What color, Matches?"

She didn't have to ask of what as she tried her best not to strip him naked right here. "I don't know that I should tell."

His hand went lower, one finger curling around the band of her thong. "There are other ways I could find out."

"We're in the middle of the personal shopper level in a department store." Which was just her damn luck.

He tugged on her lace thong, enough to make the material tight against her clit without offering any relief. "There are dressing rooms."

"Another lesson?" she asked with a flirty smile.

Hudson's jaw tensed, and he took a step back abruptly. "This is good for your date with Tyler, but what else did you pick out?"

Since screaming in frustration wasn't an option for adults—though really, somedays it should be—she gave him a wink and made her way back to the dressing room. The other option Jacqui talked her into was a crystal-blue dress with satin finished sequins, a plunging V-neck, and a tight fit. It was so not a dress Felicia would have ever normally pick out, but what had she just got done telling herself? Every once in a while, you had to change your patterns and try something new.

She stared at herself in the mirror as she did the bend and twist and pretzel yourself to get the back zipper up. Once that was done, she patted her hair back in place and reminded herself that she had three objectives in this part of the experiment: flirt, tease, seduce. Hudson wasn't going to know what hit him.

When she strolled out of the dressing room, Hudson wasn't on his phone. Gone was the predatory gleam in his eye and the gotta-have-you-now possessiveness. Instead, he'd retreated back into being the charmer, with his relaxed smile and lazy posture.

"Wow," he said, his voice just rough enough to give her hope.

She did a slow spin. "That's just the reaction I'm hoping for."

"From Tyler," he said, his tone neutral.

Fucking A. And people said she was the one who couldn't let go of something once she'd set her mind to it. It was enough to make her do something…the idea popped fully formed into her head. A quick glance around the showroom confirmed that Jacqui was helping an older woman whose look screamed rich-lady-who-lunches. Before she could rethink what had the potential to be a very bad life choice, unless it paid off like she was hoping.

"Can you come back to the dressing room with me?" she asked, not even bothering to sound like she didn't have an ulterior motive. "This zipper is a killer."

There went one corner of his mouth into a sexy half smile. "I never leave a lady in distress."

God, she was hoping not. They walked back to the luxe dressing room as if it were totally normal for both of them to go back there. Once inside the large space, she walked closer to the mirror so he had to step inside the doorway. She lifted her hair and glanced back over her shoulder. He was going to lose a molar or two if he kept clenching his jaw so tight.

"Thanks again for this," she said, fire sizzling along her skin the moment he reached for her.

The zipper started high between her shoulder blades and went down to the very base of her spine. He inched it down. Slow. Tormenting her with his absolute silence as he did. Watching him in the mirror, was even worse than closing her eyes because she could see the hunger etched into every line on his face. It was the same look he had the first time he told her he was going to taste every inch of her, the one he had before he sank his dick into her, the same one he had when she wrapped her fingers around him and licked his swollen crown. By the time he got the dress unzipped in the here and now, her thong was soaked.

He traced a finger across the upper swell of her ass, setting off a riot of sensations that made her core clench. "Black lace," he said with a strained groan.

"They're new." Her breath caught when his finger tip glided down the center piece that slipped between her ass cheeks. "You've gotta see the matching bra."

It took only a little shimmy for the dress to slide down her arms and over her hips to puddle around her heels. The whole time she watched him in the mirror. His gaze traveled down the reflection of her body as his hands stayed locked in place, one at her hip and the other curled around her thong. She took the hand at her hip and lifted it to her breast, leaning back against him as he pinched her hard nipple through the lace of her bra and rolled it to an even stiffer peak. It was so fucking hot to be here in the dressing room in her underwear and heels watching as Hudson, still fully dressed, toyed with her body with deliberate, controlling motions. His hard cock pressed against her back. At that moment, all she wanted in the world was to sink down to her knees and suck him deep into her mouth.

"I'm thinking," she said, turning in his arms. "I really need a lesson in hot dressing room sex."

God did she ever. She was on the verge of coming and he'd barely touched her.

"Matches." His tugged her nipple with just the right amount of force to almost make her knees buckle with pleasure. "I don't think there's anything left for me to teach you." Then, he let go of her as if she was covered in radiation and stepped back, stopping just on the other side of the open dressing room door. "Whichever dress you pick, make sure to have Jacqui put it on my account."

Embarrassment slammed into her. Nothing to teach her? Had she been wrong about him wanting her? No, she couldn't be, not with the way his body was responding to hers. "You don't have to do that."

"Think of it as your graduation gift," he said, a lazy, easy camaraderie in his voice. "Have fun with Tyler."

He left without saying anything else, never even looking back. Felicia stared after him, her gut churning. What the fuck? Had she read that all wrong? She'd done everything he'd taught her. She'd seduced. She'd stoked his jealousy. She'd flirted and tempted and all but begged for him to want her. Her throat tightened. Her eureka moment at the cocktail party may have been true for her, but obviously not for Hudson. Why else would he walk away unless it had all been just a *My Fair Lady* game to him? What had he told Tyler? *She's not really my type.* She'd convinced herself that he hadn't really meant it…but he had. She done it to herself again, tried to shoehorn a hope into a reality and failed miserably. Hudson may have thought he'd taught her a lot but what she really learned was that maybe the ants had it right. Maybe the males of the species should die after sex. It sure would lead to less heartbreak for idiots like herself.

...

Walking away from Felicia had been one of the hardest things he'd ever done, but Hudson knew it was the only way. She wanted Tyler. She couldn't have been more open about it. He had just been a little bit of fun before things got serious between her and Captain Clueless. If she'd been any other woman, he wouldn't have thought twice about it. He would have just figured it was no-strings-attached orgasms between friends. Nothing wrong with that. But that wasn't what it was anymore. At least not for him. And he had to see her tonight with Tyler The Idiot.

Skipping out on the event wasn't an option, and there was no way he'd make it through the night without cold-cocking the douchebag without backup. He walked out onto the busy Harbor City street and called the person who always had his back. Everly picked it up on the first ring.

"I need a solid," he said without preamble.

"You have more money for bail than I do."

He laughed despite the seriousness of the situation. "Very funny."

"I'm a fucking riot," Everly said without a hint of humor in her husky alto. "That's what everyone says about me."

No. What everyone who'd ever met Everly Ribinski said about her was that she was phenomenally gorgeous and hell on stilettos. Funny? Not so much.

"I need a date," he said, turning the corner and scanning traffic for a cab to hail.

"You're Hudson Carlyle," she scoffed. "You never need a date."

No cabs. No date. No Felicia. His day had started out crappy and ended up whatever was described beyond totally shitty. He was an artist not a word guy. "I do this time."

Everly let out a low whistle. "This sounds like end of the world stuff."

"Are you in or what?"

"Settle down." He could practically see her roll her eyes as she stood in her gallery wearing head-to-toe black. "Of course I'm in. Where are we going?"

"The Dixon Library masked ball fundraiser." He pushed the words out in a rush, knowing it was very much not her kind of event.

"Jesus," she groaned. "You realize this will test the very farthest boundaries of our friendship."

"You'll stand beside me making snarky comments about all the rich assholes who probably have shitty taste in art, and I'll smile and be charming."

"Sounds like just my kind of disaster. Text me the details later."

Relief soothed some of the burn in his gut. "Thanks, Everly. I owe you."

He pocketed his phone and turned on Powers Street. There were always cabs out here, and he needed to get as far away from Dylan's as fast as he could. If it wasn't for the fact that his dick was in love with Felicia—and he'd actually thought when given the choice she'd choose him—he would have offered to hook her up with his mom's salon for the big night. The Dixon event always brought out the press and was about as close to a Cinderella type ball as Harbor City had. *Shit.* He couldn't do that to Felicia. This was her big night, even if it was with Sir Head Up His Ass. He took out his phone and hit the first number in his contacts.

"Mom, I need a favor."

• • •

How in the world Felicia had ended up at Helene Carlyle's hair salon with the grand dame of Harbor City society sipping Earl Grey from a china cup was still a bit of a mystery—and she'd lived it. All she knew was that Jacqui stopped her before she could leave Dylan's in a huff and told her that Mrs. Carlyle's car was waiting for her and that Helene herself was on her way up. There were probably less formidable women in the world, but she hadn't met one. And that's how she'd ended up at the salon with a man making horrified expressions while examining her hair as Helene gave her what she could only assume was the rich person version of the third degree.

"It really is so nice of you to help Hudson out in his efforts to get Sawyer and Tyler to stop their silly feud," Helene said.

"I don't know that I've really done anything," Felicia said, eyeballing the stylist in the mirror as he took out his scissors. "Just a trim, please."

He gave her that smile every woman who's ever been ignored at the salon knows all too well. "But of course." And he snipped off three inches. "Just removing the split ends."

What the—

She opened her mouth to confront the stylist whose scissors were whizzing through her hair, but Helene spoke first.

"Well whatever help you gave, he sure seems taken with you."

"Hudson?" Not likely.

"Not Hudson," Helene said with a shake of her perfectly coiffed head. "Tyler."

"Of course." *Because you were just a project for Hudson.* None of the past few weeks meant anything.

"He couldn't take his eyes off you at the cocktail party," Helene went on. "He's quite the catch, that one."

"Yes. He is." One her fifteen-year-old self had imprinted on with all the devotion of an obsessed teenager. And it had stuck with her for all these years until she realized it wasn't

Tyler she'd been in love with, but her idea of him. Reality sucked that way.

"And after Charles gets done with your hair, Tyler won't be able to see any other woman at the fundraiser."

"That's the plan." Or at least it had been. Her shoulders sank. As it stood now, she didn't know what in the hell she was doing or why she was even still going.

Sure you do. You know Hudson will be there, and you just need to see him one last time when you aren't in your underwear and making a failed play for him. Pride. She needed to see him one last time to salvage her pride, that was all.

"It's a brilliant one," the other woman said before taking another sip of her tea. "Who'd have ever thought that Hudson would have a secret talent as a matchmaker?"

"He's got a lot of talents." Ugh. Stop defending him.

"Yes, he does." Helene cocked her head to the side and gave her an assessing look that reminded Felicia of Hudson's expression when he was sketching her. "I just wish he'd be a little more open about them, but that's neither here nor there because now it's time for you to make Tyler realize all he's been missing. Plus, it'll practically be a double date. Hudson is bringing Everly."

The mysterious Everly. She was probably tall and smart and funny and beautiful and perfect for Hudson in every way. Felicia wanted to throw up.

"I can't wait to meet her," she said through gritted teeth.

"You'll adore her," Helene said, a knowing smile curling her lips. "Everyone does."

Felicia just bet they did. And if she was going to have to meet the perfect Everly after making a complete fool of herself with Hudson, well, she was going to do it looking her best and have a fabulous time with Tyler while she did. If it was the hardest thing she ever did, she'd make sure Hudson never realized that what had been between them had meant something to her.

Chapter Eighteen

In the end, Helene's hair stylist had taken four inches off her hair so that it fell in that strange spot halfway between her chin and her shoulders, but Felicia couldn't deny that it looked good. She'd been wearing her hair the same way for most of her life, so the cut was a huge shock every time she walked by a mirror. Even now, after staring at it for way too long as she put on mascara—whoever invented that should be beaten with a brush covered in gobs of clumpy goo—it was like seeing a new person. The kind who wasn't going to think of Hudson every third minute. Or wonder if he'd even noticed she'd charged both dresses to his account at Dylan's in a moment of pique. Or try, and fail, to muster up any kind of excitement for finally scratching off the last item on her to-do-before-thirty list a solid week and a half before her birthday.

If nothing else, *that* part of this whole disaster should have delighted her list-loving, spreadsheet-making, nerdy self.

"I'm totally thrilled," she said to Honeypot, who just sat

on the window sill glaring at her while its tail swished angrily.

The cat was so annoyed it didn't even bother to caterwaul a warning before the doorbell rang. *Yeah. She knew the feeling.* She grabbed the purse that matched the blue sequined dress on her way to the door. When she opened it, Tyler stood on the other side in a tuxedo that made him look like a shoe-in to be the next James Bond. It was a look that did damage to women's panties across the world—just not hers, not anymore. She scooted outside and closed the door behind her before Honeypot got any ideas.

"Wow," he said, giving her a slow up and down. "You look great."

"Thank you. You, too." And he did. He looked exactly as handsome as he always did, and it did absolutely nothing for her girly bits. It was as if they'd gone on strike.

It didn't make any sense, but there it was. Logic had nothing on lust. She wouldn't use the other L-word. That was just pouring sulfuric acid into an open wound.

She followed Tyler up the steps and into the town car waiting at the curb. Then, she spent most of the ride thinking about how pissed her fifteen-year-old self would be to know that actually going out on a date with Tyler wasn't nearly as fun as spending years thinking about what it would be like to go out on a date with Tyler. Wasn't that just a real slap across the mouth? She must have uh-huhed out loud at all the right spots while totally *not* obsessing over Hudson during the drive, because the next thing she knew, the chauffeur was opening the passenger door, and then they were walking up stone steps leading to the Dixon Library and its massive first floor lobby, transformed every year into a ballroom for the fundraiser.

Tyler rested his hand on the small of her back. "You're quiet tonight."

"This isn't my usual crowd." Not a lie. Just not the whole

truth.

"You'll be amazing," he said, holding open the door. "You always are."

The newspapers and blogs always carried pictures of the library lobby when it was decorated for the fundraiser, but seeing it in person was something else. Soft lighting bounced off the limestone walls that were lined with the library's collection of Impressionist art. A quartet played classical music for those on the dance floor that was lined with Harbor City's richest and most powerful—only a third of whom wore a mask like the one Felicia held in her hand.

"I thought it was a masked ball?" she said.

Tyler shrugged. "It is, but these aren't exactly costume people."

The woman in front of them in the initial crush just inside the doorway stiffened and turned around. "You have *got* to be kidding me."

Tyler let out a string of curses under his breath. Then, the man who was with the glamazon in head-to-toe black who looked like she could kill a person with a well-placed insult turned around. Hudson. Of course. Felicia let out a mumbled curse of her own.

"Felicia. Tyler," Hudson said, his jaw tight. "This is…"

Tyler cut in. "We know each other."

"We're neighbors," the woman said with less than a zero point zero ounce of warmth. "He's beneath me."

The pieces clicked into place. Felicia glanced down. Yep. The woman was wearing perfect apartment-above-you-stomping heels so high that mere mortals got dizzy just looking at them. Plus, they probably doubled as weapons if she needed one on the quick. That was the kind of woman who was Hudson's type. Not short ant researchers with small boobs and one-eyed cats. Her mutinous attention slid over from the woman in stilettos to the man she was with. Hudson should at least have the human decency to look like he'd been hit by a crosstown bus. Instead, he looked like he belonged on the cover of Harbor City's Hottest Bachelors. What had she been thinking when she'd thought she could seduce him in a dressing room at Dylan's? Her stomach bottomed out, and she wished she were anywhere in the world but here.

Hudson relaxed the tension in his jaw and offered up a blandly charming smile. "Everly Ribinski, this is Felicia Hartigan. Felicia is an entomologist specializing in the honeypot ant, and she has a one-eyed cat with the lungs of an elephant. Everly owns The Black Heart Gallery and one of the most insane shoe closets I've ever seen."

This was Everly the gallery owner? Oh yeah. She could totally see that. "How lovely to meet you," she managed to get out before turning to Tyler. "But we better keep moving. I know Tyler had someone he needed to meet."

"Probably Satan," Everly said with an icy smile.

Tyler just glared at the woman as Felicia steered them away from the other couple. This was a major Harbor City event. She *knew* she'd see him here. She'd been planning on it. Of course, that didn't make actually *seeing* him after he'd turned her down flat any easier.

"Okay, something's up," Tyler said after swiping two glasses of champagne from a passing waiter's tray. "You might as well tell me because I'll find out one way or another."

What was it the nuns said in school? Confession is good for the soul? It was doubtful Sister Mary Thomas meant anything like Felicia's love life—or lack of one—but here it went anyway. "I've been an idiot."

Tyler laughed and punched her in the shoulder like a brother, which is pretty much *exactly* like he'd always treated her. "Now that I find hard to believe."

"Really?" And because the fates were cruel and her Hudson radar finely tuned, she asked the question as she tracked his path across the room.

Next to her, Tyler groaned, "Not him."

Her head said the same thing. Her body and heart? Well, they had differing opinions. "Him."

"And here I thought you were holding out for me."

She gulped. Okay, this was officially awkward, and she was a horrible human being. "Tyler…" The rest of whatever brilliant apology she was going to make for being a bitch died on her lips when she saw his face.

There was nothing but orneriness in his blue eyes. "Relax." He chuckled. "I'm just giving you shit. You're the little sister I've never had, and I never thought of you any other way. I just figured that Carlyle moron would have made a move by now. You're pretty fucking fabulous." He clinked his glass to hers.

It was nice of him to say, but she sure didn't feel it at the moment. They stood and sipped their champagne in silence, Felicia avoiding glancing in Hudson's direction, even though she could have pinpointed him in the room without looking his way like she was a bat or a missile guidance system or a totally miserable heartbroken moron. The crush of people in the room, the low volume chatter that nearly drowned out the band, the constant stream of masked waiters bearing appetizers and champagne—none of it made a difference. She always knew where he was. Of course, Tyler, being Tyler, never looked away from the other man.

"Actually, it makes sense that you'd fall for him," Tyler said. "It seemed like you two have been spending a lot of time together."

"Only in an effort to get you and Sawyer to put an end to whatever bullshit was between you." *Shit!* She smacked her hand over her mouth, but it was too late. "Forget you heard that."

"What? Your mission of mercy?" He grinned at her and

shook his head.

She let out the breath she'd been holding. "You don't seem surprised."

"I rarely am." He tapped a fingertip to his temple. "You forget, my business is to always know what everyone else in the room is thinking."

Of all the— "You knew the whole time? The tickets? The dinners? And you never said *anything*? You are such a jackass."

"Without a doubt." And he seemed totally okay with that. He probably was. In all the years she'd known him, she'd never seen Tyler happier than when he was busting someone's chops.

"So, what are you going to do about Hudson?" he asked.

"Nothing." She'd already wasted years of her life pining after a man. She wasn't about to repeat that mistake again. "I'm not his type."

Tyler snorted. "If you say so."

Thankfully, he let the topic drop after that, and they wandered over the to the silent auction table where people could bid on items patrons had donated. Tyler got drawn into a phone call, so she kept looking at all the items up for bid. It only took one look at the dollar amounts of the written bids, though, for her to know that she needed to keep moving. She loved her job at the museum, but there was a reason why she lived in a tiny one room.

The hint of something dangerous in the air hit her a half second before Hudson stepped up next to her. "How's the date going?"

Like she was going to tell him. She inhaled a strengthening breath and kept her attention focused on the bid sheet for a six-night stay in a Bali resort. "Fabulous."

"Then why is Tyler laughing with Sawyer instead of dancing with you?" he asked, taking her by the shoulders and turning her so she could see the other men standing behind her.

Ignoring—okay, pretending to ignore—the sparks of attraction raining down on her from his fingertips on her bare skin, she looked at Sawyer and Tyler. They were laughing. Both looked younger, happier, more at ease. She could totally picture them in prep school and college stirring up all sorts of trouble. She couldn't help but smile, despite the giant jerkwad beside her turning her panties to ash with the barest brush of his fingertips on her shoulders. Fuck. She was pathetic.

Using her annoyance with herself for something productive, she aimed her ire at Hudson. "I thought that was the entire reason for your little project with me—so those two would reforge their friendship." She added a few pounds of snottiness to her tone. "It's not like we're each other's type, right?"

One eyebrow went up, and his gaze dropped to her mouth, then lower before making it back up to her face. "I wouldn't say that."

"Really?" She would have laughed out loud at his bald-faced lie, but her chest hurt too much to make that loud a sound. Across the room, Tyler smiled and started over toward her. "Well, it doesn't matter now. We both got what we wanted."

"Yes," Hudson said, his hand slipping away from her. "We did. Exactly."

Helene's appearance a moment later saved Felicia from having to respond. Almost regal in her formal dress, the glittering half mask on a stick she held up to her face did nothing to change that impression. Together, the three of them made small talk about the items up for bid as the dancers swirled around in tuxedos and colorful dresses behind them.

When the song ended and another began, Helene gave a little gasp of delight. "Oh, I love this song. Your father and I used to dance to it all the time."

Hudson held out his arm. "Shall we?"

"Oh no, I'm not in the mood tonight," Helene said and turned her attention to Felicia. "You two go out there for me."

Team Oh Yeah and Team Fuck No revved their engines in her stomach. Dance? With Hudson? That way lay madness and ruin.

"I couldn't," she said, opting for chickening out like the smart person she was.

"I insist," Helene said, all but shoving Felicia and Hudson toward the dance floor. "Go on."

There was no graceful way of getting out of this. She looked over at Hudson. The grim line of his mouth and pinched look around his eyes said he felt exactly the same way she did, just probably not for the same reasons. He sure wasn't worried about melting into a puddle of want on the dance floor. Without a word, they walked out onto the dance floor.

. . .

Welcome to hell, Carlyle.

No talking.

No laughing.

No eye contact.

No teasing.

No flirting.

No gross ant facts.

Just two silent people moving to the music like they were dancing in fast-drying cement. It fucking sucked.

Hudson made sure to keep the socially acceptable distance between him and Felicia as they danced, but it wasn't enough. He needed at least a football field between them not to want her. Who was he kidding? He'd need to be in another solar system. Especially with her in that blue dress that managed to highlight her every curve while making him desperate to peel the material away from her soft skin so he could see everything hiding beneath. Not that it mattered. She could be in that horrible sack of a black dress that he'd first spotted her in and he'd want her. That she wasn't in that dress and that this one was bought specifically for Tyler served as the perfect reminder that this was it—their last dance. She had what she wanted. He'd done his Henry Higgins. Now it was time for them to go their separate ways.

He wanted to say something, but for once the words didn't come—and it didn't seem like she was interested in hearing him anyway. Felicia maintained her stiff body language and pointedly kept her sweet mouth shut. It gutted him.

"Matches."

Finally, she looked up at him, something a lot like hurt shining behind her glasses. Fuck. He'd screwed this all up. Right on cue, he felt the tap on his shoulder.

"Mind if I cut in?" Tyler asked.

Mind if I punch you in the face? "Of course."

Like the asshole he was, Hudson let go of the one woman he couldn't stop wanting, made way for the man she actually wanted to dance off with, and walked off to the bar for a stiff drink he could drown in. His luck was obviously holding, though, because by the time he got two fingers of scotch, his mom, Everly, Sawyer, and Clover had joined him.

"They make a lovely couple. Don't you think?" Helene asked. "Whoever fixed them up should be commended—and if he or she is single, they should definitely find the perfect match for themselves."

"They really do look good together," Everly agreed, staring at Hudson as if she knew *exactly* what he was thinking.

The shittiest part of it was that they did. They were a dark haired, blue-eyed couple moving with ease across the dance floor as if they'd always been destined to do it. It made him want to fucking puke. Instead of revisiting dinner, he downed what was left in his glass and signaled to the bartender for another. By the time they started announcing the winners of the silent auction, the alcohol had softened the edges of his reality. Then, the master of ceremonies called Felicia's name. She'd had the winning bid for an original Hughston, her choice, from his show opening next week. He knew damn well she couldn't have afforded the winning bid in the hundreds of thousands. But Tyler? That asshole had money in the bank. She must have made the same connection because she was arguing with the other man, who just shrugged. Finally, she gave him a soft smile, and unless the alcohol was making Hudson see things, Felicia leaned up and gave Tyler a kiss on the cheek.

Someone growled in disapproval. It took Hudson a second to realize he'd made the sound.

Everly wrapped her fingers around his forearm, halting his progress toward Felicia and Tyler. "You aren't going to do anything dumb, are you?"

Too late for that. He'd already done it. Like a total chump, he'd fallen in love with someone he could never have. "Like what?"

"You tell me," Everly said, taking away his mostly empty third glass of scotch and setting it down on the bar. "I'm not sure what's going on with you right now, and I've known you since we had Art Appreciation 101."

"I'm not going to do anything dumb." He picked his glass up off the bar and held it up so the bartender would see he needed another.

Everly shook her head, concern forming a V between her dark eyes. "I hope you're sure about that."

"I am." He was going to get comfortably numb while watching Felicia finally get what she'd always wanted. It's what he did. He made sure everyone around him was happy. He was a fixer. He just couldn't fix himself.

The bartender came over and poured Hudson a finger of scotch. All it took was an uncharacteristic glare from him, though, and the bartender poured another. That was more like it.

"They're leaving," Everly said.

He turned before he could stop himself and caught the sight of Felicia walking away and out of his life.

"To another successful fix-up," he said, holding his glass aloft in a toast.

Everly rolled her eyes at him but kept her comments—for once—to herself. Thank God. The voice in his head cursing him out for letting Felicia go was loud enough as it was.

Chapter Nineteen

The scotch had done its best to grind away the world's sharp edges, but they were still there, jabbing Hudson in the stomach, and there was only one way to make that feeling go away.

After the Uber driver pulled away from Everly's building, he meant to give the driver the address to his penthouse. But that's not what he told the nice lady with the spiked pink hair and the neck tattoo of a tiger. He gave her Felicia's address. That's how he ended up on the street where she lived, standing outside her apartment while Honeypot wailed in greeting.

She was probably in there with Tyler. That's why he was here. His subconscious knew that he needed to see it. See them together—not in a stalker kind of way but more in a pound your head against the wall spiked with rusty nails kind of way. So here he was. The kitchen light was off, but a dim light from somewhere deeper inside the apartment that sent enough light to outline Honeypot as she sat on the kitchen window sill. It probably came from her bedroom. That's probably where they were, on that big blue bedspread of hers with all the girlie pillows scattered on the floor.

His gut contracted and twisted itself into a knot that had him seeing red dots at the edges of his vision.

The smart thing would be to turn around and head back to his side of town, using the long walk to clear his head. Instead, the next thing he knew he was walking down the stairs to her door and knocking on it.

Felicia opened it a few seconds later with Honeypot in her arms, wearing black yoga pants and a threadbare long-sleeved T-shirt that Honeypot was in the process of shredding. She didn't have any makeup on. Her hair was yanked back into a ponytail, big, chunky strands of which had escaped. The tip of her nose was red and her eyes puffy behind her glasses.

Hudson clenched his hands into fists. "What did Captain Clueless do?" Whatever it was, he was going to pay for it.

"Tyler?" She blinked. "Nothing."

Something had happened, and he was going to do whatever it took to fix it. He just had to find out what happened first. "Then why do you look like you've been crying?"

She clamped down on Honeypot as the cat renewed its attempts to break free. "I always get that way when I'm in the middle of a fascinating article about honeypot ant queens that can lay two thousand eggs a day."

Ants. He was keeping her from reading about ants. Relief seeped through the tight knot of his shoulder muscles, knocking out some of the frustrated tension acting as a vice. Of course, that only left the Felicia-sized hole inside him, and nature abhorred a vacuum. All the want and need and bittersweet-tinged lust roared to the forefront, powerful enough to propel him through the door. He closed it behind him with a backward kick, and he cupped her face in his hands. Honeypot let out a squawk and managed to wriggle free of Felicia's hold as he backed her up so her ass was against her blue chair. The tip of her tongue snuck out and wet her lips, and he had to bite back a desperate groan.

"What are you doing?" she asked, her voice breathy as a pink flush colored her cheeks.

"Making a mistake." One he'd pay for, but he couldn't care less.

She tugged her bottom lip between her teeth as she looked up at him. "Then why not leave?"

"I can't." And it was the truth—for tonight anyway.

He crashed his mouth down on hers, desperate for her. Sex had never been more than scratching an itch for him—until Felicia. She'd changed everything. This had to be it, the last time, because there was no way he could walk away if they kept this up. Seeing her with Captain Clueless tonight had proven that.

He didn't strip her bare. There wasn't time. The need to be the only man she could want for this one moment in time was too strong.

He tore his lips from hers. "Take off those yoga pants."

She did, her eyes blazing with the same urgency blasting through him. He grabbed his wallet, had his pants shoved down around his thighs and had a condom in his hand by the time she sent the black Lycra sailing through the air.

"Are you wet for me?" he asked as he rolled it on. "Even without me even touching you?"

"Yes," she said, her voice husky with desire.

"How wet?"

She slipped her hand between her legs. Despite her wide stance, the long length of her T-shirt kept him from seeing as much as she wanted. Frustration nipped at him, making his muscles tighten as he watched her wrist push against the hem of her shirt. He wanted to holler at her to stop and keep going forever at the same time. Damn, this woman and her ability to make him insane. And just when he thought he couldn't take any more, she lifted her busy hand to her lips, mimicking his move from weeks ago, and traced her glistening finger across her lips.

Challenge gleaming in her eyes, she asked, "Why don't you kiss me and find out?"

Whatever tenuous hold he had on his sanity snapped. Whatever happened next didn't matter. It was just about right now.

He grabbed her by the waist and lifted her up at the same time as he spun around so his ass was propped against the blue chair. Demanding mouth on his, fingers yanking against his hair, she lifted her hips enough that the head of his cock was at her entrance. She didn't hesitate, didn't tease. Without even a heartbeat of a pause, she impaled herself on him, sliding down until he was buried to the hilt and her legs were wrapped snug around his waist.

"So. Fucking. Tight." And wet. Jesus the sounds their bodies made as they moved together.

He squeezed her bucking hips in his hands, helping her to raise and lower herself so fast it was nearly a blur.

"Love how you fill me up," she said, panting. "How you make me want more, even though I know I can't take it."

"Oh, you can take it. You can take it all."

And he wanted to give it to her, every inch and so much more to the woman he loved. The realization made him miss a stroke, but she wasn't having it. She arched her back and reached below them cupping his balls.

"I'm so close." She let out a yearning moan. "Just fuck me as hard as you can."

That he could do. Renewing his efforts, he plowed into her as she rode him with an almost frenzied focus. Her bouncing tits were in his face, and he sucked a nipple into his mouth, biting down with enough pressure to elicit a mewl of approval as she sped up her hips, rubbing hard against him where their bodies met on each downward stroke. He bit down again and tugged the stiff peak. She nearly pulled out his hair in response, her core squeezing his dick so tight his climax was making his balls tingle a half second later.

Desperate not to come before her, he ground her against him, making sure her clit made contact. "Matches, I—"

Before he could finish his plea, her entire body bowed, and she cried out. His body responded instantly, his orgasm slamming into him and knocking out everything except for one thought. This whole time he'd thought he was giving the lessons to Felicia, but he'd ended up the one who got schooled.

• • •

Felicia didn't know where she was. She could be floating in space for all she knew. That's what it felt like. It was like that first bite of chocolate after a really shitty day, when her entire body relaxed and she settled into as close to a Zen state of mind as she ever got. Her eyelids were heavy, but she forced herself to open them.

The first thing she saw was the curve of Hudson's jaw. The first shadow of a beard was starting to show. She wanted to trace her fingers over the coarse spikes to remind herself he was real. That they'd just had crazy hot monkey sex in her living room. That maybe…

"Felicia." Hudson lowered her feet to the floor and took a step back, taking his warmth and that fuzzy, happy feeling with him.

She took a deep breath. That did not sound like the beginning of a conversation she wanted to have wearing only a T-shirt that was half hanging off her—her yoga pants had been tossed somewhere else during the frenzy of touching, licking, sucking, and fucking.

"We need to talk," he said.

Yep. Definitely a fully-dressed type of conversation. "Let

me just put my pants back on."

She crossed over to where her yoga pants had landed on the table lamp and yanked them off the shade. Of course, her cell phone started buzzing like crazy. It was too late to be anyone but family, and she knew better than to try to ignore the Hartigans—even at a time like this. If she didn't answer, she could set the timer for the moment they'd be at her door.

"Do you mind grabbing that?" she asked. "It's probably my sister, Fallon, and she's an emergency room nurse across the harbor in Waterbury who expects me to be murdered at any moment since I live in the city."

Ramble? Her? Never.

Hudson, still soft around the edges and almost fully dressed—although the buttons on his shirt would probably never be found—walked over to the kitchen island and picked it up right as it stopped buzzing.

"It's not your sister," he said, his voice hard.

In the middle of pulling on her pants, she looked up. Hudson's face had lost the satisfied look of a minute before. Instead, it was all sharp angles and hard planes. They ended up meeting halfway, and he handed her the phone then went to work buttoning his pants. Lungs tight, she glanced down at her cell's screen.

Tyler: *Thanks for tonight. Sleep well. You're going to need that energy for tomorrow.*

"You made the right move not inviting him in," Hudson said as he slipped his belt through the buckle with jerky movements.

What was his problem? She and Tyler were going jogging tomorrow morning. It wasn't like...*oooohhhhh.* He thought something totally different. In any other circumstance, that could be a good thing if it bothered him. But with Hudson? He'd already declared she wasn't his type. The memory of hearing those words coming out of his mouth put her on guard.

"Oh really," she asked, bracing for a blow. "Why's that?"

He smoothed his belt through the loop, then turned his attention to her, giving her an assessing up and down. "After you've worked so hard for so long to get him to notice you, you don't want to just bang him right away. Gotta make him work for it."

It took a minute for her brain to make sense of his words. Was he slut shaming her? After what they'd done? After what they'd done on multiple occasions? *Oh. Hell. No.* "How dare you!"

"You dared with me on the first date." He pointed over her shoulder. "Right there on that ottoman when you came around my fingers."

"Date?" It came out shrill, and she didn't care. He wasn't getting away with that kind of bullshit. "What date? It was all just a project, remember? Operation: Bromance. Because God forbid you ever go after something or someone just because you want it."

He started. "What the hell are you talking about?"

What was she talking about? Of course he would ask that. Of. Course. Heat slammed through her as all the pieces came together and exploded inside her like an atom bomb. It wasn't just that she wasn't his type. It was that none of what had happened between them—*none of it*—had ever meant anything to him. Not even the cabin. The realizations came in short bursts like gunfire aimed right at her chest. She'd thought she'd hurt before. She was wrong. So very wrong. About so much of it. If he hadn't been standing only a foot in front of her, she would have collapsed to the floor, but he *was* here, so that wasn't an option. Instead, she grabbed ahold of every bit of spit-in-your-eye, pissed-off Irish the Hartigan family had handed down to her and turned it on Hudson.

"You like to think that you're so fucking superior, the man who sees all and knows what people really want. That's why you have that stupid secret cabin where you get to pretend to be the man behind the curtain who controls it all. And why?" She marched up to him and jabbed a finger in his unrelenting chest. "Because it makes you feel good to have that secret. *That's* the real reason you haven't told your family that you're Hughston, not some bullshit about your dad."

He brushed her hand aside and glared down at her. "You don't know what you're talking about," he snarled.

"I'm a trained scientist who observes for a living." *That's right, buddy. Undergrad. Grad. Doctoral thesis. This is what I do.* "You wanna know what I see when I step back and look at the contained and compartmentalized habitat you've created for yourself?"

His mask slid into place, and he lifted an eyebrow as if he could barely contain his boredom but had decided to indulge her. "Enlighten me, Ant Lady."

"I see a man who likes to think that he's all about sacrificing for the people he loves, but it's a lie. *You're* a lie." Just like the supposed friendship between them that had turned to something more for her. Tears burned in her eyes but she blinked them away. So much for her keen observational skills if she'd missed all of that until it was too late. It was too little, too late, but she saw it all now. "You keep your whole life, the important parts of it, secret. You wear that fake as shit Mr. Charming mask and you let people think they know you when they don't have a clue. You think you're being gallant letting people have their illusions. But you're not. You're being a total chickenshit who's too scared to show the world who he really is and what he really values."

· · ·

If Hudson looked down, there'd be a giant gaping hole in his chest. He was sure of it. He'd ached before. That had been nothing. This was like a baseball bat to the head but without the sweet relief of unconsciousness. So this was how it would end—with a bang of the non-orgasmic kind. Fine. He could do that.

Too mad to do anything but ignore the tears glimmering in her eyes, he went on the defensive. "So now it's my turn to take lessons from the woman who lives her life according to to-do lists she wrote as a fifteen-year-old?"

She gasped, her hand flying to her throat. "That's not fair."

"Matches, life isn't fair." If it were, they wouldn't be screaming at each other. "Get used to it. If I lie to the people I love, it's only because it makes everyone happier, makes their lives a little easier."

And that was *exactly* why he did it. He wasn't hiding anything, unless it was for their peace of mind. And as to being a fixer? Well, big fucking deal. He liked to help people. She could sue him.

"Sounds like rationalizing to me," she shot back, crossing her arms so that her tits rose higher under the sorry excuse of a shirt she was wearing.

Why was he even noticing that? He sure as hell shouldn't. What he needed to do was get the fuck out of here. His feet didn't move.

"I don't give two shits about what the way I live my life sounds like to a woman who spends her life in a lab surrounded by ants."

She flipped him off. "At least I know who I am and I'm honest about it."

"Oh really?" He laughed. It was a rough, mean sound that perfectly complimented the acidic anger flowing through his veins. She couldn't be right about him. She wasn't. "That's what you think?"

"It's the truth."

And she probably really thought it was. He may have been delusional when he fell for her, but she was just lying to herself. And if this was all imploding right before his eyes, he might as well go all in and watch the world burn down around him. He took in a deep breath, watching her whole body practically spark with fury as she stood in front of him, five-feet-nothing of ticked-off woman. Good. That's what he needed. She said he never took what he wanted? She was wrong. Because right now he needed her to despise him. It was the only way he could walk out that door. The only way he could stand seeing her beside Tyler at another Harbor City event. Or God forbid, at her wedding. So he ignored the voices telling him to shut the fuck up already and did what he had to do.

"I don't know whether to laugh at you, or pat you on the head and go my way, Matches, because the truth is that you don't have a fucking clue about anything, especially not what a real man and not a fifteen-year-old's fantasy of a man wants. Hell, you didn't even know what *you* wanted until I showed you."

Her eyes narrowed. "So now you're mansplaining my own wants and needs to me?"

"Someone has to." He reached out and glided his thumb across her full bottom lip. It was the wrong thing to do, but he couldn't stop himself. He needed to touch her. Righteous indignation still flared in her eyes, but her mouth softened just a bit. He could kiss her right now. It was the only fucking thing he *wanted* to do. But he couldn't. That wasn't what she needed—and to give her what she wanted he had to let loose with the napalm. "If you could've figured it out on your own then you wouldn't have fucked—repeatedly—the first guy who offered to help you learn what exactly it is that you need between your legs."

Her eyes went wide, and she inhaled a sharp breath. Her hand struck out, connecting with his cheek before he saw it coming. It hurt like a motherfucker, and he was glad it did.

"Get the fuck out of my apartment, and don't come back," she ordered, her voice shaking with emotion. "Ever."

"Gladly." He thought he couldn't feel worse. He was wrong. There were people whose parachutes hadn't opened that had experienced less pain than was breaking him from the inside out right now. But he turned his back on her, and his feet finally started to move toward the door. "You'll have to text me and let me know what Tyler thinks of that little moan you make when you come. Maybe you can give him a blowjob while you're on the ottoman. It's a good move. I taught you well."

"Just go," her voice broke.

Hudson yanked open the door and walked out, stopping halfway through, unable to keep moving without one last look at her. But it was too late. By the time he'd turned, she was already gone. Her bedroom door that had been open before was now closed. It was for the best. How else could it have ever ended for a man like him but with misery? He closed the door and headed for the only place in the world where he could escape.

Chapter Twenty

Felicia had texted in sick again. Two days in a row. This was a first. Part of her—a very tiny part—felt bad about it, the rest of her felt worse. Still in the same PJs she'd been wearing for the past seventy-two hours, she laid back in her bed and clicked start on the next episode of The Great British Bakeoff. She didn't even like to cook, but the show was soothing right up until someone's Baked Alaska melted. That was about as much drama as she could take today. Her still unfinished draft of her journal article was open on her laptop but she just couldn't force herself to do more than write a sentence and then promptly delete it so she gave in to the inevitable and clicked her laptop shut. British bakers, that was what she needed, not ants that reminded her of that first walk through the ant lab with Hudson.

Her phone buzzed on the nightstand. The Mouths group text notification lit up. Her brothers and sisters were chatting—not one day after she'd confessed all—okay, almost all because no one needed to know about the blowjob on the ottoman—to Fallon. This couldn't be good. She picked up her phone.

Frank: *I'm gonna kill him.*

Fallon: *We can use the hospital morgue to hide the body. No one will look there.*

Ford: *As an officer of the law, I am not endorsing any of this.*

Faith: *God, you've been an insufferable prick since you made detective.*

Fiona: *It's the asshole who broke your baby sister's heart we're talking about here, little brother.*

Finian: *Or did you turn in your balls in exchange for your badge? I hear that happens with cops. That's why real men become firefighters.*

Frankie: *High five!*

Faith: *What is wrong with your gender?*

Fiona: *Everything.*

Fallon: *What Fi said.*

Ford: *Some of us are too smart to go into burning buildings.*

Finian: *Good one. Like killer burn. Amazing. (Enough sarcasm in there Frankie?)*

Frankie: *Almost. He's a cop, though, so you know he's slow. A little more just to make sure he gets it.*

Finian: *Best, most amazing insult of all time.*

Frankie: *That'll do it.*

Ford: *Fuck the lot o' ya.*

Fallon: *Hello? Felicia. Broken heart. Giant asshole who needs his ass kicked. Any of this ringing a bell with you knuckleheads?*

Fiona: *Are we sure she even wants to unleash the full force of the Hartigans?*

…
…
…

Fiona: *Not one of you dipshits asked, did you?*

…
…
…

Fiona: *For the love of Mike. Don't do a fucking thing. She's a grown up. If she needs our help, she'll ask for it.*

Frankie: *You're so bossy.*

Fiona: *Pot? Kettle?*

As much sorta twisted, miserable fun as it was being a fly on the wall for this sibling conversation, it was time to set them straight.

Felicia: *Thanks, Fi and the rest of you, but I've got this.*

…
…

...

Fallon: *You didn't start a new group text stream for this convo did you, Frankie boy?*

Frankie: *Whoops.*

Faith: *And to think the entire neighborhood still thinks the Hartigan brothers are the hottest. If they only knew what idiots you were.*

Frankie: *It's not my brain they're after.*

Faith: *Ewwwwwwwwwwwwwwwwwwwwwwwwwwwwwwwwwwww!*

Fallon: *Felicia, you change your mind, let us know.*

Ford: *I was just joking about the officer of the law thing. I can be across the harbor in thirty if I use the sirens.*

That Mr. By the Book would violate procedure to make her feel better almost made her smile. He wouldn't kill Hudson. Frankie and Finian? Well, the twins had the hot heads to go with their chosen professions.

Felicia: *Thanks, guys. I'm fine.*

Finian: *You're not fine. All of those were single syllable words.*

Faith: *Butt out.*

Fiona: *What Faith said.*

Felicity: *Night. XOXO*

Felicia turned her phone over and buried it under a

pillow. Whether in person or in texts, her brothers and sisters couldn't end a conversation like normal people. There would be more smack talk and gossip, probably at least another half-hour's worth, before they'd finally be done. She loved them, but being around them right now—even if just via phone—was too much. All she wanted was to turn off her brain and watch British people baking and then, hopefully, sleep for a few hours without dreaming of Hudson like she had for the past two nights.

• • •

If it weren't for the potential of starting a massive wildfire, Hudson would have thrown a match in the mineral spirits and let the whole cabin burn down days ago. He couldn't sleep for longer than half an hour at a time. He couldn't paint. Eating wasn't even of interest so he had no idea if he could or he couldn't. All he knew was that he wanted to sit in the middle of the glorious light and stare at all the portraits for his show at Black Heart Gallery, despising each and every one. Before Felicia, he'd thought of them all as little slices of life in Harbor City. Now they just looked like lies—the kind others told him and, even worse, the kind he told himself.

The cabin had a huge fireplace. It would take all day, but he could probably take care of them all that way, and then he'd never have to come back here again.

Ten minutes later, he was still contemplating expending the energy to actually get up and start a contained blaze, when the sound of three car doors shutting came in fast succession. *Great.* He didn't need to look to see who it was, but he got up anyway and walked out onto the porch.

Linus, who had been the family's driver since time eternal, was still sitting in the black town car. However, Helene, Sawyer, and Clover were already making their way up to the stairs to the door. He knew at a glance why they were here. He should. He'd staged a similar intervention with Sawyer after he'd fucked things up royally with Clover. This was different, though. Sawyer and Clover loved each other. Hudson wasn't that fucking lucky.

Closing the door behind him, he stood in front of it and crossed his arms. "Did I forget a party invitation that I sent out?"

"You forgot to answer your phone," Sawyer said as he and Clover walked hand in hand up the steps.

"I've been busy," Hudson said, his voice sounding scratchy and used after four days by himself. "You know, with all my girlfriends."

"Excellent." Helene flashed him a brilliant smile and marched up to the porch. "Let's go meet them. I'm looking forward to being shocked. It's been decades since that happened."

One side step and there was no way his mom was getting past him. It was the smart move because once Helene, Sawyer, and Clover went through that door, there was no way to keep Hughston a secret anymore. She stopped in front of him, one steel eyebrow going up in command—an expression he'd used on her too many times to count. That's when it hit him. Helene Carlyle would take on a pack of rabid dogs for her family, and it was past time he stopped hiding this truth from her.

He let them walk in ahead of him so they could take in the room without watching their faces. All three stopped in the middle of the room as the afternoon sunlight streamed in and stared at the paintings. As usual before a show, canvases covered almost the entire space. It was worse this time because, in addition to the portraits for his show this weekend, Felicia looked out from canvas after canvas. Even after everything that had happened, he couldn't cover those paintings up. She just stared at him everywhere he walked, haunting him.

Sawyer let out a low whistle and turned around to face Hudson. "I should have brought a bottle of scotch."

Clover gave him a long look, no doubt taking in every detail of his current miserable condition. "I'm not sure forgetting is what he needs right now." She reached out and gave him a hug before pulling away, her nose wrinkled up. "But a shower has got to be up there on the list."

List.

Unbidden, an image of Felicia popped into his head. The mental image sliced through him like a rusty knife. "Right at the top of it."

"Hudson Bartholomew Carlyle." His mom's voice rang out through the open space as she stood in front of a painting of Felicia, showing how he'd seen her when she'd given him a tour of the museum art lab, right down to her messy ponytail, oversize ant shirt, and a wicked gleam in her eye. "This is your best work to date, but *this one* is my new favorite."

Clover scrunched up her face in question. Sawyer cocked his head in confusion. Hudson's stomach dropped down to his toes, and his brain went blank. His best work? How could she...

"What?" Helene said with an elegant shrug of one shoulder. "You thought I didn't know you're Hughston?"

He would have formed the obvious question if Clover didn't beat him to it. "What? Hughston? The painter?'

"So, no wild cabin orgies? Too bad." Sawyer took a closer look at the paintings then looked back at Hudson, pride obvious in his eyes. "Nicely done."

Mind still trying to process the revelation and reactions, he turned to his mom. "How did you find out?"

"Give me some credit. I *am* your mother," she said as she strolled from painting to painting, examining each one. "Do you really think every college's senior exhibition is so well attended by the critics?'

The exhibition had been packed with people, even his advisor had commented on it. And they were only there because of his family name? "You set me up?"

"No." She shook her head and crossed over to him, curling her arm around his waist. "I put the right people in the room. Everything else you did on your own."

"But Dad..." It didn't make sense. Not even a little bit. "He was adamant that I give it up. That's why I created Hughston."

Helene squeezed his waist and then walked over to the largest painting in the room. It was half finished. There was no missing who it was, though, and it just about killed him. He'd started it before...well, before. Now he could barely look at it let alone finish it.

"Your grandfather always hated this cabin," Helene said, looking around at the huge windows, stone fireplace, and timber walls.

"Why?" Clover asked. "It's gorgeous."

Helene glided her fingertips over the brushes sitting near the unfinished painting, a sad smile curling her lips. "Because this is where Michael had *his* art studio."

If she had told him his dad had been a purple dinosaur that spoke Chinese, he wouldn't have been more shocked. Not his dad. He wasn't a painter. He was a businessman. Focused. Intense. Determined to turn both of his boys into titans of the industry. An artist? It didn't make any sense.

"Your father and I met in class," Helene went on, looking at another painting but obviously seeing one that was only visible in her mind. "We always told you that but not the rest. It was a painting class, and I was the model. He was good, but not as good as you are Hudson. I wish he'd lived to see how talented you really are." Her chin trembled for the slightest of seconds before she closed her eyes and inhaled a deep breath. By the time she exhaled, she'd steadied herself. "Michael had the passion for it, but his work never found an audience, a fact that your grandfather reminded him of at every chance he got. So, when we decided to get married, your father gave up painting and turned all his attention to the business. He thought denying that part of himself was the best way to make sure his family was safe and secure." Another deep breath, her hand curled into a fist and pressed to her belly. "He sacrificed something that was important to him because he thought it was the best thing for those he loved. I tried to talk him out of it. In the beginning, I gave him brushes and paint, brought him here—but it only reminded him of what he saw as a painful failure, thanks to the way your grandfather needled him about it at every turn."

His grandfather had been a legendary asshole in the boardroom and outside of it. That he'd been a dick to his own son wasn't a shock.

"So, when you started painting," Helene said, "it brought back everything for your father, and he wanted to protect you from that disappointment. He wouldn't have ever ridiculed you, not like his father had, but he didn't want you to go through the agony of wanting something more than anything else in the world but not being able to get it. I tried to talk him out of his decision to threaten to cut you off, but he's a Carlyle, and you are all proof that the Carlyle men are an amazingly stubborn group of people."

"No argument there," Clover said, even as she snuggled in closer to Sawyer's side.

Helene strode over to Hudson, handing him the brush she'd been walking around with and curling his fingers around the wooden handle. Looking down, it was like seeing everything from far away. Maybe the anger, frustration, and sadness about all the time lost would come, but for now, all he could do was wonder what it would have been like if he'd only had the balls to tell his father the truth before he'd died.

"As parents, we want the best for our children, but sometimes we go about it in the wrong way," Helene said, tears again in her eye as she looked from him to Sawyer. "I am proof of that." She hooked her arm through his and walked him over to the unfinished painting of Felicia. "The whole time, though, your father knew he was wrong. He wanted to tell you, but he couldn't find the words. Your father's biggest regret was not going to your college exhibition. He never knew about Hughston. I couldn't tell him. It would have broken his heart if he'd known that he was forcing you into a double life. He loved you, please know that, but he thought he knew what was best for you and just wanted you to be happy. He really did think he was doing the right thing. I hope you don't ever make the same mistake your father and I did."

They stood in silence together, the kind that was almost lacking in gravity it was so pure, and looked at the half-finished painting of Felicia. He dropped the paintbrush to the floor and wrapped his arms around his mom, feeling for the first time since she'd come out of mourning just how fragile she was. She covered it up well. Like him, she was good at acting the part. But maybe now they wouldn't have to do so for each other anymore.

"Thanks for telling me, Mom," he said, his throat scratchy and raw. "I'm sorry I never told you. I should have told you both before he…"

The rest wouldn't come. It didn't matter. They both knew what he meant. After one more squeeze, Helene patted him on the back and stepped out of the hug.

"I'm going to go look around," she said. "It's been a long time."

She and Clover walked upstairs together. The fact that those two women got along as well as they did always surprised him, but it probably shouldn't—like connecting with like and all that.

Squatting down, he picked up the brush he'd dropped and put it down next to the unfinished painting, studiously avoiding looking at the bright blue of Felicia's eyes staring unblinkingly back at him. Sawyer joined him, his arms crossed over his chest as he took in the painting.

"Are you hiding out and smelling like shit because of her?" he asked.

"Who?" Hudson asked, feigning ignorance because Felicia was right, he was a chicken shit. "There are just so many women in my life."

"Cut the shit," his brother said. "It's so obvious that you're into Felicia that even I noticed during those client dinners with Tyler."

"No, that's just how we wanted it to look." Hudson's gut twisted, and all the rage at himself and the situation came back again. "It's Tyler she wants."

Sawyer mumbled something that sounded a lot like fucking dumb shit under his breath. "Is that what you're telling yourself?"

He didn't need to. It's what she'd told him—over and over and over again. "No, it's the truth."

"Since I've been with Clover, I've been trying to pay more attention to the details. You know what I just picked up on, little brother?" he asked, getting in Hudson's face. "You didn't say you hadn't fallen hard for Felicia. Shit. The evidence is right here." He jerked his chin at the row of paintings. "But if you want her, you're going to have to learn to fight for what you want. And sulking in this cabin isn't gonna solve shit."

Sulking? Anger stoked the flames of self-resentment and disappointment. He wasn't fucking sulking. She didn't want him for anything more than a hard fuck. Plain and simple. He was doing the right thing by leaving her alone. "Why don't you mind your own fucking business?"

Of course, Helene and Clover picked that moment to come back downstairs. His mom just looked from one son to the other and shook her head.

"Everything okay?" Clover asked.

"Yeah," Sawyer said, giving Hudson one last dirty look. "Someone just needs some alone time to pull his head out of his ass."

He walked them out and back to the car where Linus was reading a spy thriller. Hudson stayed out on the porch until the town car was only a speck at the end of the driveway. Fight for her. She hated him—he'd made sure of it because he knew what she wanted, what she needed. He was doing the right thing.

Two days later and he wasn't so sure doing the right thing meant shit anymore. He was a fucking mess. And he wanted Felicia more than his next breath. Worse, it took him two days to realize his brother was right. He was going to have to learn how to fight for what he wanted if he had any hope of winning her back. So what if she wanted Tyler right now? He'd made her want him, and he could do it again. Tyler would never make her happy, and her happiness was all that mattered to him.

But fuck him if he could figure out how to win her back. He'd intentionally burned a bridge with his angry words, and she'd been right all along. He was a coward. A chickenshit. Hiding out in his cabin, keeping a part of himself hidden from everyone. His heart skipped a beat thinking of his dad never knowing the man Hudson had become, never shared their love of art. All that wasted time. But he wasn't going to make that mistake again.

He was going to win Felicia back. Just as soon as he figured out how.

His mother's words came back to him and everything

crystalized in his head. Sometimes the right thing to do was the very worst move. He hurried back to the half-finished canvas, not stopping until he had a paintbrush in his hand. It was a bold move, but maybe—just maybe—it would work. Rushing around the open space, he ripped the sheets off the other paintings of Felicia. There were enough. The only question was would it be enough to make it up to her?

He grabbed his phone and hit Everly's number. She picked up right away.

"I'm trashing the show," he said, more sure about the plan with every heartbeat.

"What?" Everly squawked, losing her nothing-shocks-me Harbor City attitude for the first time in all the years he'd known her. "You can't back out. It's in three days."

"I'm not backing out," he said. "I'm giving you a whole new show. It'll be my best one yet."

It had to be. Words wouldn't be enough to make it up to Felicia. He had to show her.

. . .

Whoever Felicia thought might be on the other side of her front door, Helene Carlyle was definitely not it. She froze in surprise, and even Honeypot stopped trying to claw her way through Felicia's arms to freedom. What in the world was Hudson's mom doing in her thousand dollar Michael Kors at her basement apartment?

"Hi," she cracked out.

"Hello." Helene smiled, her nose twitched, and then she sneezed.

"Bless you." On automatic pilot as she tried to figure out what had happened, Felicia stepped aside. "Please come in."

Helene took one step inside, and Honeypot, obviously understanding a bigger, badder predator was in the room, squirmed out of Felicia's grip and sprinted into her bedroom where it was—no doubt—hiding under the bed.

From her spot just inside the closed door, Helene looked around the apartment, her gaze stopping on the Hughston print hanging on the wall. "I just had the most interesting conversation with my son, Hudson."

"Oh really? I'm not sure that's any of my business." And even if it was, she couldn't hear it. Today was the first day she'd managed to only think about him every other minute instead of every second.

One of Helene's eyebrows went up. "It is if you love him."

Okay. Mom wasn't pulling any punches. Too bad Felicia wasn't even stepping into the ring. "I don't."

"That's too bad because he's head over heels for you." Her nose twitched again and she sneezed into a delicate, pale handkerchief that she'd pulled from her pocket. "Sorry. I'm terribly allergic to cats. What's your cat's name?"

Felicia barely caught up with the quick turn of the conversation. "Honeypot."

There went that eyebrow of Helene's again. "An interesting name."

Felicia was too tired and too heartbroken to explain the origin of Honeypot's name. "She's an interesting cat."

"I just bet," Helene said. "You know, pets often take on the personality of their owner. I think that's what first caught Hudson's eye when it came to you and why he fell for you. Of course, I *could* be wrong. It has happened a time or two. But I'm sure I'm right. He's never been as happy as he has been since you two met at the museum fundraiser. I noticed that night when he couldn't take his eyes off you."

Felicia could totally see where Hudson had gotten his confidence *and* his willingness to manipulate a situation. However, this time Felicia wasn't falling for it.

"It wasn't like that between us." At least not in any way

that Hudson's mom needed to know about. She reached for the door handle. "Well, if there's nothing I can help you with…"

Helene gave her a considering look, the kind that probably turned people to nervous wrecks but only made Felicia ache because it reminded her so much of Hudson.

"No, nothing," the older woman said. "So sorry to have bothered you."

Felicia opened the door for Helene who walked through it as if she had minions to do that for her—which she probably did. However, she stopped halfway through the door.

"He's revamping his gallery show this weekend, you know," she said, turning back to face Felicia. "Everly told me he called her out of the blue and said he was changing everything. I'm not sure what the new show will focus on, but you should come. If you've never been to a Hughston show before, you're really missing out."

Felicia blinked in surprise. *His* show? She knew? Talk about burying the lead. That was the kind of information that went up front. "He told you?"

"Darling, he didn't have to tell me. We mothers always know. But yes, he finally confessed." She withdrew a postcard-sized invitation from her handbag and gave it to Felicia. "Here's a VIP invitation to the show, just in case you decide to come. You should bring Tyler. It's so nice to have him back in the family fold. Good-bye, darling."

Then without another word, Helene strode out the door and up the steps to the town car double-parked at the curb where a man in a chauffeur's uniform was waiting to open the car door for her. Felicia looked down at the invitation. It listed Hughston's name, the Black Heart Gallery, and the time. She read it over at least ten times, clenching her jaw tight to keep from crying, and then dropped it into the trash can in the kitchen and heading into her bedroom to make an early night of it.

Chapter Twenty-One

Every table in the new Grounded Coffee location down the block from Felicia's apartment was taken up by someone with a laptop or a pair of moms with strollers parked nearby. It was loud, crowded, and the last place in the world she wanted to be. She'd been to work, wasn't that enough peopling for one day?

"If you even try to make a run for it, I'm blocking the door," Tyler said, taking a step between her and her escape route.

"That's false imprisonment," she said with one last wistful look toward the exit that would get her back to her apartment sooner.

He shook his head and corralled her into the line of caffeine addicts and muffin munchers. "Felicia, you can't hide away another day. It's either coffee with me, or I call in your brothers."

Oh God. All the Hartigans crowded into her apartment was the last thing she needed. "You wouldn't."

"Not if you sit your butt down and have an espresso."

The mention of coffee reminded her of the time Hudson had brought a cardboard tray of drinks to her house because he wasn't sure what she liked. "Green tea."

"Whatever." Tyler shrugged. "Just order, and then we'll go scare off some wifi freeloader to get a table."

The simplicity of that plan—as devious as it was—made her laugh for the first time in days. "Blackmailing me isn't nice."

"Yeah." He grinned. "But it gets the job done."

They ordered and Tyler did, indeed, glare at a guy with a laptop and six empty disposable coffee cups scattered on his table. In the end, the woman next to him left her table and they snagged it. After they sat down, she grabbed the print outs she'd made for Tyler. Distraction? Her? Never.

"Here's the information you wanted on that museum donor," she said, handing them over. "What are you after anyway?"

He folded up the papers without looking at them and slid them underneath his phone on the table. "Nice try on swapping the subject."

Well, it was worth a try. "We were talking about something?"

"Yeah. You hiding."

"There's nothing to talk about." It's not like it would do any good anyway. Hudson was as good as his word. After she'd banished him from her apartment, he'd stayed away. "My love life is a topic best left buried with the salted earth."

"Don't blame yourself for falling for me," Tyler said, teasing. "It's hard not to love me when I'm hot, smart, and rich."

But there was hard not to love and then there was impossible not to love. Everything with Tyler had been built on a teenage girl's belief of what the perfect man would be like. Hot. Smart. Rich wasn't necessary but it sure didn't hurt things. It wasn't a bad list, but she should have been smart enough to realize love needed more variables than just that. Instead, she'd put that down on her list and refused to budge on it, despite all the proof that her hypothesis was wrong—until falling for Hudson had forced her to reevaluate everything. Her gut told her she was onto something, but she had to test it out.

Cheeks burning with embarrassment, she took a drink of green tea for fortification. "Ask me what color underwear I'm wearing."

Tyler blanched. "Please don't make me do that. You're like my sister and there are some things I don't want to know."

There were things she no longer wanted him to know, but that didn't matter right now. "Just ask."

He grimaced and closed his eyes. "Undies. What color?"

"None of your business." She wasn't even *tempted* to tell him that they were green.

He let out a sigh of relief. "Thank God."

Now for a question that was only slightly less embarrassing. "Call me Matches."

"I think it's time to call Fallon." He reached for his phone.

She slapped her hand down over his, holding him down. "Do. It."

His eyes went wide. "Matches."

Nothing. Not even a blip in her heart rate. She grabbed her phone and scrolled through her texts. All she had to do was see Hudson's name for her pulse to pick up, her palms to sweat, and her lungs to tighten. It had never been visceral reactions like that with Tyler. With him, it had all been about the thrill of checking something off her to-do-before-thirty list. Evidence. This was all observable fact and it meant only one possible conclusion. She hadn't just wanted Hudson. She hadn't just fallen for him. She was irrevocably in love with him.

"Oh God," she said, taking another sip. "This is worse than I thought."

"The tea?" he asked. "Of course it is. It's crap. You should switch to coffee."

Well, at least she wasn't the only one who was totally clueless. "I'm in love with Hudson."

"And this is a newsflash?" Tyler relaxed back against his chair and laughed.

Okay, maybe she was the only one. The words bubbled out of her, "I tried to use you to make him jealous. Like an immature asshole. I teased him, tried to seduce him, the whole time telling him it was because I wanted another lesson so I could catch you."

Tyler leaned forward, propping his elbows on the table and holding up a single finger. "One. TMI." A second finger joined the first. "Two. You're not the first person in the world to do something idiotic because they were in love."

"You don't understand." She swallowed past the lump in her throat. "We fought. I said horrible things to him, and he did to me."

"So write him off." Tyler shrugged. "You'll find someone else. Lots of fish in the sea. Look at how fast you got over me."

"I was never in love with you, not really." The truth her body had known faster than her thick head.

Tyler smacked his hand over his heart in a teasing gesture. "Looks like I'll need to find the first available hot chick to help me build up my fragile male ego to recover from that blow." Then he dropped his hand and got a serious look that usually meant he was in mid-scheme planning. "So you know what you need to do now."

Her brain when blank. "What?"

"What happened the first time you presented your dissertation?" he asked.

Okay, that was a total left turn—although an equally humiliating one. "They sent me home. They thought it lacked in creativity."

Tyler nodded and took a drink of his coffee. "So you just gave up?"

"No." She shook her head. "I revised and reworked it and re-presented it."

"You fought for it," he said like a lawyer leading a witness.

"Well, yeah…." The rest of the words died on her lips because the Eureka lightbulb went off again, this time with enough power to blind her to everything except what needed to happen next. "Just like I'm going to fight for Hudson, but this time I'm going to need a solid from you."

"Anything."

"We have to go see your upstairs neighbor."

His face fell. "Anything but that."

Faster than he could blink, she snatched the information she'd printed out from the museum donor database. "Help me, or I'll shred this."

He groaned and gave her a sour look. She'd just wait him out.

"Fine," he said with a snarl. "She's usually home practicing her marching drills on the day before a new show opens up at her gallery."

"You seem to know a lot about her for someone who can't stand her."

"She lives above me and her gallery takes up a good chunk of the street level part of the building," he argued, becoming suddenly fascinated with the sugar packets on the table. "Of course I know her patterns."

"And that's all there is to it?" she asked, enjoying being on the other side of the needling for once.

"Stop trying to change the subject again," he said, standing up. "Come on, let's go get our meeting with the shrew over and done with."

Fine with Felicia. The sooner she got this plan in motion, the better.

• • •

Everly had just popped the last two Tums tablets when the knock at her door sounded. Great. Only shitty news came on the day before a show opening. Kind of like how all you had to do was come into a little bit of extra money for something expensive to break—or at least that's how it always seemed. But she hadn't made her way up from the free and reduced lunch line in grade school to graduating college in four years despite working two jobs to pay for it to owning her own art gallery by hiding in her kitchen and giving into the nerves gnawing a hole in her stomach. She strode to the door in her bare feet—thank you bitching downstairs asshole Tyler Jacobson—and peeked through the peephole

Think of the conceited jerk of a neighbor and he appeared.

"Great," she mumbled to herself.

Since she didn't back down—ever—Everly slipped on the four-inch heels next to the door and opened it. "What do you want?"

The small brunette who'd wrecked Hudson—Felicia—spoke up first. "Your help."

"Sorry, I gave at the office." She started to shut the door, but Tyler's hand on the doorframe stopped her.

He thought she wouldn't smash his fingers? He was optimistic. Okay, he was also right, but she didn't need him to know that so she started to push the door shut anyway.

Tyler's size twelve foot blocked her progress. "Pretend I'm not here, and just listen to Felicia."

"Why should I?" she asked.

His sharp blue eyes narrowed like he could see right into the center of her and divine exactly what she wanted most out of life—and it wasn't a pony. "Because I can get the building owner to stop delaying and re-sign your gallery lease without the ten percent rent increase he wants."

He shoots. He scores.

"How can you swing that?"

The cocky grin on his face did a number on her panties—despite her better judgement's protests.

"Don't ask me any questions, and I won't tell you any lies," he said.

Everly had grown up in a part of Harbor City where TVs that had fallen off trucks were sold in neighborhood stores and every third kid had an uncle who *knew* people. A little funny business that could keep her gallery in the black and no one got hurt or ended up in jail? Yeah, she wasn't going to lose a minute of sleep over it.

"She comes in," she said. "You stay out."

"What?" he asked, looking every bit like a bad idea she'd end up regretting. "I don't get to see the parade grounds where you march around?"

Yep. That's right. Asshole.

She rolled her eyes. "Good one. I'm laughing on the inside."

"Really? I always figured your sense of humor was as nonexistent as your heart."

"Ouch. I might cry." If she wasn't having so much fun fighting, damn her snarly Harbor City soul.

"If you two are done flirting," Felicia said with a huff. "I'd like to get this settled. Tyler, I'll meet you down in your apartment in a little bit."

The other woman ducked under Tyler's arm and strode into the apartment, swinging the door shut behind her. Tyler got his fingers out of the way just in time. Everly would have liked her if it wasn't for the fact that Hudson was obviously in love with her and she'd stomped all over his heart to the point that he insisted on changing out the paintings for an entire show days before it was set to go on. Hudson was one of her oldest friends and—truth be told—one of only a few, which was why she'd been eating Tums like candy since he'd called with an update on the show tomorrow and asked for a favor that she definitely did not want to fulfill.

She eyeballed Felicia, giving her all the attitude she deserved. "Spit it out and leave."

"I need you to make sure Hudson shows up for his show tomorrow," Felicia said.

Now that was a record scratch moment. "*His* show?"

Felicia crossed her arms and gave as good a glare as she got. "I don't have time to pretend. Just make sure he's there."

"Why should I?" Besides the fact that Hudson's favor had been to make sure Felicia was there.

"Because I need to talk to him."

"So go to his penthouse." Like a normal person.

Her cheeks turned pink. "I can't."

"Why not?" Everly asked, actually curious.

The short brunette didn't say anything at first, then let out a deep breath. "This is bigger than just showing up at his front door."

"What, are you going to lay prostrate in front of him and beg his forgiveness for being a total bitch?" Because that is what she'd been. Hudson hadn't told her everything Felicia had said, but he'd told her enough. The fact that the other woman hadn't been totally wrong was the only reason Everly hadn't told Hudson to check his head when he'd asked her to make sure Felicia was at the show.

"Something like that." Felicia turned away, glancing out the windows overlooking the park before turning back with tears in her eyes. "Because I love him and I was too dumb to tell him when I should have."

It wasn't an exact replica of what Hudson had told Everly, but it was close. "And if he doesn't want to see you?"

"I can't give up without a fight," she said, sounding every bit as fierce as a woman in love needed to be to survive it.

"He's worth fighting for?" Everly pushed, letting her voice soften just the slightest bit.

Felicia pushed up her glasses, set her shoulders, and looked her straight in the eye. "Without a doubt."

Everly had enough experience being on the receiving end of some serious lies to know the difference. "I'll see what I can do."

"Thank you." She nodded and turned for the door.

Oh no, she wasn't getting out of here that easily. "Hey, Felicia?"

"Yeah?" she asked, pivoting to face Everly.

She didn't have brothers. Or sisters. Or very many friends. But she knew about loyalty and commitment. She knew the importance of people having your back—and she had Hudson's. "Break his heart again, and I'll break your face."

Felicia' grinned. "I'd expect nothing less."

Then she walked out, still five-feet-nothing tall but looking a lot bigger.

Everly stared at her closed door for a minute, contemplating what was going to happen tomorrow night. If she were a nicer person, she would have told Felicia that Hudson had a surprise planned for her at the gallery and had begged her to make sure Felicia showed up. Of course, she'd probably still be living in that shithole apartment she'd grown up in if she'd been a nicer person. Plus, as one of Hudson's closest friends, she wanted to see the woman who'd put him through the wringer dangled out there in uncertainty a while longer. What could she say, she was a bitch when it came to people who hurt those she loved.

She started back toward the kitchen, and her heels clicked on the wood floor. Stopping immediately, she started to take her shoes off, but then an image of Tyler's cocky smirk flashed in her mind. Jerk. Hot jerk, but still a jerk. And a slow one. If he'd been faster on the uptake, he would have thought to include no more walking around in shoes as part of his little pot sweetener to talk to Felicia.

"Score one for me."

She strutted across to the kitchen, letting her feet fall a little heavier than necessary. The answering *thunk, thunk* of a broom handle banging against his ceiling did nothing but result in a satisfied smile curling her lips.

Chapter Twenty-Two

Felicia held up the blue wrap dress. It was perfect for what needed to happen next at the gallery. Hudson would see her in the dress, think about how she'd been wearing it the first time they'd had sex, and it would give her the twenty seconds she needed to get him to talk to her. They'd both said horrible things—awful, mean, but probably true things that had hurt each other. If he wanted to keep Hughston a secret from his family, that was his choice, although it seemed like he'd finally told his mom at least. It didn't change the fact that she'd fallen in love with him and had spent the last few days realizing that life without him was way shittier than she remembered. That was gonna change. She just needed to get him to listen to her.

Holding up the dress to her body for a final look before putting it on, something else caught her eye in the mirror's reflection. A line of black in her closet wrapped in a dry cleaner's clear plastic. It was the dress she'd worn to the museum fundraiser the night she'd met Hudson. Good for parties and funerals she'd told him. It was her happy birthday early gift from her mom and tomorrow was her birthday.

Fallon had dragged her out of her apartment earlier in the week and talked her into getting it altered so it fit better. The plan had been for that to make Felicia feel better too but only one person could do that—Hudson.

Without a second thought, she rehung the blue dress and slipped on the black one. It was a bit shorter and more form fitting than before but it was still her. She left her hair down so that it dropped to almost her shoulders in soft waves. A swipe of red lipstick and she was as ready as she could be for facing the unknown without a hypothesis but with a tightly held hope.

When she walked out into the living room, she found Tyler in a tense face off with Honeypot. They eyed each other warily from opposite sides of the kitchen.

"I think it's plotting my death," Tyler said, never taking his eyes off the pacing cat.

There was exactly one person Honeypot liked on a consistent basis and the man in her kitchen wasn't him. "Probably."

She slipped her feet into her black kitten heels and grabbed her purse from the counter, her movements jittery as she tried to give herself a mental pep talk. Public declarations were so not her. Frankie? He'd kick ass at that, which was as it should be since he seemed to fuck up with women so much. Faith? As brash as she was brave, she'd do it without a second thought. But Felicia? The Hartigan who hated speaking up in staff meetings of five let alone in a room full of Harbor City art snobs? It made her want to puke.

"You sure you want to do this?" Tyler gave her shoulders a quick hug.

She didn't even have to think about it. "I've never been more sure of anything."

He grinned. "Then let's go get your man."

• • •

Exhausted and still a little paint covered, Hudson prowled the Black Heart Gallery, looking every bit like a man who hadn't slept for more than thirty minutes at a time for days. It wasn't his best look. It sure wasn't the way people expected him to look. Screw them. Finally, seeing Felicia and showing her exactly what she meant to him was the only important thing. Everly had promised that Felicia would be here.

That she would be was the one thing that had gotten him out of the cabin this morning to hand-deliver all of the paintings in a totally unprofessional, last minute move. Normally, it took days to get the artwork arranged and hung. Everly had cursed him out and called him every name in the book—all while cajoling him into eating something more than sugared up coffee—during the process.

Everly stopped next to him and stared at his favorite painting. The one that he'd stayed up most of the night like a man possessed to finish. The giant canvas said everything he'd never be able to put into words. He just hoped it would be enough.

"This is so raw," Everly said. "Are you sure you want to do this? It could backfire. She doesn't seem like the showy type."

"It could, but it's the only way I can tell her everything." For once, words had failed him.

"Well, it's definitely all in there." Everly sighed. "We would have made a killing off these."

"They're not for sale," he said, the words coming out more harsh than he'd meant.

"Believe me, I'm going to lose my voice telling that to everyone tonight." She gave him a quick hug. "Time to open the doors."

She walked away, leaving Hudson alone to stare up at

Felicia's face on the canvas. He'd painted it from one of the sketches he'd done of her at the cabin. She had just-been-fucked hair and a satisfied smile on her face. The sheet was draped around her hips, and her arm lay in front of her chest, blocking the viewer from seeing anything beyond the upper swell of her breasts. What gutted him, though, was the mixture of confidence and compassion, vulnerability and strength, the know-it-all and the curious-about-everything that came through. And it wasn't just on this canvas. Everywhere he looked she was there. The way her skin flushed when she got nervous. The strands of hair that always managed to escape her ponytail as she walked away. The new dresses. The brief hints of skin. The curve of her bottom lip. The unmistakable intelligence in her eyes. The absolutely everything he could ever hope for and more than likely didn't deserve but couldn't live without.

The chatter was starting to build as people streamed into the gallery, so he did what he always did during a Hughston show and headed for the bar. He'd made it halfway through the crowd when he spotted her across the room.

Felicia had stopped in front of a painting showing her at the museum fundraiser, her hair escaping from the ponytail and wearing that awful black dress, but with a spark of something in her bright blue eyes that drew in the viewer. In the painting, she had a shy smile. In the real world, her lips were smashed into a straight line, and a flush had climbed from her chest to her cheeks. Hudson's gut twisted. She hated it. He could tell in her clipped steps as she went from one painting to another to another until she came to a stop in front of his favorite.

He'd painted her in the ant lab, surrounded by the glass-encased colonies and wearing one of her ant T-shirts and baggy jeans. It was the exact moment she'd gone into great detail about the feeding habits of the honeypot ants. There was no missing the fire in her eyes and the absolute pleasure on her face. Her smile had been captured in the moment right before a laugh had escaped. That was it. That was the moment he should have known there was no way he could help her land another man. It was the instant he'd fallen in love with her—and right before she'd told him to go take a flying leap, ignoring his charm and money and the facade he'd projected. She was a scientist who didn't deal in white lies but in observable truth. And the reality was that she was right. He had been a chickenshit about admitting he was Hughston and about owning up to the fact that he loved her.

He took two steps toward her, but jerked to a stop when Tyler appeared at her arm and handed her a glass of champagne. She downed it in one gulp and snagged the second one the man was holding. Ignoring the possessive caveman roaring inside him when Tyler took Felicia's arm and started leading her from painting to painting, he forced himself to stay still. There was nothing he could say that the paintings didn't already. He'd brushed every emotion, every desire, every hope onto the canvas with each stroke, adding layer upon layer until it showed the depth of how he felt about Felicia.

She stopped in front of the partial nude of herself, and her entire body went stiff, her eyes going wide with mortification and her cheeks turning from pink to scarlet. Shit. That's not the reaction he'd been hoping for. Yes, it was really putting her image out there, but that's how he loved her best, fresh, unadorned, herself. In that moment, there had been no barriers between them.

Slowly, like in a horror movie, she turned, her chin up and her shoulders locked. How she'd known he was standing only a few feet behind her he had no idea. She marched toward him and the chatter around them intensified. There was no way anyone could miss that this was the woman in every painting and that she was pissed as hell.

• • •

Felicia could feel every eye in the gallery—including numerous reproductions of her own—on her, but her attention was focused solely on one man. Hudson Carlyle. He'd done this—and it had to have taken months—without ever letting on. There was no missing what he'd felt when he'd painted them—especially not the one of her in the very dress she had on at this moment. By the time she got to him, people weren't even *pretending* to look at the paintings, and she couldn't have cared less.

She stopped in front of Hudson, her heart trying to beat its way through her rib cage. "You are the most moronic, annoying, fucked up man I've ever met," she said, jabbing a finger into his chest hard enough to leave a bruise. "How dare you. You—"

"Let me explain," he interrupted.

Oh no. For once, he wasn't going to get to finesse his way through a situation. "What could there be left to say?" She waved her hand at the paintings around the room, her throat growing tight with emotion as she looked at everything he'd done, everything he'd told her without ever saying a thing. "You felt all of this, and you didn't say a word? Ever?"

The vein in his temple pulsed. "What could I say?"

She looked around at the paintings. Sure, it was more than a little uncomfortable to see herself—sometimes almost *all* of herself—but she couldn't deny that this was exactly what she'd been too scared to even dream could happen.

"That you saw what no-one else did," she said, her voice trembling. "You saw *me* from the very beginning."

"How could I not? I couldn't look away from you from the very first time I laid eyes on you," he said. "I'm sorry. I should have warned you about the paintings, but I wanted you to see for yourself. And if none of it mattered to you, then I'd know that your heart belonged to Captain Clueless."

"I'm right here," Tyler shouted from somewhere off to the left.

"Shut up, Tyler," she and Hudson called out together.

The crowd chuckled, but Felicia barely heard them. This moment wasn't about the rest of the world; it was only about her and the most frustrating man she'd ever met and fallen in love with who had nearly demolished her heart.

Raising herself up on her tiptoes so she could reach his shirt collar, she yanked him close, relief and confusion and love swirling through her like a triplet of tornadoes. "If you felt all of this, why did you push me away? Why did you say I wasn't your type? Why did you turn me down in the dressing room? Why...that last time?"

This time it was Hudson whose cheeks turned a light red. "All I wanted—and still do—was to give you what you wanted and what would make you happy."

Everything fell into place. The desperate intensity of the other night when they needed to touch each other more than they needed to breathe followed by the text from Tyler, and then that fight. She'd never expected to find these paintings when she'd walked in the gallery ready to apologize for her harsh words. All she'd wanted was a second chance with the man she loved if it was possible to move past their fight.

"I'm sorry for what I said the other night. It's your life, and you get to choose who you tell or don't tell. I just wish you'd remember that you're not only taking away other people's choices when you decide to do what's best for them, you're taking away your own, too." A tear escaped one eye and tracked its way down her cheek until she flicked it away with her wrist. "Basically, you need to stop being such a selfless asshole."

"About that night." He looked down for a half second and then back up at her. "I let my jealousy get the best of me and said some really out of line stuff. I just couldn't pretend anymore that I wasn't in love with you and it scared me."

Her heart stopped. She must have heard that wrong. "You love me?"

He laughed and gestured toward the paintings surrounding them. "Could you come to any other conclusion after seeing those?"

Maybe she went in first, maybe it was him. It didn't matter. All that did was the kiss that acted as apology, declaration, and promise all in one. It was the kind of kiss that gave a glimpse of the future, complete with family and friends and a lifelong happily ever after. It wasn't until they broke apart that the fact that everyone around them was clapping, including Tyler, who was standing with Everly, Helene, Sawyer, and Clover.

It took a second, but the meaning of all the attention sank in. "Shit. I think I just outed you as Hughston. I'm sorry."

He tucked her close to his side and brushed a kiss across the top of her head. "You obviously didn't see the placard with the name of the show."

"I was a little distracted by the giant paintings of me to everywhere." Yeah, that was putting it mildly.

"Come with me."

Hand in hand they walked through the crowd of people who were wishing them well and offering their congratulations for some reason. She'd figure out why later, right now she just wanted to enjoy being with the man she loved. Hudson stopped in front of a large black sign decorated with honeypot ants that read:

HUGHSTON (HUDSON CARLYLE) PRESENTS HIS LATEST COLLECTION: WIFE

Her heart stuttered, and she looked around at all the paintings, her gaze finally landing on Hudson, the man she'd declared Genus: Man, Family: Not for Her, and thanked God she'd so misclassified him. Not that she could let him know all of that. Charming Hudson was bad enough, Cocky Hudson would be impossible to live with, though she sure would enjoy it anyway.

She jerked her chin in the direction of the sign. "Is that a question?"

He gave her that signature, panty-melting smirk of his. "I'm hoping it will be an undeniable eventuality. After all, who can say no to a charmer like me?"

Not her, that was for sure. "I love you, Hudson Carlyle."

He dipped his head down so his mouth was almost touching hers. "I love you, too."

This time it was definitely her that kissed him because she really was a fast learner, and there was no greater lesson than learning to fall in love.

Epilogue

Three years later...

The painting hung above the fireplace in Helene Carlyle's penthouse. Four feet wide by five feet tall, it was one of his larger pieces, but instead of Hughston's well-known, if barely legible, scrawl of a signature in the bottom right-hand corner there was—in clearly visible red paint—Hudson's signature. Helene had insisted. And then Felicia had agreed. He'd known when he was on the losing end of an argument and didn't even try to charm his way out of signing one of his paintings with his real name for the first time ever.

"You know what I love most about that piece?" Felicia asked as she stepped next to him, barely avoiding the demon-speed whirlwind that was his nephew, Michael, as he ran toward the piano.

"That your soon-to-be husband at the time didn't paint you in your underwear?" he asked, pulling her close.

"They're pink tonight, by the way."

He liked that answer. *Every* part of him liked that answer.

"We can leave now."

"Oh no, you're not getting off that easily," she said, nudging him back. "Everyone's here to celebrate your show tomorrow at Everly's gallery."

And they were. Sawyer and Clover were out on the balcony looking over the city his brother helped construct as the only Carlyle brother still working at Carlyle Enterprises. Their son Michael, named after his dad, was leading Helene on a chase through the room. Clover's parents were on the couch, laughing at all the commotion. And Tyler stood with his new wife by the piano, looking every bit like they were plotting world domination.

"Yeah, including Captain Clueless." His brother may have totally made up with Tyler, but he was still holding a bit of a grudge. What could he say, he was a caveman who wanted to think he was the first and only for the woman he loved. "What she sees in him, I'll never understand."

Felicia rose onto her tiptoes and brushed a kiss across his cheek. "Hopefully the same thing I see in you."

"A man with exceedingly talented hands?" He dropped his voice to a whisper. "And tongue? And—"

She just shook her head at him and grinned. "The man I love."

"Is that why you made me ask you to marry me four hundred and eighty-two times before you said yes?" He started keeping a tally as a joke. He'd never expected it to get that high. After all, he was the charmer of the Carlyle family.

She shrugged. "I told you up-front the timing wasn't right."

"That's right. Getting married was on one of your not-to-do lists until you were thirty-three." And like the stubborn woman she was, she'd stuck to that master plan.

"Tease me all you want. I know you love my lists—especially when they involve shopping trips to La Perla."

God, did he ever. Who'd have ever thought that his

favorite ant scientist could develop such a lingerie addiction—one he was more than happy to indulge.

"Speaking of panties, if the fact that you're not in yours in the Carlyle family painting isn't your favorite part, then what is?"

Felicia looked up at the painting, her gaze going soft behind her new red glasses. "That if you look at it from just the right angle, it looks like I have the beginnings of a pregnant belly."

He suddenly felt dizzy. "You do not."

"Oh, I do." She took his hand in hers and placed it on her belly. "On canvas and soon in real life."

The rest of the world disappeared as he looked down at his wife's flat stomach, awe filling him from the bottom to the top. "When did you find out?"

"The doctor confirmed it this morning. I figured Eliza for a girl or Henry for a boy."

She could pick the name Apple Rocket for all he cared; he was too damn excited to think names at the moment. However, that didn't mean the artist in him didn't immediately fixate on the possibilities. "I can't wait to paint you in all your pregnant glory."

Her eyes went wide, and she shook her head. "No way, the world has seen more than enough of me as it is."

"Not me. I'll never get enough of you on canvas, in my bed, by my side." He dipped his head lower until his lips were nearly touching hers. "I love you, Felicia Hartigan Carlyle."

"Never as much I love you," she said as she melted into him. He'd just have to show her he loved her more later that evening.

He kissed her, not really caring if he ever successfully charmed her into posing for him again. He had something better than his muse on canvas. He had Felicia in his life. Forever. And it didn't get better than that.

Acknowledgments

There's just no way I could do any of this without the amazing people at Entangled, you guys are the best to work with. Thanks for always being there. I owe pretty much the entire company brownies and drinks by now. Someday I'll even pay up. *Grin* Liz, I try not to text before noon, but I've been up for HOURS by then and I have gifs to share. Robin and Kim, I couldn't imagine doing any of this without running it by you two first. The family Flynn, next time I'll shower during deadline week, I promise. And for the readers who make all of this possible, thank you so much for hanging out with me in this fictional world, you make it all worthwhile. Just wait until you see what happens in Harbor City next!

Ant jokes via Ants Alive (www.antsalive.com)

About the Author

Avery Flynn has three slightly wild children, loves a hockey-addicted husband, and is desperately hoping someone invents the coffee IV drip. Find out more about Avery on her Website, follow her on Twitter, like her on her Facebook page, or friend her on her Facebook profile. Join her street team, The Flynnbots, on Facebeook. Also, if you figure out how to send Oreos through the Internet, she'll be your best friend for life.

Also by Avery Flynn...

KILLER TEMPTATION

KILLER CHARM

KILLER ATTRACTION

KILLER SEDUCTION

BETTING ON THE BILLIONAIRE

ENEMIES ON TAP

DODGING TEMPTATION

HIS UNDERCOVER PRINCESS

HER ENEMY PROTECTOR

HOT ON ICE

Don't miss the companion novel to The Charmer....

THE NEGOTIATOR

a hot, romantic comedy by Avery Flynn

All workaholic billionaire Sawyer Carlyle needs is someone to act as a "buffer" between him and annoying outside distractions, not to mention from his marriage-obsessed mom. But when the free-spirited woman he hires turns out to negotiate like a pitbull and look like hot sunshine and lickable rainbows, he's soon agreeing to things straight out of his comfort zone. Good thing she's got a non-negotiable six-weeks-and-I'm-gone rule, or Sawyer may have just met this match…

Discover more Amara titles…

AGAINST ALL ODDS
an *Outback Hearts* novel by Jezz de Silva

The bomb ticking inside Abigail Williams has shadowed every moment of her adult life. With the timer counting down, Abi embarks on one final adventure into the Australian outback before returning to fight for her life. Sergeant Ryder Harper survived over a decade in Australia's military. He's ready to drag what's left of his broken body home, dreading the long flight back to Brisbane. Until he collides with the stubborn, maddening seductress sitting beside him.

SAISON FOR LOVE
a *Brewing Love* novel by Meg Benjamin

Liam Dempsey isn't long for Antero. He's not interested in forming any attachments before he leaves in a month, but after a sexy hook-up with his sister's friend, he finds himself unsure where his future stands. The last thing Ruth Colbert needs is something else on her plate, but a steamy night with Liam was just what she needed. The problem is, now she wants more, if only she could find the time for him.

DISCOVERING DANI
a *Jamesville* novel by N.J. Walters

Dani O'Rourke is raising her two brothers alone and operating the family business, O'Rourke Cleaning Services. She's never had time for men, especially none as arrogant and cynical as Burke. A brush with death has Burke questioning his priorities. He's come to Jamesville for some peace and quiet to figure out what to do with the rest of his life and is quickly caught up in Dani's family. But is there room in such a gentle woman's life for a man as hard as him?

CPSIA information can be obtained
at www.ICGtesting.com
Printed in the USA
LVOW07s1531301117
558159LV00001B/26/P